STAR TREK:
THE NEXT GENERATION NOVELS

STAR TREK:
THE NEXT GENERATION GIANT NOVELS

STAR TREK

THE NEXT GENERATION

A ROCK AND A HARD PLACE

PETER DAVID

TITAN BOOKS
LONDON

STAR TREK **THE NEXT GENERATION 10: A ROCK AND A HARD PLACE**
ISBN 1 85286 277 7

Published by
Titan Books Ltd
19 Valentine Place
London SE1 8QH

First Titan Edition January 1990
10 9 8 7 6 5 4 3 2

British edition by arrangement with Pocket Books, a division of Simon and Schuster, Inc., Under Exclusive Licence from Paramount Pictures Corporation, The Trademark Owner.

Printed and bound in Great Britain by Cox and Wyman Ltd, Reading, Berkshire.

Author's Notes, Dedications and Assorted Ramblings

A Rock and a Hard Place has a long history that I won't bore you with, except at conventions. It's gone through several name changes—anyone at a recent Creation Con who heard me mention *Space Case* or *Trouble in Paradise,* this is it. Look no further.

Be warned: I think this novel is even more serious than my last ST:TNG novel, *Strike Zone. Rock* features borderline psychotics, tragedy, loss, narrow escapes (yes, the scene with Riker on the cover is really in the book) and at least one genuine cliffhanger. But probably everyone will tell me they loved the poker game and it's another David laugh riot (just as they did with *Strike Zone,* which featured such side-splitting topics as terminal illness and nervous breakdowns.)

For those interested, DC Comics is once again publishing Star Trek comics, with the original *Enterprise* crew stories by myself, and the new guys as written by Michael Friedman. Lots of stuff that should not be missed, so don't. Also, Michael and I, along with Carmen Carter and Bob Greenberger, are teaming on *Doomsday World,* the first group ST novel. It's due out summer of 1990. You get to guess who wrote what.

Author's Notes

I thanked everyone and his brother last time out since I never thought they'd let me write another one of these things. Since they have, I want to thank, if I haven't already, Jeff Jonas who's permanently loaned me the computer I've been writing on.

Major thanks to Marina Sirtis who, at the last Shore Leave Convention, displayed extreme graciousness in answering my incessant questions about Troi. Her comments and insights were invaluable.

A special hello to my sister, Ronni Beth David, who can now show this book to disbelieving friends and say, "See, I told you I'm related to him." Why she would actually boast of this, God only knows.

Thanks also to Kevin Ryan for his usual support above and beyond, and to Dave Stern for going to the wall for this novel.

Thanks to my wife, Myra, for her continued support—although, ever since she told me that Quintin Stone was just like me, I've had a lot of sleepless nights.

And finally, this book is dedicated to Jennifer Kingsley Westburg, who personifies the message of hope and endurance that *Star Trek* is all about.

A ROCK AND A HARD PLACE

Chapter One

"STONE. IN MY QUARTERS."

Captain Borjas did not get the reaction he expected from his first officer. Actually, he got no reaction at all.

Stone just sat there, at his customary corner table in the crew lounge, and stared thoughtfully at the glass in his hand. The synthehol swirled around inside, catching the overhead lighting and glistening with the multicolor effect for which the Ferengi invention was noted.

It was not, Borjas noted, the standard-issue glass used in the lounge. Stone kept his own glasses, his own liquor supply, his own everything, as if he was determined to keep himself isolated from the rest of the crew.

Borjas stood there a moment more, composing himself. He knew that the eyes of various crew members were on him. He should have sent a subordinate down to do this. Hell, none of it would have been necessary if Stone had just answered the damned page in the first place.

Borjas leaned forward, knuckles on Stone's table. A roll of fat was just starting to develop around Borjas's waist. He was grateful for the recent redesign of Starfleet uniforms

1

that provided for the short jacket uniform top instead of the straight, simple lines of a one-piece jumpsuit. It was kinder to older officers.

Borjas had thinning black hair and eyebrows so thick that they seemed to join across the bridge of his nose. His jaw twitched in irritation. Generally, his scowl was enough to intimidate even his veteran subordinates.

Not this time, though.

"Stone, the longer you continue to ignore me, the harder you're going to make it on yourself."

Slowly, Stone looked up.

Borjas remembered the first time that he had seen Stone. The man had made him nervous since the beginning of their relationship. Stone had sturdy enough features, high cheekbones, a pointed jaw, but a long scar ran down the right side of his face. Stone's scar was odd because modern technology could remove such unpleasant blemishes in a matter of seconds. But Stone wore his like a medal.

His hair was black, cut short and spikey. Regulation, but . . . odd looking. His eyebrows were upswept, almost to the point where Borjas wondered if he had some Vulcan blood in him.

His eyes, though, had been what disturbed Borjas that first time. Those eyes could bore through you, or focus on some other part of the room, or meditate on his inner self. There was a great deal going on behind those eyes, and Borjas never knew what it was.

Stone took in a deep breath and then let it out slowly, lovingly. "Ahhhh." It was a sigh of relief. "There it is."

"There what is?"

Stone made no reply, merely smiling. It was not a smile conducive to peace of mind.

Borjas was becoming acutely aware that all other talk in the lounge had ceased. He considered ordering the lounge emptied, but decided that he would be damned if he disrupted everybody else because of Stone. Besides, let them see who was really in charge of the Starship *Nimitz*.

"Stone, I'm giving you exactly three seconds to come to my quarters."

Stone's expression said, *or what?* His mouth didn't have to.

Borjas pulled all his authority around himself and cloaked himself in it. "You are facing court-martial for insubordination, Stone."

"Court-martial?" was the calm reply.

Was he finally getting through? Borjas forged onward, leaning across the table. "Yes. Court-martial. For insubordination, and for endangering the lives and safety of this crew."

Stone seemed to be looking at a far wall. "Endangering. Endangering." He considered the word, rolled it around on his tongue. "All I remember doing is saving some crewmen's lives. Crewmen you wrote off."

"You broke regulations," Borjas said hotly, "regulations designed to guarantee the well-being of the entire crew."

"Guarantee?" said Stone. He tilted back the glass and finished the contents. Then he began to roll the glass between his palms. "Out in the middle of space, with instant death by a crushing vacuum staved off by a hull and prayers—and you want a guarantee? All right, Captain. Death is guaranteed. Nothing else."

Stone made a sweeping gesture, taking in all those around him. "These people understand that. Even if you don't."

Borjas shook his head sadly. "Stone, you are relieved of your post. That's all. I didn't want to do this in front of the crew, but . . . report to your quarters."

Stone ignored him, reached for his bottle of synthehol.

"Get up, I said!"

"Morning already?" said Stone lazily as he started to pour.

Furious, Borjas snatched the bottle away from Stone. Not so much as a flicker of surprise moved across Stone's face. Instead, he remained frozen in position, his glass in his left hand, his right hand poised as if pouring.

3

Then, very deliberately, he lowered his hand and raised his gaze staring at Borjas's head as though his glance was boring through to the back of the captain's skull.

Borjas matched his gaze. "Go to your quarters," he said. "Or to the brig. It's your choice."

"I don't like those choices," Stone replied calmly.

Borjas tapped his communicator. "Security," he said. "Report to crew lounge and escort Commander Stone to the brig."

"They can't make me go to the brig either."

Borjas folded his arms and said, "I don't see where you have much say in the matter."

Stone stared at his glass. "I'm going to sickbay."

"I beg your pardon."

"You heard me. It's more comfortable."

"You are not going to sickbay."

"Why not?"

"Because," Borjas said confidently, "you're not sick."

Stone pondered that a moment.

And then Borjas and everyone else in the lounge jumped involuntarily as a sharp crack sounded.

Borjas looked in horror at the source.

Stone had crushed the glass that he'd been holding. Unlike the unbreakable ones in the lounge, this one was actually made of real glass. The stem dropped to the table and rolled off.

Stone sat frozen in position for a moment, his fist clenched. Then he slowly opened his hand. His palm and fingers were a bloody mess.

"I am now," said Stone.

Chapter Two

O'BRIEN THREW DOWN his cards in disgust and started to get up from the table. "That's it. I've had it. I want Pulaski back."

William T. Riker placed a restraining hand on O'Brien's forearm. He knew that the transporter chief's irritation was genuine, and fought to restrain the smile that played across his lips. He was only partially successful. "Now come on, Chief," said the bearded first officer of the *Enterprise*. "You haven't been doing that badly."

"I've lost five straight hands!" said O'Brien, stabbing a finger at the seriously diminished stack of chips in front of him. "I've never lost five straight hands in my life. In my *life*."

"Everyone has a bad day," said Riker soothingly.

"It's her fault. She's cheating."

Riker looked in astonishment at the person to whom O'Brien was pointing. "Never."

"Of course you'd defend her," said O'Brien. "You and she have an 'understanding.'" He mimed quotation marks around the last word. "But I don't have an understanding. I have a cash flow problem."

"I'm not cheating," came the quiet reply.

O'Brien sagged back in his chair. "Look, Counselor, I'm not even saying it's your fault. It's my fault. You'd think I'd have learned by now—you don't play poker with an empath. That's all. You just don't."

"I don't see what the problem is," said Deanna Troi defensively from behind her massive pile of chips.

"You don't see!" said O'Brien. He placed his fingertips to his forehead and, in a fair impression of Troi's exotic accent, said, "Captain, I sense . . . great bluffing. Yes. O'Brien is talking through his hat, and in fact he has a busted flush."

Data, seated to Riker's right, frowned in curiosity. "Talking through his hat?"

"Slang for bluffing."

"Ah."

"O'Brien, if there is one thing that I know, it is my own mind," said Deanna Troi primly. The exotic-looking half-Betazoid sat with perfect posture, shoulders squared, spine straight. Riker and O'Brien slumped in their chairs. Data slumped because he was imitating the other men.

"I would not," she continued, "use my abilities in the manner you suggest."

"Maybe you can't help it."

She studied him with her large eyes. "I know you're frustrated . . ."

"You didn't have to be an *em*path to pick up on that, did you?"

"Come on, O'Brien," said Riker. "Are you going to deal or what?"

"No. Forget it. Look, at first I was nervous when we let Data in on the game." He gestured towards the white-skinned android who stared at him with open curiosity, his yellow eyes gleaming in the dimly lit room. "I thought, 'Great, how am I going to outthink a guy with a computer in his skull?' But that was before I found out I could bluff his socks off."

Automatically, Data looked at his feet, but then he looked up in understanding. "Oh. I see. Another clothing metaphor."

O'Brien nodded. "But Troi . . . look, Counselor. I'm just afraid that, even though you don't intend to, that somehow you're still picking up emotions, even subliminaly, and—"

Deanna put up a hand. "You don't have to say any more, O'Brien. I understand completely." She rose from her seat and said calmly, "Perhaps it would be best if someone new participated. I am beginning to think that poker isn't my game."

"Now come on, Deanna . . ." Riker began.

"I have things I must attend to," she said, in a tone that indicated that further discussion would be useless. She turned, and with a swish of her long green skirt, she was gone.

"That wasn't particularly nice, O'Brien," said Riker in rebuke. The expression of annoyance showed that he was not kidding.

"Okay, okay, maybe I came down a little too hard on her. I'll apologize later, okay? It doesn't change the fact that we need a fourth again."

"Certainly, there must be someone on the ship interested in participating," Data said.

"How about the captain?" said O'Brien after a moment of thought. "Bet he wouldn't mind a chance to let his hair down . . . so to speak."

Riker stared at him. "You think you can outbluff the captain?"

O'Brien conjured up a mental image of the formidable Picard, glaring at him and saying with that clipped, accented voice, "See your ten and raise you twenty." Slowly he nodded. "Good point," he said. "But then who—?"

The door hissed open at that moment and Beverly Crusher, the ship's chief medical officer, entered.

Crusher was a study in contradictions. She had an almost

7

waiflike air about her, but she gave as good as she got. The crew had quickly learned that behind her innocent demeanor was an iron will.

She had just returned to the ship after a year at Starfleet Medical, and that return was welcomed by many.

Crusher stood there a moment, glancing around the room. "I'd thought Deanna was down here. Sorry."

"She had things to do," said O'Brien.

"Oh." Crusher paused, looking at the three men around the table. "What are you playing?"

"Poker," said Data. "A card game factoring the elements of chance with—"

"Later, Data," said Riker, whose mind was already going in the same direction as O'Brien's.

O'Brien, for his part, was smiling at Crusher in the same way as Riker. Behind that beard, Riker looked almost satanic. "Have you ever played . . . poker?" said Riker.

"Many years ago," said Crusher after a moment's thought. "I was a teenager, and a couple of my girlfriends and a few guys, we played stri—"

She stopped and cleared her throat. Data wondered why her cheeks were flushing a bit. "We, uh, played a variation. But I haven't since then. I don't remember what beats what. That sort of thing."

"We have room," said O'Brien a bit too eagerly.

"Well . . . sure, why not?" said Crusher, and she walked over to the chair and sat. She smiled ingratiatingly at the others. "Now go easy on me, okay?"

O'Brien looked at Riker and made the soft, cooing sounds of a pigeon.

Data offered the only advice that came to mind. "Watch out for your socks," he said.

She looked at her feet and frowned.

Picard was frowning as well.

In his quarters, the veteran captain of the *Enterprise* stared at the image of Admiral Williams that gazed back at him from the viewscreen. "Commander Riker is an integral part of what makes the *Enterprise* function smoothly, Admiral," he said tartly. He was circling his quarters, his hands behind his back. "I cannot say that I am pleased over being summarily relieved of him."

"We regret the abruptness of this move, Captain," said Williams calmly. Williams was only a few years older than Picard, yet she had a long and illustrious history. Also, she had all the right connections in Starfleet and was very adept at making command decisions from the safety of an office. "The situation on Paradise, however, does require Commander Riker to oversee it, for the reasons I have outlined. Why is that a problem? Are you concerned that you cannot make do without your number one?"

"We have 'made do' before, Admiral," Picard told her, "as you well know. In fact, I encouraged him to leave us to take up the temporary position of Klingon first officer. This, however, seems a frivolous use of manpower and something of a waste. And, as always, a gap in the chain of command is irritating to fill."

Something about her expression at that moment made Picard think that he had just walked into something. Williams smiled pleasantly as she said, "There, I believe, we can help you, Captain. We have a temporary substitute for first officer."

Mentally, a red alert klaxon sounded in Picard's head. "A substitute?"

"That's right. A substitute."

"What sort of substitute?"

"A temporary one."

"Admiral, we are going in circles here." He paused, then took a step closer to the viewscreen and dropped his voice to a tone of confidentiality. "Karen . . . what the devil is going on?"

Admiral Karen Williams forced a smile. "Couldn't slip anything past you, Picard."

"Reassigning Riker is only part of it, isn't it?" said Picard slowly. "Just as important to Starfleet is that this temporary first officer be brought aboard the *Enterprise.* All right, Karen." He sat down as if better able to brace himself. "What's the problem with this officer?"

"Nothing extreme," said Williams. "The fact is that he's a brilliant officer. Top rate tactician. Incredible personal magnetism."

"The problem is—?"

"He's a lunatic."

Picard blinked in confusion. "I beg your pardon?"

"He's a loose cannon. A space case."

"Good lord. And this man is a Starfleet officer? How is that possible?"

"Because his psych profile is clean. His ratings are well within the norm. His stress and adaptation reactions are first-rate. According to every test we have, the man is stable."

"But—?"

"But according to every officer he's served under, the man's impossible. He does what he wants, when he wants to. Somehow it always seems to all work out . . . his instincts are absolutely dead on. But he's all instinct. He knows the rules, but he just does what he damned well feels like—the problem is that he hasn't been wrong yet. Of course, he's had several reprimands, but nothing serious enough to warrant dismissal. He lasted three months with the *Nimitz,* and that's practically a record for him."

"That's Andy Borjas's ship."

"That's right."

"Borjas is a good man."

"Well, your good man informed Starfleet that either Stone is transferred or he gets blown out a photon tube."

"Stone?"

"That's his name. Quintin Stone."

Picard scratched his head in puzzlement. "What did he do that angered Borjas that much?"

"He saved some lives."

Now Picard was really confused. "I'm not following."

Williams sighed, and Picard suspected that she had already related this story a number of times. "There was a star system where the sun was unstable, and the *Nimitz* had a geological team exploring one of the middle planets to investigate environmental impacts. The sun began to deteriorate much faster than expected, however, and the combination of magnetic radiation and solar flares rendered the transporters inoperative. Not only that, but the ship itself was in danger. Borjas, concerned about the safety of the rest of the crew, elected to move out of the area."

"Opting to sacrifice the away team for the preservation of the ship," said Picard. "Never an easy decision."

"Yes. It was not a decision Stone agreed with. Without Borjas knowing it, Stone commandeered a shuttlecraft and departed the *Nimitz* seconds before she was supposed to leave. He went down to the planet surface, found the away team after skimming the area they'd been beamed down to, got them aboard, and took off. Luckily for Stone, Borjas ordered departure at sublight speed rather than warp, or the shuttle would never have caught up with him."

"So once Stone took the initiative, Borjas decided he could not just write off the away team."

"Let's just say Borjas had his arm twisted into it and was not pleased. And when Borjas wanted to discipline Stone upon his return and have him confined to the brig, Stone . . well, it will all be in your report."

"It sounds to me as if Stone, despite his enthusiasm . . may not be Starfleet material."

"Jean-Luc, he beat the Kobayashi Maru Simulation."

Picard wasn't quite sure he had heard properly. "What? Without cheating?"

"Yes. Stone blew it out of the water. Programmers were in mourning for a week."

"I'm impressed."

"We're all impressed. Stone is an impressive officer. But he lacks discipline. And we need someone who can teach him that."

"And I'm elected."

"Starfleet isn't exactly a democracy, Captain, but . . . yes. You're elected."

Chapter Three

MARK MASTERS STALKED AROUND the inside of Jackson Carter's office. Masters fit the description of most terraformers—sturdy, wiry, and grizzled. The soft-soled boots made no noise on Carter's polished floor. Carter simply watched without comment.

"It stinks!" Masters said at length.

Carter nodded agreeably. "There is that."

"We contracted with the Federation! Contracted exclusively for terraforming privileges."

"I know we did," said Carter. "I was one of the ones who signed the contract. You're not telling me anything I don't know."

"Well, I'll tell you what *I* don't know! We've been doing a fine job! Sure it's been going slower than planned. But why in hell do we need the Federation shipping us a monitoring and research group?"

"Why not? It's a big planet."

"You're kidding, right? Ninety-five percent uninhabitable and he calls it a big planet."

Masters strode to the window of Carter's office. The office

was on the third floor, which was as tall as a building got in Starlight.

Through the window was a beautiful view of a hell called Paradise.

Once, barely years ago, there had been no life on the planet at all. It hadn't even had a name, merely an identification number. Once it had had population, life. But that was many centuries ago, and the populace had obliterated themselves through environmental atrocities and pointless war. To this day, the planet had been uninhabitable by humanoid life.

It was the perfect type of planet for terraformers.

They had laid their claim with the Federation, guaranteeing that the planet was being developed for colonizing, and that any activities would involve only those intended for benefiting peaceful coexistence. In other words, no making use of the desolate area for developing weapons.

The Federation had agreed, and the terraformers—112 in all—had dubbed their new home "Paradise." With the furious winds, perpetual snowfall, hard-to-breathe air, heavily ionized atmosphere, and inhospitable land, it was definitely a misnomer.

The first thing had been construction of an atmosphere processing plant, slowly supplying a small area with proper atmospheric conditions. This alone had taken long, arduous months, and the result had been Starlight, the first city on the surface of Paradise in who-knew-how-many centuries. It was only a few miles square, and there was a definite grunginess about it. But it was home.

The buildings were stark and functional, and there was a constant dim haze in the air—a result of the interaction between the reconditioned atmosphere and the natural one. Buildings wore a coat of perpetual grime, and the terraformers had given up trying to keep them clean long ago. Instead, the buildings had names or off-color messages etched in the dirt on a daily basis. By the next day, new dirt, and new messages, replaced the old.

14

The city had been laid out helter-skelter, which had never been a problem since everyone there knew where everything was. At night there were glowing, flashing signs on the buildings to summon the terraformers to the pub for relaxation and recreation.

Once Starlight had been established, the skeleton crew of terraformers swelled to its full complement of 112. The buildings had gone up, and scientific research bases were established. Plans were well under way to create other atmosphere centers, other cities. Feasibility studies of networking tunnels, for quicker, safer access to future cities, were conducted. All of it, however, took time.

And there were the setbacks . . .

"It's the Wild Things, isn't it?" said Masters, still looking out the window. "They heard about the Wild Things and they're upset."

"No one anticipated the Wild Things," replied Carter soothingly. "A genetic mishap, that's all."

"They shouldn't have escaped. I'm head scientist. It's my fault." He turned towards Carter. "I'll resign. The Federation is probably looking for a head to roll, and it'll be mine. If I go willingly, me and the family, then maybe they'll—"

Carter put a hand up comfortingly. There was something about Carter that radiated calm. He had a thatch of graying hair, a rounded, bearded jaw, and a smile so perpetual that at first you thought he must not have understood the gravity of the situation. But Carter always knew every aspect, every angle. Because of that, he was able to focus on the positive side of things. And he did so without a Pollyanna-like attitude.

"No heads are going to roll. Everything is going to be fine. The Federation isn't looking to take over anything. That's not how they operate. All they want to do is help."

"What if we don't want their help?"

"Then we'd be idiots. Mark, this isn't a race. This isn't even a matter of pride. We all have a common goal," Carter said affably. "Besides, it turns out the guy who is going to be

15

commanding the Federation team is none other than Commander William T. Riker."

Masters stared at him blankly and shrugged.

Carter let out a sigh and shook his head disappointedly. "I've told you about him. The guy I grew up in Valdez with?"

Carter frowned. "I don't remember you mentioning any . . ." Then his face cleared. "Wait. The guy you called Thunderball?"

"Right, that's him."

"The guy who—"

"That's right. The same."

Masters grinned. "Oh, I've got to meet this guy."

"You'll like him."

"He'll hate me."

Carter smiled reassuringly. "Don't worry, Mark. We all do."

The *Enterprise* cut gracefully through space, her sleekness of movement in apparent contradiction to the massiveness of her build.

In the captain's ready room, however, William Riker was feeling anything but graceful. He turned so quickly that he almost knocked over the captain's model of the *Stargazer*.

"Transferred?" he said again. The word had such a nasty sound to it.

"Only for a month. It's purely temporary, Number One, I can assure you. And certainly no reflection on the job you've done here."

"Captain . . ." Riker paced the ready room like a caged cat. Picard sat serenely behind his desk, sympathizing with his second-in-command's feeling of disorientation. "If this has something to do with your concerns about my overworking . . ."

"No." Picard shook his head. "Obviously I have not been clear. This is a Starfleet order. They feel that growing up in the rugged terrain of Alaska makes you suited to head a science and advisory team to a terraforming world."

"I'm not a scientist."

Picard's lips thinned. "Then you'll have to advise, won't you?"

Riker swung a chair around and straddled it. "Terraformers are noted for knowing their own mind and not taking well to advice from outsiders."

Glancing at the specs on the world of Paradise, Picard nodded slowly. "That has usually been my experience with them. However, the leader, Jackson Carter, has a reputation for—"

"Hold it. Jackson Carter?"

"Yes. Why? You know him?"

"Do you have his bio there?"

All of the pertinent records regarding Paradise and key personnel had been forwarded to Picard. He called up Carter's biography on the screen now. "Yes."

"Birthplace?"

Picard's gaze flickered towards the appropriate line and his eyes widened. "Valdez, Alaska."

Riker slapped the table. "I don't believe it! Squibby!"

"I take it by the fact that you were born in the same place as Mr. Carter, and that you appear to know him by an absurd nickname, that you were friends."

A grin split Riker's face. "Good deduction, Captain."

"Well, I am a detective in my spare time," Picard said modestly.

Riker's thoughts were a million miles—and several decades—away. "My God . . . Squibby. After all these years."

"Why 'Squibby'?"

"Because he looked like a Squibby, whatever the hell that was," he said. "That kind of face, that kind of personality. Everything about him just said Squibby. Someone tagged him with the name and it stuck."

17

"That someone being—?"

"Me," Riker admitted sheepishly. "He hated the name, too. He got back at me, though, when he called me—"

His voice trailed off and Picard, interest piqued, said, "Called you what?"

"Nothing. It was silly."

Picard had not seen Riker this off balance since number one had learned Troi had fibbed about Betazoid sex drive. So often had his first officer seemed endlessly self-assured, that Picard could not resist the temptation to engage in some harmless needling. "You don't have to tell me, Number One, if you don't wish to."

"Good."

"However—"

"Uh oh."

"I could order you, of course."

Riker winced. "Captain, I'd really rather you didn't force me to—"

"Force you?" Picard seemed shocked, and he said stiffly, "Number One, if there is one thing that I can respect, it is my crew's need for, and right to, individual privacy."

"Thank you sir," said Riker gratefully.

"However—"

"Oh, God . . ."

Deanna Troi tapped her communicator in response to the page. "Troi here."

"Deanna? It's Bev. Where are you?"

"Deck eight holodeck."

"I'm sorry, I didn't mean to interrupt—"

"It's quite all right. I had intended to just spend some quiet time alone."

"Oh."

Deanna smiled at the pause. "Would you care to join me alone?"

"If you don't mind."

"Not at all."

Moments later, Beverly walked in and slowly came to a halt.

A dazzling vista spread out before her. The land stretched as far as she could see, rugged and cratered, with vast mountain ranges curving upward like fingers of a world caressing itself. The sky was a shimmering rainbow, the bands of light actually trembling.

Crusher glanced over and saw Deanna Troi sitting calmly, cross-legged, on a narrow outcropping. Deanna was not looking at her, but straight out at the undulating sky.

Afraid to say anything that might break the spell, Beverly walked slowly over and sat down several feet behind Troi. They remained that way for an undetermined amount of time, for time seemed to have slowed down or perhaps even vanished altogether.

"The Singing Skies," said Troi at length.

"Singing? I don't hear anything."

"You could not," was Deanna's reply. "You have to listen to yourself."

"What?"

"It is a place on my world for thought and contemplation. It provides beautiful harmonies . . . but only in the mind." She turned towards Crusher, her dark eyes wide. Bev could almost imagine she saw patterns of music dancing behind them. "To hear the tune . . . you must be in tune."

Bev closed her eyes, cleared her mind, tried to turn herself inward.

Nothing. And out loud, she admitted, "Nothing."

"No one can hear the music immediately. You must work your way towards that. Hearing the music is a blend of harmony with the world and with yourself. Only when the two are together can the music play within your head. It is a way of testing empathic powers."

Bev sensed an incomplete thought hanging in the air. "And how are yours testing today?"

Slowly Troi uncrossed her long legs and stood, shaking out her hair. "The music is faint today," she admitted.

"What's the problem? If it's the card game, then I'm sorry. I didn't mean to suddenly wind up taking your place like that—"

Troi looked at her in amusement. "You took my place?"

Bev nodded unhappily.

"You did poorly."

"I don't want to talk about it."

"As you wish."

"Fortunately, the game broke up when Captain Picard summoned Commander Riker about something."

Troi slowly sat down, as if she were a doll deflating of air. "He will be leaving."

"Who?"

"Commander Riker."

Bev frowned and sat next to Troi. "How do you know?"

"I sensed the Captain's thoughts in turmoil, which was the reason I left the game. The captain told me what was happening, and asked me not to speak to Will of it until he had."

"And has he?"

Troi seemed to be reaching outside herself once more. "Yes. And Will is ambivalent. But he will go. It is what he must do."

"And how does that make you feel?"

"That does not matter."

"It does to me."

Troi smiled at that, and patted Bev's hand. "You know . . . for so long, I did not see Will, and I thought I had put him out of my mind. Then we met again, and it was like the time apart had never happened . . . and yet it did. It is so frustrating. All of it is."

"All of what?"

"All of everything. O'Brien, for example. He didn't want me in the game because he thought I could not control my empathic abilities for something as routine as a poker game. That is how humans are, Beverly. Their thoughts are their private refuge. They think things that they would never

20

dream of acting upon. So when they encounter someone who can sense their thoughts, they become frightened of that person."

"I'm not frightened of you," said Bev. "And the captain . . . my God, he depends on you."

"He's come to know me and trust me. For many others on the ship, I'm a mystery. They don't know what my capabilities are. They don't understand, for example, that if they don't want me to know what they're thinking, I can be blocked. And that I receive empathic feelings only if I do certain mental preparation. It can't happen 'accidentally.' Empathy is a cooperative endeavor, not a . . . I don't know . . . a 'mind rape' or something."

"Give them time. They'll come around. People are only nervous about things they don't fully understand." Bev smiled. "It was only a few centuries ago that, if there was something unknown, humans would automatically deal with it in one of three ways: kill it, pollute it, or try to make money from it. We've progressed far beyond that, thank heavens. But no matter how far we come, it only seems to indicate how much further we have to go."

Troi nodded at that as she continued to stare out at the lights. The rainbows danced in the luminous darkness of her eyes.

Bev stared out also, straining her hearing. Still not so much as a note. "I would really love to hear the music," she said.

"Try for something easier first."

"Like what?"

"Your heartbeat. You're a doctor. When you can hear your heartbeat, that will be the first step to hearing the music of the Singing Skies." She smiled. "Not to mention winning at poker."

Riker was in his quarters packing his gear when there was a tone at the door.

"Come." But he already knew who it would be.

He nodded to Deanna as she stepped in. The door hissed shut behind her. "Word spread quickly, Counselor?"

"News has a way of traveling aboard a Starship."

"A very formal way of putting it," he smiled.

She walked toward him, and then veered off slightly and sat in a chair nearby. "It sounds very rugged, where you're going."

"It is."

"We shall all miss you."

He placed two more shirts in his bag. "You took an opinion poll?"

"I shall miss you."

"Ah." He turned and grinned widely at that. "Well . . . missing me shouldn't be all that difficult. We had a stretch of years where we didn't see each other at all."

"Are you under the impression, Commander Riker, that you occupied my thoughts every day of our separation?" she said teasingly.

"Of course not," was the stiff response. "After all, I never thought of you."

"Nor I you."

A smile played across his lips. Then, what he wanted to say flashed through his mind. He did not speak, of course. He could not say to her: *I never thought of you. Not your silken hair or sweet voice. I never thought of the tender caress of your words. The dark eyes you can get lost in. Never for a moment did that cross my mind.*

She walked toward him slowly, and then several feet away she stopped, her arms folded. She made no reply, for he had said nothing . . . merely smiled in that way he had. Thoughts flitted across her mind, which she did not voice. She did not say: *You were a barely distinguishable memory. I could barely recall the strength of your heart beating against mine. The way your powerful hands could make me feel. The way your eyes crinkled when you laughed. These are but the dimmest flutterings of fast-fading memory.*

All of it remained unsaid.

22

They stood there a moment and then Riker stuck out a hand. Troi took it and shook it firmly. "Good-bye, Commander. Be careful. I shall continue not to think about you in the same way."

"Take care, Counselor. Thoughts of you will occupy me no more than they ever have."

Light years away, somewhere in the Hidden Hills of Paradise, the Leader of the Wild Things screamed in anticipation.

Chapter Four

THE FIRST WORDS out of Borjas's mouth were "I'm sorry."

Picard had gone down to greet Borjas when he beamed over. He had not seen Andrew Borjas for quite some time, and was surprised by how haggard his old friend seemed now. The apology had been simultaneous with his stepping off the platform, as if he were concerned that Picard wouldn't let him on the ship if he didn't apologize.

Picard blinked in surprise even as he shook Borjas's hand. "You're sorry, Andy? Good lord, what for?"

"For dragging you into this. I can assure you that if I had known Starfleet was sticking you with that nut, I'd never have requested his transfer. I'd have just put him in the transporter and set it on maximum dispersal."

"Andy!" Picard was shocked. Borjas was as peace loving an individual as Picard had ever known. Such talk from him was wildly out of character.

It was also potentially damaging. Picard noticed that O'Brien, naturally, was all ears. The last thing Picard

24

needed was advance word of a maverick first officer spreading through the ship.

"Let's discuss it in my quarters," said Picard.

"Tea? No . . . you take coffee. Light, no sugar."

"Decaffinated. My nerves are shot enough as it is."

Within moments, Borjas was sipping the coffee with delicacy and glancing around Picard's quarters in admiration. "Some setup you've got here."

"I feel like I hardly spend any time in it," Picard admitted. He sat down across from Borjas, eyebrows arched, waiting for Borjas to say something. Nothing was forthcoming, however, and at length Picard offered, "So this man has been giving you problems."

"Problems! Nothing but. He is unreasonable, stubborn, insubordinate . . ."

"Those are very serious charges. Are you saying he actually disobeys orders?"

"Yes. Well," and he amended it, "not exactly."

"Andy," Picard said slowly, trying to understand, "this shouldn't be a difficult question. Either he disobeys orders or he doesn't."

"I can't deal with him, Jean-Luc!" said Borjas desperately, spilling some of the coffee. Picard quickly produced a cloth to clean it up. "On an exploratory ship like the *Nimitz,* every officer needs to be a team player. He's *not* a team player. At least, not on my team. He's totally self-directed."

Picard nodded. It went without saying that on the *Enterprise* (indeed, on any starship) Stone would have to be a team player as well.

"Would you mind," Picard asked, "if I brought him over here? So we could all discuss matters?"

"I'm not taking him back, Jean-Luc. As badly as I feel about your getting stuck with him, I'm not taking him back."

Picard rested a hand soothingly on Borjas's shoulder.

"I'm not saying you have to. Starfleet's wishes were quite specific and I, of course, shall honor them. I would hope, however, that if we have the opportunity to bring things out in the open beforehand, we can perhaps avoid some of the mishaps that led to your breakdown in communication."

"Fine." He tapped his communicator. "Borjas to *Nimitz.*"

"Nimitz," came the crisp reply. "Neilson here."

"Have Commander Stone beamed aboard *Enterprise.*"

As Borjas issued orders to his own ship, Picard contacted the bridge. "Lieutenant Worf, our temporary replacement for Mr. Riker will be coming aboard. Please greet him at the main transporter room and escort him to my quarters."

"Yes, sir."

"I hope your man can handle him," said Borjas cautiously. "Stone can be something of a wild man."

"In that case, Worf is just the one for the job," replied Picard, smiling slightly.

Worf waited in the transporter room with mild impatience and annoyance. He had not liked seeing Riker leave.

"Receiving the signal," O'Brien said in his most businesslike voice.

"Energize," said Worf.

Within moments, the sparkling had faded, and Quintin Stone stood on the platform, glancing around. He seemed to be taking in everything and then mentally filing it away for possible future reference.

His gaze got to Worf and stopped dead.

They stared at each other. Then Stone said, "I didn't know this was a Klingon ship."

"I am the only one," rumbled Worf.

"I see." He paused, as if collecting his thoughts. "And how did a Klingon come to serve aboard a starship?"

"I might ask the same of you."

Stone smiled, but the smile did not touch his eyes. He stuck out a hand as he stepped off the platform. "Commander Quintin Stone."

"Lieutenant Worf." He took Stone's hand and shook it firmly.

"A pleasure to be working with you, Lieutenant," said Stone calmly. "You strike me as an officer I can respect."

Worf released his grip.

"Thank you," said Worf.

Stone appeared satisfied with whatever he had wanted to see in the transporter room. "I assume your captain wants to see me."

"He requested I bring you to his quarters."

"Ah."

"I believe Captain Borjas is there as well."

"Ah." He smiled again, and this time it did touch his eyes. For some reason Worf found this less pleasant than before. "We should not keep him waiting."

Borjas had finished his coffee and was nervously pacing Picard's quarters. "Maybe," he was saying upon reflection, "it's not too late to halt this whole thing."

"I'm afraid it is," said Picard. "Commander Riker has already been dropped off at Starbase 42, where his team has been assembled and a transport ship is to bring them to the terraforming planet. The hole is already there in my command structure."

"Certainly you have officers who could fill that hole."

"Oh, quite capably, I assure you."

"Well, then—" Borjas gestured as if that should be the end of the discussion.

"That was not Starfleet's request, however," Picard reminded him.

Borjas sighed heavily, just as the door sounded.

"Come," Picard called out.

The door hissed open and Stone stood there, arms behind his back in traditional parade rest stance. Worf was visible behind him.

"Thank you, Lieutenant," said Picard. "I believe we can handle things from here." The remark was intended for Worf, but Picard looked at Borjas as he said it. Borjas blanched slightly, clearly displeased. The door hissed shut.

Stone walked in slowly, and Picard realized that it wasn't just slowness . . . it was caution. Despite the fact that he was entering the cabin of a commanding officer on a starship, Stone was taking absolutely nothing for granted. He was entering a strange place and was assuming that there could be a trap.

Overcautious? Paranoid, even? Then again, Picard recalled the events involving parasitic invaders that had usurped the bodies of Starfleet personnel. When dealing with the unknown every minute of your life, caution was mandatory.

But where did one draw the line between healthy and unhealthy concern?

Stone's gaze flickered in the direction of the connecting rooms that comprised the rest of Picard's quarters. He couldn't see into them but was clearly making the internal snap judgment that all was fine. Finally, he looked at Picard and nodded.

"Captain," he said, with the slightest of bows. Then he glanced at Borjas and performed the exact same movement and repeated, "Captain."

Picard was quiet for a long moment. Letting silence hang could be an excellent indicator of personality. A nervous, defensive type of person would feel the need to fill the silence with words, as if afraid to give another person time to think.

Stone said absolutely nothing. He merely waited, calmly. Picard got the impression that they could have remained that way for an hour. Stone's face was expressionless.

It was Borjas who broke the silence. "Aren't you going to

say anything to your new commanding officer, Stone?" he demanded.

Stone looked at him blandly. "I already did, sir."

"Yes, quite right," said Picard. He glanced at Borjas, who seemed to be steeling himself, and then said, "Do you know why you're being transferred to the *Enterprise,* Commander?"

"Starfleet orders, sir."

"And do you know what prompted those orders?"

Stone did not appear remotely interested. "I would not presume to second-guess Starfleet, sir."

Borjas snorted disdainfully. "When was the last time you cared about rules, Stone?" demanded Borjas.

"Always," was the calm reply.

"Captain Borjas feels," Picard interjected, deciding that nothing would be gained by pussyfooting around, "that you have nothing but disdain for regulations in general and for him in particular. Now this is an open forum. Nothing goes beyond these doors. I ask you to speak freely with no concern about recriminations. How do you perceive Captain Borjas?"

Borjas gave Picard a look that said, *here it comes.*

"I think Captain Borjas has done a capable job," said Stone.

Borjas's jaw dropped. If it was two inches lower, it would have hit the floor.

"He has carried out his duties in accordance with regulations, and his personal behavior and conduct have been beyond reproach." Stone raised an eyebrow and added, "I'm sorry to be so blunt, but that's how I feel."

"You are incredible!" exploded Borjas. "To stand there and pretend that you don't think I'm incompetent!"

Picard couldn't believe what he was seeing. Borjas was one of the calmest, most level-headed individuals he knew. And here he was acting . . . well, as crazed as he accused Stone of being.

"I know what you're doing," said Borjas. "You're trying

to make me seem crazy while you stand there, the picture of calm. But it won't work. You're not fooling me."

Picard looked from one to the other. He harrumphed loudly. "Captain Borjas, perhaps now would be a good time for you to go back to your ship. We both have our respective assignments—"

Borjas looked as if he'd been slapped. "Jean-Luc, you can't be falling for this. You can't be taking his side."

"I'm taking no one's side. I am simply trying to do my job." Picard felt like the only sane man in the room.

Borjas suddenly seemed seized by inspiration. "Stone, show him your hand. That's an order."

"Which hand, sir?"

"You know damned well which one. The right one."

Stone obediently held out his hand, palm down.

"Turn it over!"

"Captain, this has gone on far enough," began Picard in exasperation.

Without a word, Stone turned his hand over and immediately Borjas pointed and said, "See! Look at that, Jean-Luc! He did that to annoy me!"

Picard looked in surprise at the thin scars that crisscrossed Stone's hand. "How did that happen, Commander?"

Stone shrugged. "A glass broke in my hand, sir. Not much to tell."

"Not much to tell!" Borjas's voice went up an octave. "He did it on purpose so he could go to sickbay rather than the brig."

Stone's mouth twitched. "Sir, if that's what you wish to believe, I will certainly not contradict you."

"You see, Jean-Luc! You see!"

"Thank you, Captain Borjas. We will speak again."

Borjas stood there with his mouth hanging open. Then, almost as an afterthought, he closed it again. He looked frigidly at Picard and said stiffly, "Thank you, *Captain*

Picard. A pleasure as always. Enjoy your new second-in-command."

He squared his shoulders and walked stiffly out of Picard's quarters.

Picard watched him go and then turned toward Stone. Stone eyed him innocently and Picard gestured for him to sit. Picard sat as well, the desk between them. The *Enterprise* captain steepled his fingers and looked at Stone appraisingly.

"I'm not certain what just went on in here," Picard said slowly, "but Andrew Borjas is a good man. He claims that you bear watching. Starfleet agrees. Would you agree?"

"Of course," replied Stone.

"Why?"

"Everyone bears watching. Anyone could crack, any-time."

"Not people who have gone through Starfleet training," said Picard flatly.

"Training." Stone talked to Picard, but his attention seemed elsewhere. "Training to face the unknown. But if they're facing the unknown, they can't know what they're training for. Anytime." He snapped his fingers. "Just like that."

"I don't agree," replied Picard.

Stone shrugged. "The ones who are the most confident are the first ones to crack."

"You are of course excepting yourself."

"No," said Stone.

"Then how do you explain your own confidence?"

There was a thoughtful pause. "Perhaps I've cracked already," said Stone.

Picard stood and slowly walked around the desk, arms behind his back. Stone did not follow him with his gaze but continued to stare straight ahead. "You saved some men on a planet," he said at length.

"Yes."

31

"Ignoring your captain's orders."

"The captain did not say I couldn't take out a shuttlecraft."

Picard stopped in midstep and turned towards Stone. "Did he say you could?"

"No."

"What did he say?"

"He was occupied with departing the area. I didn't wish to interrupt him. So I took it upon myself."

"Meaning you didn't ask since you knew he would say no."

"I don't know what he would have said," replied Stone.

Each word frozen in ice, Picard said, "You had a hunch."

"I don't like hunches. They're messy. Like leaving crewmen behind." He turned and for the first time fixed Picard with a direct stare. "That's messy too."

Picard leaned over, putting one hand on the back of Stone's chair and the other on his desk. He was now leaning over Stone, face practically in the commander's face. "What counts on this ship," he said tightly, "is communication. That should be simple enough. You have a communicator on your uniform at all times. It's there for a reason."

Stone looked at it with no overt interest and Picard continued, "If you have a plan, you clear it. A question, you ask it. A thought, you voice it. I am open at all times to any suggestions. This ship, this crew, is a unit, and will function as one. Is that clear?"

"Yes, sir," said Stone.

"The notion that something can be done because it has not been expressly forbidden is a childish one, and I will not tolerate it from my first officer. Is *that* clear?"

Stone still did not look especially cowed or in awe. If anything, he seemed a bit bored. "Yes, sir," he said again.

Picard stepped back. "You have been sent here as a learning experience."

"It will be an honor, sir."

Picard wasn't sure whether Stone was being sarcastic or not. "What do you mean by that?"

"Nothing more than what I said, Captain."

"I see," Picard said, a note of annoyance in his voice. "Very well, Commander. I'll have your personal belongings beamed aboard, and see that you're assigned quarters. Shortly thereafter I will have a general meeting to introduce you to my key personnel. That will be all."

"Yes, sir."

Stone stood and started toward the door. Just as it slid open, Picard said, "Stone."

Stone turned.

"Commander Riker was a very popular figure on this ship. He will not be easily replaced, even temporarily. You will be under a magnifying glass."

"Thank you for the warning," said Stone diffidently.

"Good luck with your tenure on the *Enterprise*."

Stone walked out of the captain's quarters. As the doors hissed shut behind his new first officer, Picard could not help but feel the first pangs of concern.

Riker had indeed left very large shoes to fill.

Chapter Five

"WIPE YOUR SHOES, RIKER."

The command had been issued in a very pre-emptory tone, and Riker grinned when he heard it. "This," he said, "from the man who kept a room so sloppy his parents said they'd forgotten the color of the floor."

Carter rose and came from around his desk, smiling. Riker had just entered his office, wearing heavy thermal gear so padded that he looked like a polar bear. Carter embraced him, pounding him on the back, and the bulky jacket made *woomf* noises with each slap of his hand.

"Thunderball!" he said joyously.

"Oh, God," Riker winced, "please don't call me that, Jack. Please? What's it worth to you?"

"More than you can cough up, Thunderball . . . all right, Will," he said laughingly, upon seeing Riker's genuinely distressed expression. He stepped back and grabbed Riker by the shoulders, studying him up and down. "What in hell are you wearing that get-up for? It's plenty warm in Starlight."

"That's for certain," said Riker. He made a sweeping

gesture that seemed to encompass the planet. "Atmosphere generator's working tiptop. But we were shuttled in, and standard procedure is to dress as if anticipating that the shuttle is going to break down."

"Caution is a good thing. Keeps you alive."

He gestured for Riker to sit as he stepped back around his desk. Riker swung the chair around and straddled it, and then said, "I'd never have recognized you if I hadn't known. Grizzled, snow up top to match the snow outside," he gestured to the grayish white hair that was just starting to thin atop his friend's head. "Salt and pepper beard—Christ, Jack, you're practically an old man."

"I'm only a couple years older than you," protested Carter.

"But I've had quality years," Riker deadpanned.

"Oh, right. Riker, you were a smartass when we were growing up in Alaska, ever since you hung that Squibby tag on me. And you're a smartass now, the only difference being you're a smartass with a beard. Although frankly, anything that covers that mug of yours is an improvement."

"This mug served me in good stead," Riker replied. In the far distance he heard the winds of Paradise howling. It reminded him a bit of the old days in Valdez. "Every woman in Valdez was sweet on this mug. Even Eleanor Buch. Remember her?"

Carter frowned. "Buch. Eleanor Buch? I don't—"

"Come on!" Riker reached out and prodded his shoulder. "You remember. We called her Buch the bookworm; the brainiest girl around, plainest thing you ever saw, uncoordinated, too. Couldn't hit water if she fell off a boat."

Carter was rolling his eyes, trying to recall her. "Eleanor Buch, Eleanor Buch, God, I haven't thought about her in . . ."

Riker turned as the door to Carter's small, cluttered office opened. A striking woman entered, and Riker felt the blood drain from his face.

35

". . . in about five minutes, at least," finished Carter, savoring the moment. "Ellie, you remember Will Riker. Will, Eleanor Carter. Formerly Eleanor Buch."

Riker looked from one to the other. His manners on autopilot, Riker stood without hesitating and extended a hand. Eleanor shook it firmly, smiling. "Commander Riker," she said with a touch of bemused formality. "We've followed your career quite attentively. It's nice to know that a local boy has cut such an important figure in the annals of Starfleet."

Riker managed to get his mouth working again. "You two are married?"

"No, Will," said Carter dryly. "After you left for Starfleet, I adopted her."

"Now Jack, be nice," Eleanor remonstrated. "Tell me, Commander . . . do they still call you Thunderball?"

"Oh lord," sighed Riker. "No, my friends call me Will. Although on the *Enterprise* I'm sometimes called Number One."

"Number One?" said Carter. "Then that means you're in charge."

"No, I'm not in charge," said Riker. "I'm the second in command."

"Then why aren't you called Number Two?" asked Carter.

"Because that's the way it is," answered Riker, starting to feel a little confused.

"I get it. If you're the number two man, you're Number One. Who's the number one man on your ship then?"

"Captain Picard," said Riker.

"Then do you get to call him Number Two?" asked Carter. "Because if you don't, then I think you have grounds for a complaint."

Riker shot an exasperated look at his friend, then took his glance to Eleanor with a silent plea for help. He was starting to wish he'd gotten another assignment, like walking the border of the Neutral Zone stark naked.

"Please accept my apologies for my soon-to-be late husband's comments," said Eleanor. "I love him dearly, but sometimes he says stupid things. Like when he's awake, for instance."

Carter mimed being shot to the heart.

"No, it's quite all right," Riker sighed. "No one can quite embarrass you like an old friend. And no one quite has the same right to do so."

"Spoken like a true victim," said Carter graciously.

"I'm the assistant engineer," Eleanor said formally, hitching herself up to a seated position on the top of Carter's desk. She moved with an easy grace that Riker was amazed he hadn't noticed as a young man. Obviously, Carter had. "I've already seen to it that the scientific team you arrived with has been settled in. They're going over our records and list of experiments now. You've got three good people there. It's fortunate that Starfleet didn't send more; we're not exactly bursting with guest facilities down here."

"As it is, you'll be bunking with us," said Carter cheerfully.

Riker tried to keep his enthusiasm down. It was easy. "I am?"

"Well sure," said Carter. "Where else?"

"I wouldn't want to put you out . . ."

"No problem at all," said Carter. He leaned forward and gave a genuine smile. "We'll be happy to have you, Will . . . presuming I can call you that. We are still friends, aren't we?"

Riker grinned. He was starting to recall the daffy, offbeat pleasantness of Carter that had made him such a valued pal. "Of course we are. Don't worry, Eleanor," he said, "we'll try not to keep you up too late with bawdy recountings of our exploits."

"Well, we'll have to keep it clean," said Carter. "After all, I have to set an example for the kid."

Riker blinked. "Kid?"

"Our kid. Mine and Ellie's." He smiled. "Boggles the mind, doesn't it?"

"Fortunately," said Eleanor archly, "she takes after her mother." And then she writhed, giggling, as Carter prodded her waist, tickling her. She squirmed off the desk and said, "I'll get things ready at home."

"You do that," said Carter, "and lock Stephy up."

"Who's Stephy? A pet or something?"

"Stephy is our daughter," Eleanor informed him.

"How old is she? Eight? Nine?"

"Fifteen."

Riker gasped. "My God! You have a teenaged daughter? Jackson . . . I'm only thirty-two. That's obscene! Now I feel ancient. Couldn't you have waited a few years before having her?"

Carter glanced at Eleanor. "No."

Riker looked from one to the other and said quietly, "Oh."

"Anyway, she's fifteen," said Eleanor, "going on thirty-two. Kids grow up very very fast on Paradise. They have to. Jack, why should we lock her up? To protect Will from her?"

"Or protect her from Will," Carter corrected. "After all, Will . . . we wouldn't want people to find out just why they call you Thunderball, would we?"

Riker sighed again deeply. A month. Just his time in the office already seemed a month.

The three scientists had already been given the walking tour of Starlight when Carter brought Riker around. Riker refrained from commenting on the general disarray that was a direct contrast to the spic-and-span environment of the *Enterprise*. The narrow roads were pockmarked with small craters and potholes, and all around them people seemed to be in a hurry. They had to keep their eyes open to avoid collisions on two occasions.

They stopped in front of one low-slung building and

Carter gestured proudly. "We built this first, right after the atmosphere plant."

"Resource center?"

"Nope."

"Med facility?"

"Nah."

"Dormitory?"

"Of course not." Carter sniffed disdainfully. "Saloon."

"How foolish of me," said Riker.

Carter gestured towards it. "Would you care to—?"

Riker put up a hand and nodded graciously. "Maybe later. After the inspection. What's that place?" He pointed towards a large building with ventilated windows.

"You don't want to know."

"If I didn't before, I certainly do now."

Carter sighed. "Genetic engineering lab. We were trying to develop an animal that could survive in that." He pointed east.

Riker half glanced towards the horizon line. The atmosphere plant had created a bubble of habitability within which Starlite was situated, a mile-wide eye in a hurricane. But that hurricane was quite visible beyond the city's perimeter. The harsh, unpleasant surface of Paradise was dark, stormy, and uninviting. The skies undulated in a miasmic whirl, and lightning was dancing across the heavily ionized skies. At the moment, it didn't seem to be snowing, but the wind was clearly blowing fiercely.

No wonder that transporters and sensors had little effectiveness on this type of planet. Who would want to know what was down on the surface of such an inhospitable world, much less go down to it.

"Survive in that?" Riker said in disbelief.

Carter nodded. "Most beings in harsh climates have some kind of animal to be a beast of burden or form of transportation. Something you can count on when the machinery goes kablooey, which happens with alarming regularity around this place. Camels, Huskies, Goo-jibs . . . all products of their environment and all useful to humans and humanoids. Now this place,"—he waved—"produced nothing for us. In fact, if there were indigenous life, we wouldn't have been able to colonize."

"So instead, you tried to make your own."

"Can't blame a guy for trying," said Carter.

"And? . . ."

Carter took a deep breath and shrugged. "Didn't work out. Turns out genetic engineering wasn't our specialty. Win some, lose some, that kind of thing."

Riker eyed his friend closely. Was there something else?

"Come on," Carter said, clapping him on the back. "Wife's waiting for us."

They walked on toward Carter's small but sturdy home.

And somewhere in the shadows of starlight, something growled.

Chapter Six

HE GROWLED deep in his throat.

Beverly Crusher was momentarily startled. She actually took one step back from Stone before saying again, slowly, "It's just a routine physical, Commander. Now remove your uniform top."

Stone eyed her up and down. "You first."

Crusher blew out air between her teeth. "Not on a first date. Now grow up, Commander. We both have things to do. This is standard operating procedure, and we both know it."

"Other exams have been more cursory," he said.

"On this starship the regulations are more stringent," she said tightly. "Now let's go."

He considered her statement a moment and then undid his jacket. Moments later, he pulled the black T-shirt over his head.

Beverly had had her back turned to him, calibrating some readings on the diagnostic table. She turned back toward him, starting to say, "Let's start with . . ." and then her breath caught in her throat.

His chest had a thin mat of black hair that could not begin

to cover up the scars crisscrossing his torso. He stared straight ahead as Beverly walked slowly around him and saw similar vicious lacerations on his back. She took several more moments to resume her professional demeanor. When she had, she finished the circle to face Stone once more.

"This isn't on your medical record," she said.

"So?"

"So?" She couldn't conceal her disbelief. "These are serious scars."

He didn't even seem to hear her.

She decided to try a different approach. "I could remove those scars for you. Any competent doctor could. Don't you understand that?"

He had not been looking directly at her; his gaze had been turned inward until that moment. But now he examined her straight on, and she felt uncomfortable with the intensity of his stare. Then slowly, in that deliberate manner that marked all his movements, he tapped his forehead. "Can you remove the scars here?"

Beverly realized she'd been holding her clipboard in front of her as if it were a shield. She was quickly beginning to take the measure of this individual and realized that he was someone who appreciated forthrightness. She lowered the clipboard, sending out a silent message that said: *I'm here for you. You can speak to me. I'm open to you.* She walked over to him and ran her fingers across his torn back.

"How?" she whispered.

He took in a deep breath and let it out in a long, unsteady sigh. "Orion pirates," he said softly. "It's what led me to join Starfleet."

"I've heard they can be vicious."

"You heard right." His mind seemed to drift back. "My parents are both wealthy, powerful people. So when I was growing up, I had everything. I was spoiled rotten. I had no particular ambition, didn't care about anything. I had six personal cruisers, can you believe that? Six."

Crusher let out a low whistle. Personal cruisers were a luxury item at best. Six was simply ludicrous.

"I had everything. I had my ships. I had my parents, my wealth. And I had my girlfriend"—His eyes misted over—"Gloria. We were going to be married. A week before our wedding, we decided to take an extended trip. You know, our last time together before we became old married folks. Are you married, Dr. Crusher?"

She took a breath. "Widowed."

"Oh." He looked deeply sympathetic. "Maybe you don't want to hear this . . ."

"No, it's all right." She put a hand on his forearm. "I do. That is . . . if it will make you feel better. I want to help you."

"That's . . . that's very kind of you." His face hardened. "Kindness was something those Orion bastards knew nothing about."

"You were ambushed by them?"

He nodded. "It was a joy ride, nothing more. We were still well within the boundaries of Federation territory. And the Orion pirates just . . . suddenly, they were there. Their captain, his name was Wynsteen . . . I'll never forget the leer in that monster's face when he saw Gloria.

"They took us both, took the ship. We were . . ."

He broke off, his chest heaving. Stone put a hand on her shoulder, trying to steady himself, steady the recollections that seemed to be slamming through his brain. "I'm sorry. I can't. I can't tell you the details. Every night I dream of them, remember Gloria begging me, screaming my name, pleading for me to do something. But I was helpless. They kept her so that I could watch, they forced me to watch while they . . ."

Stone leaned forward, covering his face with his hands. "My father, very influential, as I said. He wielded power. He got the Federation to intercede, but it took time. Too much time. Me, they kept around to see how much suffering I could withstand."

Slowly he removed his hands, smiling up at her. "I surprised them. I surprised myself. Gloria . . . she didn't last at all . . ."

"They killed her?" whispered Beverly.

He nodded. "Gave her to the Orion slave girls, with instructions that they were to . . . break her in. They did. Into pieces." He stared off into nothing for a moment and then turned his eyes toward Beverly. "I carry these scars," he whispered, "for Gloria. Can you understand that, Doctor?"

She wrapped one of his hands in both of hers. She was impressed by the strength of it, the size. Controlled power seemed to flow through him. She remembered the face of her own beloved Jack, and the searing of her heart his death had inflicted on her.

And Wesley. She remembered when Wes had seen her go ashen upon hearing the news. He had looked up at her with those young, innocent eyes, and said—"

"Mom?"

Crusher turned, startled.

Acting Ensign Wesley Crusher had entered sickbay, a question poised on his lips. But there was another one in his eyes as he looked at Stone and his mother, quite close, sharing what appeared to be a rather intimate moment.

Next to Wesley was a friend of his, Paul Estin, although the nickname he'd acquired around the ship was Scooter. Sturdy and compact, Scooter was a direct contrast to the tall, lanky, Wesley. Indeed, Wes had so matured during her time away from the *Enterprise* that Bev Crusher had hardly recognized him, not realizing until just then how like a young Jack Crusher he was becoming.

Scooter snickered. "Did we come at a bad time . . ." Then his voice trailed off. "Holy Kolker! What happened to you?"

Stone made no reply. Instead, he started to pull on his shirt, saying, "Doctor . . . maybe this could wait until another time . . ."

"No," she said firmly. "Now. Wesley, can you come back later?"

"Sure. Uh . . ." Automatically, he extended a hand. "Wesley Crusher."

Stone took it, shaking it firmly and glancing towards Bev. "You have a teenage son? I'm amazed."

Bev flashed a quick grin.

"Stone," he said to Wesley. "Quintin Stone."

"The new first officer," Wesley said.

Stone gave him a quick nod.

He shook Scooter's hand in turn and said briskly, "Come on, boy, you have a stronger grip than that. That's it." Scooter increased the pressure as best he could. "That's right. You're judged on your handshake. The handshake was originally a way of making sure your opponent wasn't carrying a weapon. But it's also a way of showing that you can defend yourself without a weapon."

Wesley nodded towards the scars. "Looks like you could have defended yourself better."

"Wesley!" Beverly remonstrated.

Stone smiled thinly. "Boy's right. We all have fights we wish we could have won. All right, Doctor, let's get this exam over with."

Wesley and Scooter quickly withdrew from sickbay as Stone leaned back on the examination table. The moment the door had closed behind them, Scooter said, "Did you *see* that guy? His body looked like a roadmap!"

"That's enough, Scooter," said Wesley quickly. "Medical stuff is all confidential. We shouldn't be spreading it around. Understand?"

"Oh, absolutely," said Scooter. He mimed zipping his mouth and tossing a key away, and spread his hands in a gesture that said, *not a word out of me.*

Stone was walking past Worf's cabin when he heard someone dying.

45

At least that's what it sounded like. Stone could swear the floor was rumbling under him as a chorus of voices screamed for death to release them from the torture they were undergoing.

Amazingly, other people were just walking past as if nothing was happening. What the blazes was wrong with these people?

Ignoring the door signal, Stone started to pound on the door. "This is Commander Stone!" he shouted. "Hang on! I'll get security here right away!"

From inside, the awful wailing stopped, and a sharp voice command cancelled the lock. The door hissed open and Stone was standing there, first poised to pound some more.

Worf was sitting in the room, cradling what appeared to be some sort of stringed instrument. But the bow was so large, resting across the strings, that it looked more like a weapon. Indeed, if that thing had been making the sounds he'd just heard, it was more weapon than instrument.

Stone looked from the instrument to Worf. "What the hell *was* that?"

"ChuS'ugh," replied Worf.

"Did you just sneeze?" said Stone.

Worf scowled even more deeply than he usually did. "Had I sneezed, you would not be standing."

Stone took a step in, the door hissing shut behind him. He was still staring incredulously at the instrument. "I thought someone was being slaughtered."

"I see that first officers share a lack of appreciation for quality sound," said Worf. "Commander Riker is a superb second-in-command, but he also does not understand the power of Klingon music."

"ChuS'ugh." Stone rolled the word around in his mouth a moment. " 'Heavy noise,' right?"

Worf blinked. "That is a crude translation, yes. You know Klingonese?"

He shrugged. "A smattering. I can understand a little but can't speak it worth a damn."

"I could tell by the way you pronounced *chuS'ugh*."

Stone actually laughed at that. It was the first time he'd laughed since he'd come on board the ship.

It wasn't a pleasant sound.

"I would imagine," said Stone, "that mere humans are not able to comprehend the majesty of Klingon music."

"Most humans, yes," said Worf.

"I would not think of impugning the skills of so fine a warrior as yourself."

Worf nodded approvingly at this. "Word around the ship is that you carry the scars of battle yourself."

Stone raised an eyebrow at this. "Word gets around quickly. I am surprised at Dr. Crusher, that she would—"

"I doubt she was the source," said Worf.

"Ah," said Stone thoughtfully. "There were two young men. Crusher's son, I believe, and a 'Scooter' . . ."

"That would explain it," said Worf. He paused a moment. "It is rare to find a human proud of his scars."

Stone nodded slowly. "They help me . . . to remember my parents . . . and their untimely death."

Worf had been tuning his *chuS'ugh,* but now he stopped and looked up. "Your parents."

"That's right." Stone picked up a curious piece of statuary. "What's this?"

"Klingon erotica."

Stone put it down again, quickly.

Worf never took his eyes off him as he circled Worf's cabin. Worf couldn't help but get the feeling that Stone was checking it for possible traps. Commendable.

"How were your parents killed?" Worf asked.

He shot Worf a sidelong glance. "I didn't think Klingons were interested in matters of a personal nature."

"I am interested," replied Worf. "I lost my parents at a young age."

Stone surveyed Worf with new interest. "Raised by parents in the Federation?" At Worf's slow nod, Stone said, "Well that explains that. My parents—" he hesitated. "My parents were settlers. Trying to carve a new life for themselves after difficulties." He smiled. "Hardly had two credits to scratch together, but they always seemed happy somehow. Never gave up hope. My father, he would see one of those fancy, personal cruisers go by and say, 'Someday . . . someday that's where we'll be.'"

He then said sadly, "Never to be. We were on an outpost planet . . . my father was a hydrofarmer. Federation patrol ships only got out there every so often. *They* knew that."

"They?" prompted Worf.

"Romulan raiding party."

Worf felt a chill go through him. But he said nothing as Stone continued, "I'll never forget the sounds . . . I was twelve, maybe thirteen, and I thought the sky was falling. Sounds of phaser blasts . . . you know, you never realize what the phaser blast of a ship sounds like until you're on the ground and they're exploding around you. I was running towards home, as if that would have provided me shelter. The next thing I knew, the ground seemed to just blow up right from under me. I was flying," Stone was half smiling, "and I remember thinking, 'I guess I'm dead and I'm flying up to heaven now.' And the next thing I knew . . ." He stopped, as if trying to find words. "You know plexicore?"

"Of course," said Worf. "It's two grades less dense than the material we use for our own viewports on the *Enterprise*. Still, very durable."

"Unbreakable, right?"

Worf nodded.

Stone laughed unpleasantly. "Want to hear something? Plexicore can be shattered by the hurtling body of an adolescent when he's propelled by a Romulan explosion."

Worf's eyes opened wide at this as he envisioned the impact. "You lived through that?"

"Well, obviously," chuckled Stone, sounding remarkably pleasant about such a traumatic experience. "I don't remember much . . . I lay there for several days, I'm not sure how long. I flitted in and out of consciousness. Between the blood loss and the shock it's a miracle I didn't die."

"To put it mildly," said Worf.

"But I didn't. Eventually, I was found, my body practically ripped apart. Some locals found me, kind of stitched me back together until Federation ships arrived. Federation surgeons had far more sophisticated techniques, of course, and offered to treat my injuries in a more . . . aesthetic . . . manner. But I refused."

"Because your parents had been killed."

He turned to look at Worf. "You think I'm crazy?"

"No," said Worf. "I know firsthand of the trauma such events can bring about."

"I see."

Stone had walked over to a stand upon which Worf's large, silver sash was hanging. He fingered it a moment and, turning to Worf, said, "Isn't it uncomfortable?"

"Yes."

"Then why wear it?"

"Because it *is* uncomfortable."

Stone stood, aiding himself by placing his hand against the small of his back. "I don't get it."

"Klingon uniforms are made of metal and leathers. They are sweaty and unpleasant. Such irritation keeps a warrior on edge at all times. Starfleet uniforms are designed for,"—he made a slight face of distaste—"ease of wearing. Far too easy to become complacent."

"So you wear it to keep you in a nasty mood."

"That's correct."

Stone nodded. "It does its job."

"Thank you."

At that moment, the communicator on Worf's uniform beeped at him. Worf tapped it and responded.

"Picard here," came the crisp summons. "I know you're off duty, Lieutenant, but you're needed on the bridge. We have a crisis situation on our hands."

"I will be there momentarily," said Worf. He had already put down his instrument and reached for the sash.

"Good," Picard said. Then he added, "I wish Commander Riker was here. This is the kind of situation that he excels in. Picard out."

Worf glanced at Stone, whose expression now matched his name.

A second later, Stone's communicator beeped. Stone stood there, his arms at his side, making no effort to return the page.

Worf, adjusting the sash (and surreptitiously checking to make sure the hidden dagger was still in place), scowled at Stone. "You shouldn't ignore a page."

The communicator beeped again.

"Of course," Stone said icily. "I wouldn't want to risk offending the captain." He tapped the communicator and said briskly, "Stone here."

"Commander Stone," came the stern reply. "I am not accustomed to waiting quite that long for a response to a page."

"Yes, *sir*. Sorry, *sir*."

"You're needed on the bridge." He paused. "Commander Riker understood the need for alacrity at all times. I trust you do as well."

"Thank you for making that clear to me, Captain," he said. "Riker . . . I'm sorry. *Stone* out."

He stood there for a moment, his face an expressionless mask. Worf said to him, "Commander Riker was a very popular officer."

"Really," said Stone with only distant interest. "I'll tell you something, Worf. I've never met the guy . . . and already I'm not crazy about him."

Chapter Seven

"GOD, COMMANDER RIKER IS *GORGEOUS*."

Eleanor Carter saw that familiar glint in the eye of her daughter. Many, many years ago (although she would never admit it) she herself had the same look in her eye when beholding a young William Riker. Still, she had never regretted the life decision she had made when Riker had left for Starfleet and the older, but equally as interesting Jackson Carter, had turned a speculative eye her way.

There was a major difference between Riker and her Jack, she had come to realize. Riker was self-sufficient, but Carter definitely needed somebody to help keep mind and body together. And Eleanor "Bookworm" had been more than happy to step in and fill that need, as well as all his others.

She removed the vegetables from the flame. "Eyes to yourself, Stephy," she said sternly, fighting the twitching muscles that sought to bend her mouth into a smile. "He's old enough to be . . . your father's friend."

"Uh huh."

Stephy, thankfully, did not remind Eleanor of herself at that age in looks or personality. Eleanor had been, to put it charitably, a late bloomer. Stephy, on the other hand, was a pleasant combination of vivaciousness and intelligence. She was slendor, yet round in the right places. Her black hair was cut short, but somehow she always managed to have her bangs covering one eye to give her an additional bit of alure.

She could go from flirting to all business in an instant, depending on the situation. Indeed, when technical matters were being discussed, Carter was just as likely to call on his daughter for advice as his wife.

On the planet Paradise, Carter was fond of saying that no individual could be a wasted one. Everyone had to serve a function. The line between childhood and adulthood was, therefore, appropriately blurred, as teenagers were given adult responsibilities and treated as if their contributions mattered.

On Paradise, adulthood came as soon as one could handle it.

Riker and Carter were in the living room of Carter's simple, functional home. The living room was spartan, the furniture made of solid, dependable materials and not particularly decorative. Riker was paging through an old book, *Captain Blood* by Sabatini, and turned toward Carter who was going through plans for the next day's activities.

"Construction on the next atgen is coming along on schedule," said Carter idly. Riker glanced at him, a question on his face, and Carter amended, "Atmosphere generator."

Riker shook his head. "How can you have the patience for it?" he asked. "You realize that you've embarked on a project that can't be completed in your lifetime?"

"Oh, I don't know," said Carter. "I personally am planning to live forever."

"Oh really."

"Yes, really."

"And these," Riker held up the book. "Don't you know printed matter is passé?"

Carter sighed loudly at that. He rose, shaking his head

slowly. He spoke as if chiding a child as he crossed to Riker and took the book from him. "Will, Will, Will," he sighed. "You don't understand anything about anything, do you?"

Riker smiled and leaned against a table. "Indulge me," he said. "Explain it to me in words of one syllable."

At that moment the kitchen door opened and Eleanor and Stephy walked out, carrying two platefuls of food. "Dinner's up," called Eleanor.

Moments later, they were seated around the dinner table and Riker looked with forced interest at the array of vegetables that were in front of them. "It looks excellent," he said.

"Bull," said Carter.

His wife looked up at him with undisguised annoyance. "Jack! I worked hard on this!"

"I know that, Ellie," he said. "I'm not speaking on my behalf. But as I recall, Will here was always something of a meat and potatoes man."

"Oh, I'm sorry," said Ellie. "Will, we could have the synthesizer whip up something for you. I just thought that you would prefer something that was grown on the planet."

"On the *planet,"* reemphasized Carter, holding up a rather curiously colored carrot. "We actually managed to reintroduce nutrients into the ground. Once the land could have provided nothing. Now we have acres of things growing."

Smiling at his friend's enthusiasm, Riker took the carrot and bit it in half. "Excellent."

"That's how it has to be done, Will," said Carter. "Man against the planet, a little bit at a time. Mankind saw what happened decades ago," he added darkly, "with the concept of terraforming all in one shot. It goes to show how technology can so easily be perverted."

"You an antitech now, Jackson?" asked Riker as vegetables were spooned on to his plate by an overly cheerful Stephy. "Claiming that man is too mechanized? Too much done for him by machines?"

"No, I'm not antitech," scoffed Carter. "I know we couldn't even begin to develop this world without atgens, for example. And I'll admit I'll synthesize up a good steak every now and then. Machines as supplemental are fine, but not as something that supplants. You probably don't understand that."

"Of course I do," retorted Riker.

"Suuuure you do."

"I do!" said Riker, piqued.

"Now Jack," Ellie began, putting down her serving spoon.

But Carter wasn't listening. Instead, he reached over and took Riker's right hand and held it out. "Look at that," he said, poking it. "I remember when your hands were as tough as anybody's. Now look. Skin nice and soft. No hardness or cracks to it. Your problem is that your ship makes things too cushy for you."

"That is hardly the case," replied Riker, withdrawing his hand.

"Sure it's the case. I've read up about those things. You're on a Galaxy-class ship now, right?"

"The *Enterprise*," he nodded.

"Right, right, whatever. Everything is voice activated, except some panels, which are smooth. No nasty buttons to mess with." Carter grinned ear to ear. "Crew lounges, swimming pools, holodecks. World's cushiest job."

He knew his friend was just ribbing him, and yet Riker couldn't help but feel the slightest bit defensive. "You wouldn't last a week, Jackson."

"Right, right. I might die of boredom. Here, there's always something going on that makes you have to get your hands dirty."

Just then the thin, translucent front door exploded inward.

Riker leaped from his chair and spun around, in time to see a growling mass of fur charge at him, mouth open and displaying a hideous double row of sharp teeth.

The monster landed flat on Riker's chest, knocking him to the ground. Riker lashed out blindly, grabbed the creature's neck, and shoved upward. The jaws snapped viciously mere inches in front of his face.

"Shit!" yelled Carter, leaping to his feet. Everything had happened within perhaps three seconds, during which time Carter had been frozen. Now he came around and threw his arms around the creature from behind, trying to drag it off the struggling Riker.

Stephy, screaming, fell back, and Ellie upended the round table, making it a shield between the struggling beast and her daughter.

Riker couldn't see the beast clearly. All he could see were the jaws snapping at him, a mouth as wide as his face. Its fetid breath washed over him, its growling as deep as the throbbing of warp engines. He pounded on it, curling his legs up underneath and then shoved back like an uncoiled spring.

But Carter, who was still yanking on its back, didn't have time to get out of the way as it fell backwards on top of him.

Suddenly, Stephy and Ellie were there, long electric prods in their hands. With perfect coordination, their momentary hysteria forgotten, they jabbed the prods into the creature's side. It writhed and howled, falling back off of Carter, who was gasping and clutching his side.

The creature spun on its four feet, snarling, trying to dart one way and the other while being countered by the prods.

By that time Riker had his phaser out. It had not seemed a dangerous assignment, but he had nevertheless packed it.

"Back away!" he shouted, and they immediately complied. The creature sighted him, started its leap, and Riker fired using heavy stun.

It blasted the creature back, end over end, slamming it against a far wall. Shelving fell, books tumbling over it.

The creature lunged to its feet and charged again.

Again Riker fired, this time a sustained blast. The creature staggered under the withering barrage, and Ellie stuffed her fingers in her ears to block out the high-pitched whining of the phaser.

It fell over and stopped moving with one final, angered snarl. Riker released the firing button and the phaser barrage ceased.

There was dead silence. Riker stared at the creature for a long moment. Covered with brown fur shot through with gray, it was as big as two large huskies, with a body that appeared to be solid muscle. Its triangular head seemed to be entirely jaw. Its short tail twitched spasmodically.

"What the hell is it?" said Riker.

The creature was suddenly on its feet. Momentarily disoriented, it smashed into a couch, knocking it over. "Kill it! Kill it!" Stephy screamed.

Riker quickly moved the phaser to a lethal setting as the creature, drawn by Stephy's cries, turned and focused its attention on her. Carter, still clutching at his side, tried to get in the way.

"Stay down!" shouted Riker. He fired.

The creature howled once and then vanished.

They all stood there for a long moment, gasping, trying to compose themselves.

Slowly Riker turned towards his friend. "Care to tell me about it? Like how the hell did it get in, for example. Where is your security?"

"We thought we'd killed them all," Carter answered. "And with nothing alive on this planet but us, we don't need much security."

Ellie was just finishing the bandages on Carter's side. Mark Masters, the head scientist of Starlight, also doubled as the chief medical officer. He had just finished scanning Carter and confirmed that there were no broken bones or other serious injuries.

A replacement door had already been synthesized and installed. Except for the broken furniture and general air of disconsolation, no one would have been able to tell that people had been fighting for their lives there barely an hour ago.

"Was that an example of the animals you were trying to create?" asked Riker.

Carter nodded slowly. "My own damn fault. I tried to play God and we produced those monsters."

"We did what we thought was right," said Masters testily, glancing at Riker. It was clear to the *Enterprise* first officer that Masters felt extremely defensive. "Everybody has twenty-twenty hindsight."

"It didn't take much foresight," replied Riker.

"What is that supposed to mean?" snapped Masters.

"It means that when you bioengineer something that vicious, you can only expect it to turn on you."

Masters started to get to his feet, his hands balled into fists, but Carter brought him up short with a sharp word. Still scowling at Riker, Masters slowly sat down again.

"We weren't dealing with particularly fierce animals when we started, Will," said Carter slowly. "We gene spliced from several different types of creatures, noted for their durability and their ability to be domesticated. Primarily, they're Hukors, although we've crossed spliced in—"

Riker put up a hand. "You can explain the details to the other scientists," he said. "Just tell me this: what was the result?"

"The result was what you saw," said Masters in irritation.

"In a way, we accomplished what we set out to do," said Carter. "The animals we created were capable of surviving in the wilds of Paradise. Durable, tireless, and they go from newborn to full grown in a little under four weeks. Yet they have remarkable facility for storing food. Just like camels."

"But? . . ." Riker waited for them to finish.

Masters and Carter looked at each other. Carter finally said, "The first ones were fine, but something in the mix, I don't know . . . they turned vicious. Uncontrollable. We started calling them Wild Things, and it stuck."

"Why didn't you destroy them?"

"We were going to," said Masters. "But then one of our power generators went down. It dampened the fields penning the Wild Things, and a bunch of them escaped, into the wilds."

"That was over a year ago," Carter told him. "We went out to hunt them down, and I thought we'd gotten them all. The one you blew into atoms, for which I'm grateful, by the way, was clearly an old one. Probably the last, and he somehow slipped through our sweeps."

"I don't understand one thing," said Riker.

"Only one?" asked Masters innocently.

Riker ignored him. "How did they survive at all out there? What in the world did they eat?"

Once again Carter and Masters exchanged a look, and then Masters said slowly, "Each other."

"What?" whispered Riker.

"When they breed, they have very large litters," said Masters, trying to sound very removed and scholarly. "Far more than they need to perpetuate the species. So the adults eat the smallest ones, and the mothers nurse the others to adulthood at which point the offspring . . ."

"Complete the cycle," said Carter. "Sometimes. They might also consume members of the pack that are too old to run or defend themselves. Or others of their groups that have become ill, or injured, or whatever."

"It's really very efficient," said Masters, "in a grotesque sort of way."

"That's putting it mildly!" said Riker. "Jackson, I can't believe that you would be a party to this!"

"A party!" Carter slammed a fist down on his armrest and winced at the pain the motion caused in his side. "This isn't a party! Terraforming is a fight for survival against a planet that is making it abundantly clear that it doesn't want you there. And you have to do whatever you can to survive."

"Even if it means creating a race of cannibals?" said Riker distastefully.

"That certainly was not our intention," protested Carter, "and I think you know that. Besides, we thought we had rectified it. Obviously, we were wrong, but I'm positive that no more of them remain."

There was a long pause.

"Are you going to report this to Starfleet?" asked Masters.

"What do you think?" replied Riker.

Masters threw up his hands. "I knew it. I knew you couldn't trust them." He got up, started to pace furiously. "He's your old pal, you said. You said you could control him."

Riker looked in bemusement at Carter. "Control *moi?*"

"Just a passing thought," Carter said.

"They're going to close us down," said Masters. "I know it. That's the way they work."

"We're not going to close anybody down," said Riker tiredly. "Jackson, does this guy ever shut up?"

Carter cast a glance at Masters. "Rarely."

"Thanks, friend," said Masters sourly.

"Now look," Riker said, leaning forward. "Certainly, this whole business has to go into a report. I'd be derelict in my duty if I just made no mention of it. But the extent to which it's mentioned, and the severity of it, is certainly up to my discretion."

"And what does that mean?" Masters was still on the defensive.

"It means I have the leeway to give old friends a break," said Riker. "It means I'm here for a month, remember? That I'll have plenty of time to see how things are done, to see how the entire operation is being run. Then I can make whatever recommendations are necessary. And if the Wild Things are really no longer a consideration, and if you people can really handle things, then I'm sure that there will be no thought of breach of contract."

He paused for a second and then spread wide his hands toward Masters. "Satisfied?"

Masters smiled slowly. "That seems fair." He looked at

Carter and said, "I'm impressed. Your friend seems the straightforward type."

"Thank you," said Riker, even though the comment was not addressed to him.

"You're welcome," he said. "Considering that they called you Thunderball . . ."

There was distinctly female laughter from behind him and Riker covered his face. "You're never going to let that drop, are you, Squibby?"

"Not as long as it gets the kind of reactions I've come to know and enjoy," replied Carter.

Stephy was looking from one adult to the other. "I don't get it. Why do they call you Thunderball?"

"When you're older," said Carter.

Stephy made an annoyed whistling sound. "I'm grown up enough to do everything else around here. Why can't I hear the good stuff?"

And all three adults in the room chorused, "When you're older."

Chapter Eight

DEANNA TROI COULD READ the captain's mood. So could everybody else in the room.

"Where in hell is Stone?" he demanded.

It was an open question to everyone in the conference room. Worf, who was already seated, said, "I saw him several minutes ago. He said he would be right along."

"Right along." The words somehow had a more ominous sound to them when Picard said them. "He'll be right along."

Troi glanced around the room. There was a great deal of free-floating emotion, and she tried to pin it to the source. She sensed annoyance from the captain, puzzlement from Geordi La Forge, sympathy (sympathy for who?) from Beverly Crusher, and from Worf . . .

Her mind shied away from Worf. There was something about the Klingon, something that disturbed her. It had not always been there . . .

No. She knew exactly when it had occurred, when that wall between Worf and her had first been erected. She decided not to dwell on it, for the memories were still too painful.

At that moment the door to the conference room hissed open and Stone walked in.

Geordi, Worf, and Data, out of courtesy, half rose from their chairs. Picard remained icily frozen to his.

"I requested your presence with due speed, Commander," said Picard sharply.

"Yes, sir," was Stone's calm reply. "My apologies."

Slowly, deliberately, he walked along the side of the conference table to a vacant chair. Then he folded his hands and placed them on the table, looking expectantly to the captain.

Immediately, Deanna tried to get a surface impression from him, a general sketchy idea of the type of man he was.

"I imagine," Picard was saying slowly, "that introductions are in order." Quickly, even naming those that Stone had already met in order to fulfill protocol, Picard introduced each of his officers to Stone and Stone in return to them.

Stone inclined his head slightly to each one. His gaze, however, rested with Deanna.

His hard gaze locked with hers.

She felt waves of empathy. She got the overwhelming sense that there was so much to Stone, so much there, remarkable depths . . .

And it slammed shut. He blocked her. Blocked . . . her!

She didn't know whether to laugh out loud or gasp. The entire exchange had taken only a moment, but already a wealth of information had been exchanged.

But not everything.

She could force her way in. Humans could block her, yes, but if she put her mind to it, if she concentrated, she could overwhelm those blocks. Indeed, in crisis situations where the captain needed information to make a life or death decision, that was precisely what she would do.

This was not that, however. And for her to force her way into Stone's mind . . . it was just wrong. She would not, *could not* do something like that. To so override the wishes of another would be the equivalent of assault.

If she did something like that, it would destroy her inner peace. She would not have balance or the ability to hear the Singing Skies.

Stone seemed to be smiling at her discomfiture, a pain that only he understood. Troi forced herself to smile and meet his gaze, but he already seemed to be looking elsewhere, as if his mind had wandered. Yet instinctively, she knew it had not.

"Counselor?" It was Picard, sensing something was wrong.

She turned to him. "Yes, Captain?"

"Problem?"

"None at all."

"That's good to hear." He paused. "I certainly wish that I could say we did not have a problem, but such is not the case. A situation has arisen on the planet Culinan that demands our immediate attention.

"Culinan has been a monarchy for many years now, and the people were eager for a change. Many had felt that the current monarch, Ryne, had become far too oppressive."

"Recently," he continued, "Culinan's monarch decided he was willing to hold free elections for the first time in his planet's history. He asked the Federation for aid in implementing the election. A team of diplomats was sent in to aid them—strictly as observers and for guidance, you understand."

"Of course," said Troi.

"So," said Picard, "the election was held, Ryne was voted out—" he put his hands flat on the table "—and decided that he wasn't ready to go. He declared the election null and void and stated he was the winner. This brought his people to the point of revolt. Ryne promptly took the ambassadors hostage and is now stating that if the Federation does not aid him in quelling the uprising, he is going to kill the hostages."

"Nice guy," muttered Geordi.

"So we have been dispatched. We should be there within thirty-six hours at warp six, if that isn't a problem, Mr. La Forge."

"The *Enterprise* is humming along beautifully, Captain," said La Forge, adding with a smile, "thanks to her chief engineer."

"I wouldn't think of giving the credit to anyone else. Now then, since this is a serious diplomatic situation, I am considering leading the away team myself. Comments?"

"A poor move tactically," said Worf immediately. "Risking the captain is always to be avoided if at all possible."

"I'm not sure how possible that may be in this instance." He turned towards Stone and said, very deliberately, "What are your thoughts on this subject . . . Number One?"

There. He'd actually said it. Taken a step towards accepting Stone as Riker's replacement, albeit temporarily, by using that holdover military term that he'd so comfortably and casually applied to Riker.

Deanna Troi looked from the captain to Stone with great interest. This was exactly the type of situation where Riker would stridently try to curb Picard's instinct for leading his men in all ways, in all instances. Most of the time, Riker argued him out of it. Occasionally not, in which instances Riker seemed to get a little sulky.

Stone pursed his lips and then shrugged. "Go ahead. You're entitled to risk getting killed."

Dead silence.

"Are you saying," Picard said slowly, trying to comprehend what he'd just heard, "that you do not wish to head the away team?"

"No. I'm saying that if you want to do it instead, that's your right." He frowned. "Are you saying it's not, Captain?"

"Of course I'm not saying that!" said Picard, voice sharper than he would have liked.

"I'm saying," said Stone, "that if you wish to lead the away team, fine."

"And how would you view that?"

"As an indication of how little you trust me." He leaned forward, suddenly whipcord tense. He said tightly, "Because if Riker were here, you wouldn't hesitate to send him down. Correct?"

Picard's instinct was to reject the insinuation out of hand. And then, almost to his surprise, he realized he was nodding.

"All right," said Picard. "You think you can handle it? This situation on Culinan?"

"That's not the question, is it? The question is, do *you* think I can?"

The other members of the crew kept looking from Stone to Picard to Stone and back again. It was like watching a tennis match.

"I won't send you into a situation you feel you can't handle," said Picard.

"There isn't any such animal."

Picard suppressed an amazed chuckle. "You are that confident."

"Yes."

Stone's expression had never changed, never showed the slightest flickering of emotion. *Stone faced,* thought Troi.

For a long moment, Picard said nothing. Then he leaned back and said, "Make it so. You choose the away team, Commander, and you will lead it."

Stone inclined his head slightly. That was all.

Picard turned towards Beverly. "Dr. Crusher, prepare sickbay for potential casualties, although hopefully there won't be any. Above all, we want to get those diplomats out safely, without violating the Prime Directive. It will be something of a balancing act—without a net."

When the meeting adjourned minutes later, Picard made a silent nod towards Troi. Deanna was already so attuned to the captain that she had sensed his desire to talk with her in private before he even indicated it.

The moment the doors shut behind the others, Picard said to Troi, "Well, Counselor? Impressions?"

He didn't even have to specify impressions of what or of whom. They both knew what they were talking about.

"Commander Stone has a very powerful mind," she said slowly. "Very strong-willed. In a way, almost as strong-willed as you. But lacking your willingness to open up. He's very guarded."

"Secretive?"

"Cautious."

"He's hiding something."

She smiled. "Aren't we all."

He nodded at that, and rose from his chair. He walked the edge of the room slowly. Coming to the viewport he looked out as the stars raced away from them. "How much further could you probe with him?"

"I will not do it in such a way that it would violate his right to privacy," she said stiffly. "You could not ask me to do that, Captain."

"Nor would I," he said with assurance.

He hesitated, and Troi said, "You are still troubled."

Nodding, Picard turned toward her and said, "The general buzz in Starfleet is that our Commander Stone is a space case."

Her eyebrows knit at that. "They think he's insane?"

"Some hold that opinion, yes."

"Then what in heaven's name is he doing in a position of power on a starship?"

"Because," Picard said, "they have no proof. What is your feeling on it, Counselor. Best estimate. Is Commander Stone sane?"

"Yes."

"Is he crazy?"

"No."

He blinked at that and smiled slightly. "You sound quite certain considering that you only have surface impressions."

66

"Don't misread that term, Captain. What is surface for me would take three months of steady probing for a non-Betazoid to learn. And not quite as reliably." She paused, sensing that the captain was still having misgivings. "Insanity in a human is very easy to detect. Thought patterns are random or uncontrolled. Either that, or certain aspects are out of proportion to others . . . paranoia, for example. Even my surface reading of Commander Stone would detect that. His way of handling matters may be original, perhaps even outrageous, but he is not insane."

"Original," mused Picard. "For example, reverse psychology. He wants to make damned sure I stay on the ship, so instead, he urges me to go to the surface."

"There is that," Troi said with a smile.

"You think that's what he did."

"It presents itself as a possibility. Certainly, he was not intimidated by the thought of leading the away team. Nothing intimidates him, really. It's as if . . ." Her voice trailed off as she realized something. "He's not afraid of pain."

"I beg your pardon, Counselor?"

She tried to find words to phrase it and once again wished she were full Betazoid so that she could communicate telepathically and not be limited to clumsy verbiage. "Pain takes on many forms in humans," she said. "The pain of death, the pain of embarrassment, the pain of social ostracism . . . it's a very powerful emotion, and one of the most easily sensed. And . . . I didn't sense that from him."

"Meaning he doesn't have it?"

"Meaning he represses it so far down that it's not easily touched. And that is unusual."

"Odd," said Picard. "There's a human colloquial expression of 'feeling no pain,' generally meaning the individual is inebriated or otherwise in a pleasant, foggy haze."

"Commander Stone is definitely not 'foggy,' Captain."

"That is very true," said Picard. "And I cannot shake the

feeling that I should proceed with the utmost caution in how I deal with him."

Picard turned and headed for the bridge, and Troi followed him. For one moment she started when she saw Stone seated in Will Riker's chair. Then she realized that it wasn't Riker's chair, it was the chair of the second-in-command. Naturally, that would be where Stone should sit.

Still, it jabbed at her like a pin in her heart. She cleared her mind, regained her mental balance, and walked to her seat on the other side.

Picard went to his command chair, but did not yet sit. He never did when about to issue orders. "Mr. Crusher," he said to Wesley, "set course for Culinan, warp six."

Wesley's fingers flew over the board and he nodded surely. "Course laid in, sir."

Picard pointed with a slight snapping motion. "Engage."

Smoothly, the *Enterprise* angled off and kicked into the increased warp.

Picard eased down into his seat and turned toward Stone. He watched as the silent commander surveyed the bridge, taking in every detail. At length, Picard said, "What do you think of the bridge, Commander?"

Still looking straight ahead, Stone said, "Technically, very impressive, Captain."

Picard leaned forward quizzically. "I can't help but notice your emphasis on the word 'technically.' Is there some other aspect of the bridge that you find deficient?"

Slowly, Stone shook his head. "You don't want to know, sir. It'll make you angry."

All heads turned at this, and Picard was the most confused of all. "Commander Stone," he said carefully, "whatever disagreements you may have had with Captain Borjas, we do things differently on board the *Enterprise*. If we have concerns on our mind, we discuss them freely, without fear of reprisal. *That* is the sort of communication I was discussing earlier. I assure you, whatever you have to say, if it is presented in a calm and thoughtful manner, I will not get angry."

Calmly and thoughtfully, Stone said, "For one thing, the boy has to go."

Wesley went dead white.

From behind Stone, Worf rumbled, *"The boy?"*

"And the machine," Stone added.

Data turned around and looked at Stone.

"In the Ready Room, *now,*" said Picard angrily.

"I don't think we should go in the Ready Room," said Stone.

"Why not?"

"I'm not ready."

Picard slowly stood, towering over Stone. Stone, wisely, did not stand as well. "We have to talk," grated Picard.

Troi looked from one to the other. The waves of fury from Picard almost buffeted her like something living. And Stone—

Tranquil. At peace. Balanced.

But his voice was like iron as he said, "Captain, you asked for my opinion. I warned you. You disregarded it. I told you. And now you're upset with me."

Troi knew instinctively what was going through her captain's mind. Picard was blocked. He could order Stone into privacy, even have Worf pick him up and carry him there, which Worf seemed ready to do. But Stone was openly challenging him. All right, then. Open challenge, openly met. "You," said Picard tightly, "will learn respect for other crewmen."

"I have respect," shot back Stone. "I also have doubts. The bridge of a starship is no place for a kid, and I'm sorry, Mr. Crusher, but that's how I feel. You're an 'acting ensign,' whatever the hell that is. I don't know. Does anybody here know?"

Sharply, Picard said, "It means that Mr. Crusher, by his actions, has earned a position of responsibility on the bridge—"

"A position which could, and should, be filled by any of five dozen people on this ship, all of whom have been through Starfleet academy. And as for the android at Ops—"

Picard intensely disliked being in the position of defending his bridge crew, but Stone was clearly not going to let it drop. "Mr. Data is a valued member of the bridge crew."

"I don't like it, sir," said Stone. "I don't like having machines, no matter how sophisticated—sorry, Data—having positions of authority. Are you aware of the debacle over the M5 experiments, when they tried to put a computer in charge of a ship in lieu of a captain?"

"That was decades ago," retorted Picard. "Mr. Data is far more advanced than the M5 was."

"Even now, Starfleet is doing research to understand my makeup and capacity," Data added helpfully.

It didn't help. "Oh, that's wonderful!" said Stone. "He's in charge of Ops, and we don't even completely understand how he *works!*"

And now Stone stood, body language directly challenging Picard. "Commander," Picard said with dangerous quiet, "the sentiments you are expressing are completely out of line for someone wearing that uniform."

"Captain," Data spoke up thoughtfully, "you and Commander Riker voiced the same concerns."

Picard stopped in mid-thought and turned toward Data.

"In the past you quite clearly stated that children had no place on the bridge," said Data.

"Yes, but . . ." Picard found suddenly that he couldn't meet Wesley's look. "That was before I knew of Mr. Crusher's capabilities."

"And," continued Data thoughtfully, "as I recall, Commander Riker, as did Commander Stone, cited concerns about working with a machine. So although I obviously do not agree with Commander Stone's assessments, they would certainly seem consistent with earlier human reactions."

"Yes, but," Picard gestured helplessly, "it was the way in which Commander Stone said it."

And now Stone slowly sat, looking contrite. "I'm sorry, Captain," he said sincerely. "I'll try to be more tactful when giving my opinions in the future."

It was some time later when Troi entered Picard's ready room. The captain was sitting there, staring into empty space. Troi stood there, her hands folded in front of her, until Picard spoke.

"He did it to me, didn't he?"

She raised an eyebrow. "'It?' Captain."

"Made me look like a fool in front of my crew."

"They know you were standing up for them, sir."

He stood up and came around the desk, "So why is it that it seemed that I was some sort of bully?"

"You lost your sense of balance."

"Yes, I did, didn't I," he said. He sighed. "Thinking of how Stone so rattled Andy Borjas put me even more on my guard than I should have been. Made me overreact. Counselor, is Stone trying to make me lose my temper?"

She considered it. "I believe it's a control effort. He wants to have command of a situation. That, and also he may just want to see if he *can* make you lose your temper."

"Why?"

"I don't know." She paused, and then said, "There are ways to find out, though. Ways besides mental probes."

"Sounds like you need a detective," said Picard. He half smiled. "Where is Dixon Hill when you really need him?"

"Or Sherlock Holmes." She returned the smile. "But there are ways. And I will find them."

Troi came out of the ready room and saw Stone in the command chair, looking secure. He did not even look around when she emerged, and went past and up the ramp to the turbolift without so much as a word.

She returned to her quarters and pondered the situation for long minutes.

What was Stone trying to accomplish? Did he have some actual sort of plan? Was he simply reacting instinctively?

"Space case," she said out loud. A cheerful throwaway term to give gloss to a concept that was frightening: someone for whom the mysteries of space, the oppressiveness of the everlasting dark, the constant need for artificial protection, had become overwhelming. Something had just snapped, despite all the psychological preparation, all the certainties.

How could the unknown really be tested when it was, by definition, unknown?

But Stone wasn't insane. She was certain of it.

She went to her computer monitor, called up Stone's service record, and went to work.

Chapter Nine

ALTHOUGH THE TERRAIN of Starlight had naturally been smoothed out for the creation of the so-called tourist center of Paradise, there were still some rocky areas.

William T. Riker was seated on one now, gazing heavenward thoughtfully.

He remembered ancient legends of gods who had offended their superiors and been cast out, nevermore to share the kingdom of heaven. Riker, of course, didn't have enough of an inflated ego to think he was a god. But he had walked among the stars, seen them race past him in a dazzling array that he had come to accept as an everyday occurance. He'd taken it for granted.

Now, to look up into the sky and see the stars just sitting there, unmoving blobs of light against a black background; it just seemed *wrong* somehow.

Riker wanted to urge the planet to kick into warp two, leap forward toward the stars, and bring them close enough to touch once more.

No, not a god. Merely a mortal who was getting a taste of what it was like for a god to be sentenced to the world of mortals.

A soft voice spoke suddenly from behind him. "Commander?"

Riker turned, knowing who he would see before he saw her. "Hello, Stephy."

She smiled shyly as she approached him. "You want to be alone or something?"

"You mean do I mind if you join me?" She bobbed her head. "Go right ahead."

She sat down next to him on the rock, a little too close. He slid over a few inches to provide a discreet amount of distance between the two of them.

"What do you think of the planet so far?" she asked.

"Well, aside from the Wild Thing trying to eat me yesterday, it's been pretty calm," he said agreeably. "Your father's quite a man, trying to carve out a life for people here."

She half shrugged. "I guess."

Riker smiled at that. Somehow the children of great people always seemed underwhelmed by their parents; no matter what their accomplishments, there was still the attitude of "yeah, but it's just dad" or "but it's only mom."

"You miss your ship?" she said.

"How can you tell?"

"The way you stare off into the skies like that. Like the stars are your home."

He nodded. "They are, really. In a way, the history of space travel and exploration is the same as what is happening on this planet."

She looked around skeptically. Far in the distance, beyond the friendly confines of the metamorphosed atmosphere, lightning crackled in the sky. "You're kidding, right?"

"No, I'm not kidding," he said with a laugh.

"Space travel is glamorous," she said wistfully. "Go to strange, far-off planets and meet exotic life forms—"

"That want to eat you," he finished.

She shook her head and poked him in the shoulder. "Now you're making fun of me. Come on. Space exploration is nothing like this."

"You're looking at space traveling as it is now, and comparing it to this world as it is now. That's hardly fair. Space exploration in its early days was so dangerous they only sent animals up."

She blinked at that. "Animals flew the starships?"

"There were no starships!" he laughed. He held his hands out, palms facing each other about a foot apart. "There were space capsules about this big. Well, that's an exaggeration, but not much bigger than that. All that the early space explorer—they were called astronauts—could do was sit, for days at a time, and all the capsules could do was orbit the earth. When they landed on the moon, it was a major event."

"Do you have a girlfriend?"

Riker blinked in surprise. He had forgotten that talking with Wesley Crusher, who spoke casually on linear tracks, was not the typical interaction one had with a teenager. Stephy was suddenly no longer interested in discussing the relative merits of early versus modern space travel. Indeed, from the direction of the topic drift, it seemed likely that she hadn't been all that interested in the first place.

"A girlfriend?" he asked.

"Back on your ship," she said. "You know, a girlfriend. Or," she hesitated, "a fiancee. Or wife. Or wives."

He laughed at that. "No, no wife or wives."

"No girls you're close to."

"Oh, there's women I'm close to."

"How close?"

He looked at her curiously. "What, do you want names and dates?"

She gazed off into the sky. "I'm just curious as to how a guy who looks like you isn't hooked with any one woman, that's all. I mean, I would have thought that someone would have . . ."

"Well . . ." His voice trailed off.

Now she leaned forward eagerly. "There is someone, isn't there?" Her tone was a mixture of eagerness and . . . disappointment? Could that be?

"There's someone who has an . . . emotional grasp, let's say."

"Meaning she's always in your thoughts."

He nodded. "That's a very apt way of putting it."

"So you and she are together now."

"We were. Now we're friends. Well, more than friends, but . . . it's kind of complicated."

"I'm good at complicated things."

He sighed. "Let's just say that we had something and we're reluctant to rekindle it because . . . the timing's not right."

"For who?"

Riker laughed and shook his head. "You're like a dog with his teeth in a bone. You're not easy to shake loose, are you?"

"Nope."

"And what about you?" said Riker, hoping to turn things around a bit. "You have anyone?"

"In this place?" She made a derisive sound. "You're kidding, right?"

"There isn't anyone else here your age?"

"Well, sure there is, yeah. But the guys are so . . . immature."

"That will change."

"Not soon enough for me," she said forcefully.

She put a hand on Riker's knee.

Riker looked at it for a moment and then very gently removed her hand from his knee.

"Stephy . . ." he said.

"The kids call me Stephanie," she said hopefully. "It sounds more grown-up."

"But the adults call you Stephy," Riker said as kindly as

he could. "I'm an adult. And your father's friend. And . . . well, I prefer a more mature woman."

The minute he said it he wished he'd thought of a better phrase.

"Mature," she said, quietly smoldering. "Do you have any idea what my responsibilities are around here? How hard I work? How I'm out there breaking my butt, day in, day out, alongside the adults? But if you can't look beyond age, Commander Riker, then that is your problem." She stood. "For that matter, I'm not sure what you thought I was implying by my paying polite interest to you. If you'll excuse me, I have ground samplings I should be reviewing. You, of course, are more than welcome to remain here and continue to think about the more mature women in your life." And she turned and stalked off.

Riker sighed. Why was it that every single teenager he encountered seemed to be in such a damned hurry to grow up?

Wesley Crusher, his irritation evident, sat on the edge of one of the sickbay beds and said, "I can't believe you're on his side, mom. You didn't hear the things he said."

"Wes, not now, *please.*" Beverly Crusher was working on the forehead of a sobbing four-year-old girl, Jenny, who was lying flat and trembling. Her mother stood anxiously nearby, her hands fluttering nervously.

"All that blood," her mother wailed. "I thought she was—"

"She's fine. Aren't you fine, sweetheart?" Beverly smiled down at the child. The doctor had just finished wiping away the last of the blood that had covered the child's face. Her blond hair was still matted with it, but that could be attended to shortly.

The child sniffled in response.

"I told her not to run," her mother said for the tenth time since she'd dashed into sickbay, the hysterically crying child

77

in her arms. The mother's blouse still had blood stains on it, mixed with tears.

"It's really going to be all right," Beverly said again. It seemed to her that the mother was far more upset than the child. "Head wounds always look much worse than they are. There's a lot of bleeding, but—now see, there. There's the laceration."

And indeed, there was the source of the bleeding, high on the child's forehead. It was about a half-inch long, nasty looking and inflamed, but not especially serious.

Beverly reached for a small device that was shaped like an orange peel. She held it over the girl's head and a faint glowing from within the device highlighted the child for a moment. "This won't hurt at all," said Crusher.

"Really?" sniffed the girl.

"Really?" sniffed her mother.

"Really," confirmed Beverly. She placed the device on the girl's forehead. The child winced reflexively, anticipating pain, but there was none. Within minutes, Beverly removed it and there was no more cut; merely a pinkish line that was already fading and blending in with her skin.

"There," said Beverly. "All done."

"No more?" asked Jenny.

"No more," said the doctor. "You can get up . . ."

"But slowly," Wesley warned from nearby. "Wouldn't want your head to fall off."

A brief look of alarm crossed the child's face and Bev shot her boy genius son an annoyed glance. "He's kidding, Jenny."

"I'm kidding," confirmed Wesley.

Jenny sat up carefully, checking her neck just in case to affirm that her head was still attached.

"I tried to watch her," her mother said, feeling guilty.

"It's all right," said Beverly. "No matter how carefully they build a starship, a running child is always going to find some sharp edge somewhere to crack her head against. You slow down from now on, okay?" she said to Jenny, who nodded eagerly.

Bev watched the two of them go, shaking her head. "Centuries ago," she said, "for a minor thing like that, first they would have had to inject, with metal needles, an anesthetic that would have given her a lump in her skull like this." She made a circle with her thumb and forefinger. "Then they would sew it up with sutures. Then they'd have to cut them off. And it would leave scars."

"Sounds nice," said Wesley.

"As nice as you sounded," she said, remembering that she was annoyed with him. She slapped him lightly on the knee. "'Your head will fall off.' Good lord, Wesley, where's your bedside manner? Here I hear all these things about how you've become so mature and responsible in my absence, and then you say brilliant things like that."

"I was just kidding. Besides, not everyone thinks I'm so mature."

"No one will if you keep acting the way you did." She was briskly putting her instruments away.

"You should have heard him, mom. Commander Stone was saying I shouldn't be on the bridge."

"Commander Stone doesn't know you, or what you're capable of," his mother said calmly.

"Well he shouldn't jump to conclusions. He should trust Captain Picard's judgment that I belong there."

She slid the drawer closed and looked a bit sad. "To be honest, Wes . . . I don't think Commander Stone trusts much of anyone. He's been through a lot."

Wes tilted his head curiously. "Like what?"

"Like things I can't discuss," his mother said primly. "Like things that are protected by doctor-patient confidentiality. Like shouldn't you be somewhere else," she added, ruffling his hair fondly. "I have things to do."

"Right, right." He slid off the bed and started to head out. Then he turned and said, "By the way, O'Brien was very anxious to know if you would be at next week's poker game."

She winced and shooed her son away.

Wesley went up to the Ten-Forward lounge intending to talk with Guinan. His mother had been right, of course, but still he had the feeling she didn't quite understand. In his mother's absence, Wes had found that the Ten-Forward's hostess had always had a sympathetic and understanding ear. Even better than his mother, in a way. When Guinan gave advice, Wesley felt that he could take it or not, at his discretion. With his mother, however, there always seemed to be an attitude of "if you don't take my advice, what did you ask me for?"

He breezed into Ten-Forward and stopped short.

Stone was sitting there, nursing a drink. He glanced up, caught Wesley's eye. Wanting to avoid a fight, Wesley started to back up.

Stone didn't move, except his hand. He waggled a finger at Wes, making quite clear that he wanted Wes to join him.

He outranks me, Wes thought unhappily. Gulping deeply, he walked over and sat down across the table from Stone.

Stone eyed him thoughtfully for a moment and then said, "I've been checking up on you."

"Really?" Wes didn't know what to make of that.

Stone nodded. "Pretty impressive. They call you the Brain Trust, I hear."

Wesley sighed. "I hate that name."

"Why? Because it makes you ashamed of your accomplishments?"

Wes looked up in surprise. "That's it exactly."

"Never let anyone do that to you," Stone said flatly. "Always make them come up to your level. Never descend to theirs."

He sipped his drink and Wes watched him, filled with curiosity. Wes remembered the little girl and said, indicating Stone's face, "My mom could fix up those scars. Like the one on your face."

"What, this?" He pointed at it. "Heidelberg fencing scar. My father was a fencing instructor there, in fact. He taught me everything I know . . . not everything he knew, of course." He paused. "He didn't have the chance."

"Why?" said Wes.

Stone paused and seemed to be visually dissecting Wes.

"Can I trust you?" he said at length.

"Uh . . . sure," said Wes.

"I mean *really* trust you. For example, I don't need any of this getting back to your mother."

"I wouldn't mention it if you didn't want me to," said Wes. He was now totally confused. He had thought that Stone couldn't stand him, and now Stone was acting as if Wes was his long lost brother or something.

"I don't . . ." Stone stopped, and then started again hesitantly. "I don't talk about myself much. Never a good idea. Don't give out pieces of yourself."

"I understand," said Wes, who didn't.

"But you,"—he looked at him appraisingly—"you remind me of myself when I was your age."

Wes squinted, trying to see the resemblance. It was not readily apparent. "If you say so, sir."

"I say so." He nodded. "Stupid, stupid accident. You know, when you fence, you're supposed to have safety tips on the points."

"So that you don't stab somebody," Wesley said.

Stone smiled thinly. "Exactly. So that you don't stab somebody." He paused. "My father's best student and he were having a marvelous match. Dazzling. Blades moved so quickly they were a blur. You heard the duel rather than saw."

Stone stopped speaking for a long moment, and Wesley prompted, "And? . . ."

"And the student's safety tip fell off during one particular engagement. They didn't notice, and the student riposted

81

and thrust, fully extending. The blade slipped in under the bib of the mask, right here." He tapped the base of his throat at the collarbone. "And kept on going. Came out the back of dad's neck." He made a slight whistling sound and mimed the action.

Wesley felt the blood drain from his face. "Oh man," he whispered. "Did you . . . were you there?"

"Of course I was there," said Stone, sounding distant. "I saw my father slide down off the sword and I ran forward, screaming. And the student was so horrified that he stepped back, yanking the sword away. He didn't see that I was right behind him, the sword whipped around . . ."

"And that's how you got the scar on your face," Wes said in sudden understanding.

Stone nodded. "I was lucky, really. Fraction of an inch one way, my eye is gone. Another way, my ear is lopped off. As it was . . ." He shrugged.

"That must have been awful. How old were you?"

"I was a kid." He paused and slid closer to Wes. "That's why I reacted the way I did. I saw something horrible when I was young, before I was ready, and I can tell you I was never the same. So I was alarmed at the thought of hurrying you along. Enjoy being a kid. Don't be in a rush to grow up. It's not all it's cracked up to be."

"It's not, huh?" said Wes with a small laugh. He felt himself beginning to relax with Stone.

"No, it's not. When you're young you think that you grow up and all the answers to everything appear in your head. You won't be stupid anymore. Adulthood is the realization that stupidity is permanent and terminal."

"Oh, I don't know," said Wes. "I know lots of smart adults. Like my mom. And Captain Picard."

"Everyone is stupid," he repeated more firmly. "There's different degrees, and some people are better at hiding it than others. But it's congenital."

Then slowly, he shook his head. "See. See what happens when bad things happen to you when you're young? You become cranky and cynical like me. You're lucky you don't have to deal with that."

Wesley looked down hesitantly and then up again. "I know what it's like," he said. "My dad died when I was little."

Stone looked stricken. "No. Aw, kid, I'm sorry. I had no idea. I assumed your father was an officer somewhere on the ship. So it's just you and your mother?"

Wes nodded. "For a while it was just me, but mom came back to the *Enterprise.* It's really great having her back, but, you know, you get to a point where she's still trying to treat me like I'm a kid. And I've had so much responsibility while she was gone, that it's hard to be what she expects and what Captain Picard expects, and switch back and forth."

"Be what you expect and let others switch back and forth," said Stone firmly.

Suddenly, Wes realized the time. "Uh oh. I have a lesson in astrodynamics I have to get to."

"Then you better get to it," Stone smiled that same, damned weird smile, but Wes decided to think nothing of it. So Stone was a little offbeat. Everyone had their little quirks. Wes stood and, to his surprise, Stone stood with him and extended a hand. Wesley shook it, endeavoring to squeeze as hard as he could, and Stone nodded curtly.

Wes grinned. There was nothing like a firm, man-to-man handshake to kick you up a few notches in your personal self-esteem. Wes walked out feeling pretty pleased with himself. He stopped, turned, and said, "You're nothing like Commander Riker." He walked out.

Stone sat back down and immediately all the signs of relaxation vanished from his body. It reverted to a tense, whipcord posture. He sat broodingly until he detected rather than heard a soft footfall behind him.

He glanced around at the odd woman behind him. "And you are—?"

"Guinan," she replied, her voice pleasantly melodic. "I'm the hostess."

He frowned and said, "You aren't in the ship's records."

"I'm flattered you checked." She seated herself opposite him. She was dressed in long, flowing blue robes that gave no hint of the shape of her body. A hat of matching color that looked like a flying saucer sat perched precariously on her head.

He had seen her smiling at others, from the corner of his eye, and it had been warm and genuine. But now there was the same sort of mirthlessness that was in his own smile.

He found it stimulating.

Continuing, she asked, "You've been researching the ship's personnel."

"The main officers, yes, as soon as I learned I'd be coming aboard. The others I've been looking up when I've found time."

"Yet," she said, "you act as if things that are told to you are revelations."

He took her measure and found her intriguing. He lowered his guard a fraction, which was as much as he ever lowered it. "People like to talk about themselves. They can't do that if they know you know it all."

Slowly, she shook her head. "It's a game to you, isn't it?"

He made no reply.

Then her voice changed, became lower and more intense. "These people are my friends."

Still he made no reply.

"Stay away from Beverly Crusher."

At that he blinked, then sighed in relief. "There it is," he said.

"The challenge."

"Yes."

"The threat."

"You are threatening, then?" he asked with detached amusement.

"Promising. Promising trouble."

"You could make trouble now."

"You could make more. And you could make great good,

84

but you have to do it yourself. If I stop you, you'll never get better."

He looked at her askance. "What are you saying?"

"I'm saying stay away from Beverly. She's off limits in whatever mind games you're playing."

"Mind games," he said tightly. "Is that what you think?"

"She's in mourning."

"For her husband?" There was open incredulity on his face. "It's been a decade. More."

"And every day for every year of that decade, she hasn't shaken the notion that somehow her husband is going to walk through the door. Even though she watched them put his body in the ground. She still hasn't admitted the unfairness of it all."

"You know a great deal about matters," said Stone.

"I know everything," she replied.

"Everything?"

"Yes. It's easier. That way I don't have to be selective." She paused. "Beverly is a walking open wound. Don't touch her."

"Or what? You'll sick Picard on me?" he laughed.

"Worse. Troi."

Stone leaned back, looked at Guinan as if trying to figure whether she was joking or not. "Troi."

"Yes. You've built enough walls that Picard can't get to you. But Troi could."

"You have a vivid imagination, Guinan," replied Stone. "Walls, eh?"

She nodded. "Stone walls. But deep inside those walls, where you're hiding, you know what Troi could do."

"Burn."

She tilted her head slightly in curiosity. "What?"

"Burn," he repeated. "Troy . . . burned. When something entered that great city, something that had things hidden within, it overran Troy. And Troy burned with a glorious light that left nothing but ruins."

"The Trojan horse."

He nodded. "The Trojan horse."

He rose from his seat, looked down at Guinan. "You think she could handle me."

"Easily."

"You'd warn her."

"I wouldn't have to," said Guinan. "There's nothing I could tell her that she doesn't already know."

"Oh," said Stone. "I see. She knows everything, too."

"No. But she's not lazy, like me. She's selective. And she knows the right things."

"That's comforting," he said. He turned and started to head out of the Ten-Forward lounge.

From behind him, Guinan called, "It wouldn't hurt you to learn the difference between right things and wrong things, too."

He stopped, turned, and smiled that bizarre smile.

"I know them," he said. "I just don't believe them."

Chapter Ten

DEANNA TROI SAT BACK in her chair and rubbed her eyes. She felt as if she had been at it for hours. She probably had been.

She pulled her legs up onto the chair and sat serenely in a precarious lotus position. Troi stared straight ahead but her eyes began to lose their focus. She sensed the beating of her heart, a soft, rhythmic sound, and concentrated until it filled the whole of her being. Then she let the sound fade, lull her, and she was floating as if in the womb, her mother's heartbeat providing a steady and distant lullaby.

Her mind wandered.

Stone.

A very impressive record. Very impressive—and eclectic. Commendations of valor, ingenuity, heroism, interspersed with complaints, charges—*anger, fury*—

With his record, he could be a captain. The youngest captain in the fleet in eighty years—but he wasn't. He could be popular with all officers—but he wasn't.

Why?

Why was his life so totally out of control? How could an officer so sharp, so intelligent, let things develop in this way?

All he was doing was hurting himself. Why was he letting this happen?

His psych profile was clean.

Which either meant that the psych profile was wrong, which was highly unlikely, or that something had happened. Something that had triggered a change.

Or . . .

He actually was totally in control.

Or a combination of both.

But if he was in control of his mind to that degree, how could his life spin out of control?

What if—

What if it wasn't out of control? What if he was doing exactly what he wanted to do?

Be only a commander, be unpopular, be a space case.

Why? It didn't make sense.

Humans valued the acceptance of their peers. But not Stone.

Stone not human?

She paused, considering that one. Some sort of disguised alien? Heaven help them, *Q?*

She considered and dismissed it. She'd sensed his thoughts, albeit briefly. He was human. She would stake her life on that.

Which left her with exactly what? That Stone was acting contrary to established human norms.

Which could mean he was crazy.

But he wasn't. She would stake her life on that, too.

His thoughts were too orderly, concise, controlled.

There was that word again. *Controlled.*

Was he in control, or wasn't he?

Did something happen, or didn't it? Did he want to be accepted, or not? If not, why not?

She slowed down the beating of her heart, regulating the flow of blood to her mind.

Premise: Stone was not crazy.

Premise: Stone was in control.

Observation: Stone was not popular and/or accepted with a number of people.

Supposition: Stone could be popular and/or accepted if he so desired.

Conclusion: He did not so desire.

Question: Why?

Because he: wants to prove a point? Wants to show his independence? Is afraid of losing those things once attained? Feels he doesn't deserve them? Feels they're unimportant? Feels they're dangerous?

What?

What could it be?

What could it *be?*

Slowly, Deanna brought the beating of her heart back up to normal speeds. Her eyelids fluttered, her eyes snapped back into focus.

Eyes looked back at her.

She jumped slightly, gasping in surprise, as Stone's rugged features filled her field of vision. And then were gone.

She shook her head, trying to pull together her scrambled thoughts. Her head snapped around just in time to see the doors of her quarters hiss shut.

She had not imagined it. Stone had been in there, in her quarters, watching her.

For how long? She wasn't sure how long she herself had been in her meditative trance, much less how long Stone had been observing her.

She rose, stretching her legs which were tingling from the lack of circulation. And then she saw something on her table that hadn't been there before.

Two chess pieces.

A white queen and a black king.

She picked them up in her hand and examined them. They were exquisitely made, and she knew instinctively that they hadn't been made on the ship. These had been carved by hand. And they were beautiful.

The message was not lost on her. Female and male, light

and dark, each one capable of conquering the other. But it would require strategy, maneuvering.

She held the king up to the light, admired the way it glistened off the smooth coolness of the surface. She looked at it for long moments, certain that there was something else there that she should be seeing, but not certain what it could be.

Then she noticed something in the base of the king. It was a small crack, so small that casual inspection would not have revealed it.

Accidental? An oversight? Or was Stone dropping a hint?

The appearance of perfection, but actually with a minute flaw that one had to look carefully to find.

"Opening gambit," she said softly.

"You wanted to see me, Counselor?" asked Data.

"Yes, Data," said Deanna, sitting back in her chair. Data sat across from her, waiting patiently. She couldn't help but notice that others who came to her quarters would invariably let their attentions wander, looking at the fascinating artifacts and treasures from her travels she kept on display. Not to mention the more exotic items from Betazed.

But for all that, Data's attention did not wander. He merely sat there, waiting for her to continue, his golden eyes gleaming in the pleasant dimness in which she kept her quarters.

"I was wondering," she said, "what you know about the planet Ianni."

Data's eyes seemed to look inward for a fraction of a second, as if he were visually scanning printed matter from his brain. "Ianni, fifth planet of seven in the Roze system," he said promptly. "A member of the Federation. Oxygen/nitrogen atmosphere, breathable. Humanoid population, at last census count—"

He went on for five minutes, and could not help but feel the merest flicker of surprise. Counselor Troi was not interrupting him. That was most unusual. Nine times out of ten, whenever he was asked for information, he was stopped before he could complete the narrative. It was a curious human habit.

He remembered that once, in trying to act more human, he had taken to interrupting people while they were talking to him by saying "Thank you, that's all," or even better, "Shut up." It was a very short-lived experiment.

When he finished, Troi nodded. "Thank you, Data. Very comprehensive. However, much of what you told me was already in the ship's records."

"That does not surprise me," said Data. "May I ask, Counselor, why you are interested? If it is not prying."

She paused, weighing matters. "In confidence, Data?"

"If that is your desire," he replied.

"Three years ago, Commander Stone was in command of an away team that had contact with Ianni, while he was serving aboard the *Moniter*. It was shortly after that that the complaints about his being difficult to work with began to surface."

"Difficult to work with." Data nodded slowly. "I must admit, Counselor, that my first encounters with Dr. Pulaski were . . . strained. Now it seems Commander Stone displays the same technological biases."

"It is hard to tell with Commander Stone," said Troi. "He seems more concerned with the results of what he says rather than with the actual statements he makes."

"I see." Data paused. "Are there any records as to what happened on Ianni?"

"The only records that we have," she said, "are the notations that were made on Commander Stone's files." She leaned forward, the files in question still on her viewer. "'Commander Stone acted in the best interests of the Federation and solidly followed Starfleet regulations in the face of a difficult situation.'" She sat back. "Not exactly a stinging indictment."

"We need to obtain the *Moniter* ship's logs for more information," said Data. "Starfleet itself would have to be contacted for that. It will take time. Of course, we could always ask Commander Stone."

She smiled thinly. "That," she said, "is not the best option in my opinion. You will find, Data, that in psychology, the best question to ask is the one to which you already know the answer."

Data looked at her in curiosity, tilting his head. "Why is that? It would seem that asking such questions serves little purpose."

"Oh, it serves a tremendous purpose," she said. "It gets people talking."

"Some complain," Data said with a sigh, "that that is my main fault. I talk too easily. And at length."

"They don't understand what makes you special, Data."

Data nodded at that. "I am very complex."

"If you could contact Starfleet for me—?"

"I shall attend to it immediately."

In Jackson Carter's living room, Riker eased himself slowly out of the chair, moaning softly. Carter stood above him, grinning. "Told you that you were out of shape."

Ellie was bringing tea to the two of them as Carter pulled off the heavily lined gear he'd been wearing. Riker had already removed his own and was slumped back, shaking his head. "On the *Enterprise* I'm one of the most fit men on the ship. Ellie, you're a lifesaver," he said and took the tea.

"Standards must be different there," said Carter as he dropped down into the chair opposite.

"Don't listen to him, Will," said Ellie as she brought tea over to Carter. He grabbed at her impishly and she spun away, laughing and saying, "Oh, that's brilliant, Jack! Fool around while I'm holding hot tea."

She approached him again and handed him the cup of tea. He took it graciously, then suddenly put it down on the table next to him and grabbed her by the waist. "Got you this time!" he shouted, and Ellie gave a mock shriek of mirth as he pulled her down on top of him.

Stephy stuck her head out of the kitchen and made disapproving, clucking noise. "Act your age, you guys," she scolded them and retreated back to the kitchen.

"We have to act our age," said Carter contritely, and kissed Ellie on the bridge of her nose. She swung her legs up and was now comfortably seated across his lap, looking as if she was going to be there for some time.

"You have a special someone back on your ship?" asked Ellie.

Riker put the tea down and laughed. "This seems to be a running thing in your family."

"Why? Who else asked?"

Riker inclined his head in the direction of the kitchen.

"Aaaaaah," said Ellie, understanding. "She wanted to know if you were unattached for her own, nefarious needs."

"Isn't that why you wanted to know?" asked Carter.

"What, for my own nefarious needs?"

"Right."

She stared at her husband thoughtfully. "I should've spilled the tea on you when I had the chance. It could only have been an improvement."

"So what did you tell her?" asked Carter. "Although you are aware, of course, that should you lay a finger on her, I'd break your kneecaps."

"Don't be ridiculous," laughed Riker.

"What, you think I couldn't break your kneecaps?" Carter deadpanned.

"Hey, anyone who can handle what we just went through with as little trouble as you could probably take me on," said Riker. "But you know that I would never—"

"Of course I know," said Carter. "I remember you didn't like younger women even when *you* were that young. And besides that, since Will is going to be here for a month, he wouldn't want to get involved with anyone. He's more a love 'em and leave 'em kind of guy. Always looking for variety, right, Thunderball?"

"That's one way of looking at it," said Riker dryly.

"But he's got the gift," said Carter. "No woman was ever able to resist him. Right, guy?"

"Well . . ."

"Ohhhh," said Ellie. "The truth revealed now." She slid off Carter's lap and onto the arm of the chair. "There's somebody on board the *Enterprise* playing hard to get?"

"Let's just say," said Riker, pausing to find the phrase that would be the least embarrassing. "She's special and if I were inclined to settle down, she'd probably be the one."

"Of course," Carter started to laugh, "what she'd want with a corpse I haven't got the foggiest. 'Cause that's the only thing I can see that would cool your nacelles."

"This" said Ellie, "from the man who, the day of our wedding, was dropped off half-drunk at the chapel with the words 'Better dead than wed' stencilled on his forehead."

"A wedding gift from some friends," explained Carter ingenuously, "of which you were not among, Will, I might add. Hot shot who had to run off early to get into the Academy."

"I had a lot of eagerness back then," said Riker thoughtfully.

"And a lot of anger," added Carter, suddenly serious. "Tell me, did you ever get things sorted out with your father?"

"We've . . . found a common ground," said Riker.

"I'm glad to hear that," said Carter with genuine concern.

"So what did you two big, strong men do today, anyway?" asked Ellie.

"Mountain climbing."

"Mountain climbing?" She suddenly looked nervous. "Oh Jack, not the Hidden Hills."

"No, no, of course not," he retorted. "Total other direction. Went up the side of Umbo Mountain. It was fairly balmy today."

"Balmy! It was just above freezing!" said Riker.

"Right. Balmy. Usually it's just below freezing. C'mon,

Will, that place was an anthill next to some of the babies we used to scale."

Riker continued to sip his tea, feeling the warmth spreading through his chest. "What's this Hidden Hills place?"

"Dangerous," said Ellie succinctly.

"Pretty nasty stuff," agreed Carter. "Lots of hidden crevices. You could be walking along and suddenly find yourself buried under two hundred feet of snow. Or fall off a cliff that the wind blinded you to. And the weather gets particularly nasty over there. Not that the weather is any great shakes anyplace else on this Godforsaken pile of rock, but Hidden Hills has a special place in our hearts."

"Thanks for not taking me over there."

"My pleasure."

The three of them talked until very late that evening. When Riker finally went to bed, he fell asleep the moment his head hit the pillow.

By the time he woke up the following noontime, the family had vanished.

Chapter Eleven

THE *ENTERPRISE*'S FIRST COMMUNICATIONS with Culinan were less than promising.

Picard emerged from the ready room as Wesley Crusher brought the great starship into orbit. Wordlessly, Stone rose from the command chair and slid into the first officer's place next to it. Picard and Stone exchanged a glance, and Picard noted that his first officer's look was carefully, guardedly neutral.

At a summons from Picard, Deanna Troi appeared on the bridge a moment later. Stone looked her way momentarily and nodded before looking back at the viewscreen.

"Hailing frequencies," Picard said.

"Open," replied Worf, and a channel was established to the planet below.

"Culinan, this is the *Enterprise*," Picard said with authority. "Come in please. We are here in regards to the individuals you've captured."

After a moment, Worf said, "Receiving a reply, Captain."

"On visual, Lieutenant."

An image shimmered into existence on the screen. The individual had a thick Vandyke beard, and his closely shaven black hair hugged his head in an eccentrically cut pattern. His eyes were thin, narrow slits, and when he spoke, it was with a low, deep rasp. "This is Ryne. I am the Praedor of Culinan."

Picard inclined his head slightly. "We have come to discuss the release of the hostages you have taken."

"In our great square," said Ryne, "are massed millions of people. They insist I step down."

"Praedor Ryne," said Picard, "I understand your concern . . ."

"Do you?" said Ryne sarcastically. "You have many people on your ship, Captain?"

"Yes," said Picard, "but I don't—"

"Have you ever been in a position where they all wanted you relieved of your command?"

"Praedor, we can discuss our mutual feelings on this matter at our leisure. As it is, the most pressing concern we have is the hostages."

"Your pressing concern is not mine. Here is what I want, Captain. You are to turn your ship's weapons onto the coordinates I specify, and open fire. That will dispatch those who would have me out and will help solidify my position. Once you have done that, we can discuss terms."

"That is out of the question," said Picard tightly, jaw set.

"Not at all. For me, that *is* the question. Just how determined are you to save these people of yours?"

"We will not bow to pressure from you," Picard replied. "We will not kill or even stun your people. Even if our Prime Directive did not exist, it would be completely unethical for us to do as you suggest."

"I don't recall any suggestions," said Praedor Ryne. "Simply a statement of what must be done. And I shall tell you something further, Captain. You have precisely one hour in which to act. After that I shall kill one of the hostages. And another, and another. One an hour. There are four hostages in all, and within five hours they will all be dead."

"That is unacceptable," said Picard.

Ryne actually smiled. "I'm not asking for your acceptance. I'm asking for your power. And you will provide it. If you wish to discuss this further, I expect you or your people down here in short order. But I would not wait too long a time."

The image blinked out.

In the Conference Lounge just off the bridge, the mood was tense among the senior officers. Picard turned towards Stone and said, "Your first assignment seems to have its sticking points."

"I can handle it," said Stone calmly.

Picard turned his attention to Troi. "Counselor, what is your feeling of Ryne? Is he frightened? Desperate?"

Slowly, she shook her head. "It may seem like an act of desperation," she said. "But the praedor is quite calm. Confident, in fact. He has been in power for so long that he is quite convinced he will never be removed from it. He is certain that he has thoroughly analyzed the situation."

"Does he really think we will just dispatch his people for him?" Picard asked incredulously.

"I cannot determine the specifics," she said. "Merely that he is confident of an outcome in his favor."

"We'll rattle his confidence a little," said Stone.

"Mr. Data," Picard was now addressing his second officer, "I want you to be scanning the planet surface. The ideal situation would be for us to lock onto the ambassadors via their life readings, transport them up and be done with it."

"I agree, sir," said Data. "However, the life signs of the ambassadors are quite close to those of Culinan residents. It is not as if I were scanning for, say, a Horta. In this instance, I am forced to scan every individual in hopes of pinpointing the handful we need."

"Keep at it, nevertheless. Commander Stone," he stepped forward to face the new number one, "operate with extreme tact."

"Tact. Yes, sir."

"Keep the Prime Directive in mind at all times. No interference with the development of the society."

"Prime Directive. No interference. Got it."

Stone sounded entirely too flip for Picard's taste, and for a moment Picard considered reversing his decision and heading the away team himself. He dismissed the idea for two reasons.

First, nothing was going to be accomplished in terms of Stone's development as an officer if Picard did not put him into the customary situations that a first officer faced.

Second, the prime rule of command was: Make a decision and stick to it. Any decision, even one subsequently proven to be wrong, can be defended on the basis that, with all the available information at the time, it seemed like the correct move. But vascilating on a decision would be ultimately destructive to crew morale and confidence in the commanding officer.

Picard was not about to let that happen. Especially with the space case on board.

"Have you selected your away team?" he asked.

Stone nodded. "I felt, considering that this is a dangerous situation, that it would be best to keep the away team small."

Data half turned in his chair. "To minimize the number of potential losses?"

There was actual amusement in Stone's eye at that, and Picard winced.

"Data," said Picard slowly. "You simply must find a more delicate way of phrasing things."

"Oh." Data thought about it a moment. "Is it to minimize the number of people who might not be coming back?"

The thought flashed unbidden through Picard's mind: *Please, Stone, for God's sake, take him with you.* But he didn't say it.

Stone glanced around. "I'd like to bring Lieutenant Worf, Counselor Troi, and an additional security man, chosen at your discretion, Lieutenant." Worf nodded in silent approval, and Stone continued, "We'll meet in five minutes in the transporter room."

"Be careful," Picard said, "when dealing with Praedor Ryne."

Stone said nothing, and Picard had the sudden feeling that Praedor Ryne would best be the one to be careful.

As he approached the transporter room, Stone heard a female voice call his name. He slowed his stride just enough to allow Deanna Troi to catch up.

"Are you excited about your first mission as *Enterprise* first officer?" she asked as they walked briskly towards the transporter.

"Can't you tell?" he replied.

"You seem calm."

"There's your answer, then."

"But you should be excited."

"You mean I'm not living up to your expectations?" He shook his head. "That is really more your problem than my problem, don't you think?"

"I see. So you have a different problem, then."

"You'll just have to dig a little deeper to find out, eh?"

"Perhaps I will." She paused just outside the transporter room door. Stone stopped and said, "Coming?"

"I would imagine," said Troi with careful casualness, "that this type of mission should be routine for you . . . after the business on Ianni."

She got what she wanted.

For just a moment, his calm, icy demeanor slipped, and she was buffeted by a wave of emotion unleashed by the mention of that planet.

It was as if a cork had been shot explosively from a bottle of champagne, but what bubbled up was not a pleasantly festive liquid to tickle one's nose and celebrate a momentus occasion.

There was the pain she had wondered about, the hurt,

and . . . blood. My God, all the blood. So much blood. *Blood on my hands* Troi thought wildly, *so much blood on my hands.* She held her palms up in front of her.

Nothing. The emotional torrent subsided as if a lever had been turned, the flow shut off.

Her chest was heaving wildly and she put her hand against it to calm herself. She searched in herself for the neutral place, for balance, and was still disoriented.

She looked up. Stone was watching her from what seemed a long, long way away, as if he were at the end of a long tunnel. From a great distance his voice said softly, "You've been reading up on me. I'm flattered."

Controlled. Calm. Barriers in place once more.

Deanna pulled herself together as she said, her voice rough, "It's my responsibility as counselor to be familiar with everyone on the ship."

"How familiar?" he asked, taking a step closer.

"Familiar enough."

"And who defines 'familiar enough'?"

"I do," was the sharp reply.

He nodded, and then spoke. "For now."

He turned and walked into the transporter room and Troi, after taking a moment longer to compose herself, followed him in.

O'Brien was at the transporter console and Troi paused there a moment, watching him work briskly. He was busy setting coordinates so that the away team would be beamed down to the point of origin of Ryne's transmission. Troi glanced over toward the transporter pads, where Stone was in deep conversation with Worf, Captain Picard (who had obviously come down to see them off), and security officer Buchanan. She was a compact, muscular woman who reminded Troi faintly of Tasha Yar.

In a voice too soft for anyone to hear except Troi, O'Brien muttered, "You know what I like about being transporter chief?"

Troi smiled at him. By striking up a casual conversation,

O'Brien was clearly trying to show that there were no hard feelings as a result of the poker difficulties. "What would that be?" she asked.

"The transporter is the great equalizer," he said, still keeping his voice down so that only Troi could hear him. "And I'm in charge of it all. Y'see, to me, everybody is just molecules, that's all. And nobody's molecules are more important than anybody else's."

And to O'Brien's shock, Picard suddenly turned and said dryly, "Speak for yourself, Chief."

Troi stifled a laugh as Picard turned back to Stone. O'Brien looked at Troi in shock and mouthed, *He hears everything.*

Picard was saying to Stone, "Remember, exhibit caution. The main concern is the safety of the ambassadors, but we cannot let that override the Prime Directive."

"No interference in development, yes sir, I know," said Stone. If he was exasperated with the repetition, he didn't let it show. In fact, Troi thought he sounded oddly distant, as if his mind were already leaping forward in anticipation of other matters. "We'll be fine."

"Stay in constant touch."

Stone nodded, his mind apparently elsewhere.

And then they were gone.

On the planet's surface, the away team materialized in the communications center of the capital building.

The first thing they reacted to was heard rather than seen. Chanting, yelling, and hatred were all around them. It was so overwhelming that for a brief moment they thought they were surrounded.

But the communications center was relatively empty. Only a skeleton staff was on duty, and one of them, a tall, lean individual who identified himself as Clarke, bowed slightly to each of them upon introduction.

"I apologize for the disturbances," said Clarke, "and the

unfortunate circumstances of your arrival." He had to speak loudly to be heard over the chanting.

Stone glanced around. "What the hell is going on?"

Clarke gestured towards a large window and the away team approached it cautiously. Stone started to step up to it but Worf interceded, placing himself between the window and the first officer. He gave Stone a look that said, *stay there,* and peered out first.

What he saw was a massive gathering of people, the most he'd ever seen in one place. A mob composed of individuals, but which seemed to have taken on a life all its own. A massive, throbbing life, swaying and moving like a headless serpent. They were shouting, chanting, demanding the removal of Ryne as the monarch and praedor.

Worf sensed Stone looking over his shoulder. "Doesn't look good," Worf observed. Stone nodded curtly.

Stone turned towards Troi and immediately sensed the Counselor's distress. Her body was rigid and tense, her gaze locked. Stone went to her, put his hands on her shoulders, and said "What's wrong?"

Troi closed her eyes a moment, trying to block out the chanting. "So much emotion," she whispered. "Overwhelming. I'm just—it will take a moment or two, that's all. I have to adjust."

"Take your time," said Stone. He moved behind her and then Troi felt his fingers digging into the tense muscles of her shoulders. "Just relax," he murmured. "You'll be fine."

Indeed, the manipulation of her muscles was easing the tension. Her eyes were half-closed, her shoulders now moving in slow rhythm with Stone's fingers, and then through her half-shut eyes she saw Worf looking at her curiously.

She cleared her throat and straightened herself, shrugging away Stone's fingers. "That will be fine, thank you, Commander," she said formally.

"Do you wish to see the praedor?" asked Clarke.

"Yes," Stone said. "Immediately."

Clarke walked away briskly, leaving the handful of communications monitors at their posts.

Stone was studying the room carefully, taking in every corner and crack. Troi couldn't help but notice the way his gaze darted about, taking in everything. He was a most intriguing individual.

Now why did she feel guilty thinking that? Even disloyal?

An image of Riker popped unbidden into her mind and she promptly dismissed it. Now was not the time to go off on a tangent.

Worf stepped up to Stone and said in a low voice, "Not the most technologically advanced of equipment."

Stone nodded slowly. "Whatever works," he said.

"I have always been of that opinion," said Worf.

"Really." Stone studied him carefully. "Good."

Clarke walked back in and said briskly, "The praedor will see you now."

They followed Clarke out of the communications center.

The walls and floor of the building gleamed with purest white marble, and their boots clacked smartly on the floor, echoing off the walls. The shouting of the crowd outside also echoed throughout the building, and Troi could not help but feel, albeit deep down, a sympathy for the praedor. To have that sound, that constant, pounding condemnation of you reverberating in your ears . . . well, it couldn't be the most pleasant of mental states to be in.

They entered a large and very ornate room, studded with hanging furs and the heads of dead animals, none of which the away team recognized. Worf breathed silent thanks that Data wasn't along—he would have started naming every one of the damned things.

A large, furred rug that, grotesquely, was the fur of an animal with the head still attached, covered the floor directly in front of a raised dais. On the dais, two steps led up to a throne on which sat the praedor Ryne. He was swathed in a large cape that was also fur lined. He was almost as muscled as Worf, and was clearly accustomed to having his way in all matters. Several guards surrounded the praedor, standing at stiff attention.

There was no sound of shouting people here, Troi quickly realized, because there were no windows. Obviously, the praedor had chosen to make himself less of a target to any potential hostiles, of which there seemed to be many at present.

"You are the people from the *Enterprise?*" said Ryne. He looked at them appraisingly, and his gaze stopped on Deanna. She shifted uncomfortably in place. The feeling she was reading from him was personally discomforting.

"Commander Quintin Stone," said Stone. He made no move toward Ryne, nor Ryne toward him. "We want our ambassadors back."

"I'm sure you do," said Ryne. Slowly, he rose from his throne and descended the steps. He seemed to loom over Stone as he stopped a foot or two away from him and said, "What do you intend to do about it?"

"Get them back."

"Indeed. By acquiescing to my desires?"

Stone pursed his lips a moment, as if trying to determine the best way to proceed. "We could not, even if we wanted to. Prime Directive. You understand."

"I do not understand."

"We can't interfere. We can't turn our weapons on your people for you."

"Then you will not do as I wish."

"That is correct."

"And if I were to kill your ambassadors?"

Stone said nothing.

Slowly the praedor walked around Stone, studying him up and down. He laughed low in his throat. "You seem less than impressive. Where is your captain?"

"On the ship."

"Hiding?"

Stone turned slowly around to face him, his eyes

105

narrowed, and Troi sensed a palpable unpleasantness in the air. "He had more important things to do," he said.

The insult hung in the air a moment. "More important than the lives of your ambassadors?" said Ryne incredulously.

Again, Stone made no reply. His attention was totally focused on Ryne, as if there were nothing else in the room.

Ryne stopped in front of the rest of the away team, standing most closely to Troi. "And who are these?" he asked, although he was not looking at anyone besides Deanna.

Stone said their names in a clipped fashion, Ryne nodding at each one. It was clear, though, that Troi had captured his attention.

"We must find some common ground," said Ryne, half turning away from Troi. "My people do not know what is best for them. They are unhappy with their lot, and think that removing me will remove their problems. They are wrong. I will not be moved. And you will help me."

"We will not."

"Because you will not interfere. You will take no action." He paused. "So if I ordered my guards to open fire on you, you would just stand there."

"We can, of course, defend ourselves."

"Ah. So you can interfere when it suits your purposes." In a quick move he put his arm around Troi's waist and pulled her towards him.

With a growl, Worf started toward him and all the guards brought their weapons up. Buchanan was already reaching for her weapon.

"Hold it!" snapped Stone. "Don't move."

Worf froze, his body quivering with rage.

Ryne had his arms around Troi, and Deanna said quickly to Stone, "Don't interfere! He's just trying to provoke you. He means no harm toward me. I'm perfectly safe."

If Stone heard what the empath had said, he didn't indicate it. However, he made no move toward his own phaser. "Get your hands off her." The tone was flat, without threat to it.

"Or what?"

"Or I'll kill you."

Ryne roared out loud. Then he swung Troi around and kissed her roughly on the mouth. Troi's eyes opened wide in shock and she tried to shove him away, but he was too strong. Then he released her, sending her away with a spin, and Worf caught her before she could fall. "I'm . . . all right," she gasped.

"Hah!" Ryne was saying, as he strode towards Stone, swaggering and full of confidence. "You hypocrites! You won't even protect your women—or yourselves!" He drew back a hand and swung at Stone. Stone did not flinch, did not move, and the hand cracked across his face with a jarring slap.

Ryne smiled. So did Stone. Ryne stopped smiling.

Stone's hand moved so quickly that no one even saw him reach for his phaser. One moment his hand was empty, the next his phaser was in it.

"I was going to kill you for manhandling Troi," he said. "All that slap did was determine how painful it will be."

Ryne stopped, his face going white.

From the corner of his eye, Stone saw a guard moving. Calmly, he swung the phaser around and fired. A beam lashed out, blasting the guard back. He slammed against the wall and slid to the ground.

Stone's phaser was already back in place, aimed straight at the praedor.

Worf and Buchanan had their phasers out and had stepped in front of Troi, shielding her with their weapons and bodies. The guards were momentarily confused, not sure whether to react to the security people, to the threat against the praedor, or to their fallen fellow.

And the praedor's mouth twisted into a sneer. "You're bluffing," he said. "You dare threaten the praedor? The mightiest hunter, the greatest monarch of—"

Like lightning, Stone slammed his foot up into the praedor's stomach. Ryne gasped and doubled over, wretching. His face set, his eyes crazed, Stone grabbed the praedor by his ear and yanked forward viciously. The praedor screamed as Stone twisted him around. The entire thing had taken no more than seconds, but within that time the praedor found himself twisted backwards, Stone's powerful arm in a choke-hold across his throat.

Stone had his phaser pointed directly at the bridge of the praedor's nose. His head was directly behind the praedor's, and now his voice dropped to a harsh, demented whisper that still carried throughout the room. The closeness to Ryne's ear, though, made it feel as if it filled his entire head.

"You messed up," said Stone. "You could have slapped me around, wouldn't have mattered. I don't care. But touching her first . . . she matters. And you stepped over the line."

"Let go of me, you lunatic!" gasped out the praedor.

"I'll kill you." Stone was speaking faster and faster, one word tumbling over the next. "You think I won't? You think I give a damn whether you live or die?"

"Your Prime Directive—"

"Your society wants you out," said Stone. "I'm not interfering."

"If you kill me, your ambassadors die," gasped out Ryne.

Stone laughed. He actually laughed, a high-pitched, nervous-sounding giggle. "Go ahead. Kill them. We've got lots of others."

Worf started to move towards Stone, and to his amazement, Troi's hand restrained him. "There's no danger," she whispered, looking confused. "I don't know how, or why, but there's no danger. I'm certain of it."

Worf looked down at her, and it was clear that he was hardly convinced. He turned towards Stone. "Commander." Worf's voice was deathly serious, but he made no move. "You can't do this."

And now Troi spoke up, her voice soft and soothing.

"Please . . . Quintin . . . you would be court-martialed if you killed the praedor." Even as she spoke, she tried to sense what was coming from him.

And he was calm, as always. No frenzy. No hurry. Despite the outward appearance of a desperate, crazed man, inwardly Stone was completely composed. He had decided on a course of action and was clearly going to see it through. Did the course of action involve murder? She didn't think so. She was certain it didn't.

But my God, she thought . . . look at him.

The guards stayed bolt still, afraid to make any move that might result in Stone pulling the trigger.

Ryne struggled in Stone's grasp and Stone drew his arm tighter in the choke hold. Ryne gagged as Stone dragged him toward the dais, where he then dropped down onto the steps. One leg was on either side of the praedor now. He had him completely immobilized. And the phaser had not wavered so much as an inch.

Stone appeared to be considering Troi's words. "You think so?" he asked.

She nodded vigorously.

"I couldn't live with that," he said in all seriousness, and then spoke softly into Ryne's ear, with a pleasantness that was in horrific contrast to the tension of the moment. "If I failed my mission, *and* was court-martialed for killing you, that's no good. No good. No damned good. So you'll have to let the ambassadors go."

The praedor gurgled.

"What?" said Stone.

The praedor gurgled once more.

"Oh. Sorry," Stone said, easing up minutely.

It was enough for the praedor to draw sufficient breath to say, "Never."

"Let them go, I'll let you go."

"You're bluffing. You won't kill me. Your phaser is only set on stun."

Very quickly, Stone swung his phaser around and aimed

at the head of one of the animals mounted on the wall. He fired and the head exploded.

Just as quickly the phaser was once again pointed at the praedor's face. "Think what that would do to your head."

The praedor suddenly realized . . . and he started to laugh.

"Care to share the joke?" asked Stone.

"You are bluffing!" laughed the praedor. "From this close range, the way your phaser is pointed, you'd kill yourself too. You'd have to push me away to get distance, and if you do that, my guards will kill you."

The laughter continued, until it was cut short by Stone's quiet response: *"Don't you think I know that?"*

The praedor stopped laughing. "Wh—what do you mean?"

"I'd rather die than fail. We both go, you and me. I won't be court-martialed. I won't live with failure. So we both go."

"You wouldn't dare!" he gasped out.

"By the count of ten, free the ambassadors."

"You're bluffing!"

"No. I'm counting. One . . ."

"Commander," said Worf urgently, "this—"

"Don't do it!" cried out Deanna.

"Quiet," he snapped. "I'll lose my place. Right, then. One . . ."

"I'm not impressed by this," said Ryne.

"Two."

"I'm not fooled."

Stone's manner was calm and unhurried. "Three."

"I won't do it."

"Four."

"You can't make me."

"Five."

"The people need me."

"Six."

Ryne tried to struggle, didn't succeed. "Shoot him!" he shouted at the guards.

"Then you die a few seconds sooner," replied Stone. "Seven."

"Let me go! You won't do this!"

"Eight."

"Stop this! *Now!*"

"Nine."

"You'll die too!"

The scar on Stone's cheek flared a furious red, and the whispered answer chilled everyone in the room as Stone snarled viciously, *"I died years ago. Ten."*

His finger started to squeeze the trigger.

"All right!"

Stone froze. "All right what?"

"Guards! Get the ambassadors! Bring them here!" gasped Ryne. "Make sure they're not harmed!"

Immediately, relieved to be taking some sort of action at last, two of the guards bolted from the room.

"They're . . ." Ryne, ashen, gulped and started again. The phaser had not wavered from its place. "They're some distance from here. It will take awhile."

"We've got time," said Stone.

It was close to an hour later when the ambassadors were hustled into the throne room. They looked in astonishment at the scene before them.

Stone had not moved from the spot. He still had the choke hold around Ryne, the phaser at his face. Ryne had lost the feeling in both arms and legs, but Stone's endurance had been superhuman. His hand had remained elevated and level, never budging an inch to the left or right, neither up nor down. It was as if his mind had disconnected from his body—but the reflex to kill was still present and deadly.

The rest of the away team had hardly uttered a word during the long seige. Twice during that time Stone had been contacted by the *Enterprise,* and each time he had responded calmly that everything was under control and he would be reporting back shortly.

Troi had tried to determine something of what was running through Stone's mind, but as always it was locked tight, calm and dispassionate.

I died years ago. What did that mean?

The ambassadors looked somewhat disheveled, but otherwise none the worse for wear. Stone glanced up at them, his eyes not really focusing on them but looking in their general direction. "You okay?" he asked.

The ambassadors nodded as one, still confused. Slowly, Stone rose, holding the praedor tightly against him as he said to the others, "Get close. We're getting ready to leave."

"You're not taking me!" shouted the praedor.

Stone said nothing to Ryne, but instead, addressed Worf briskly, saying, "Lieutenant, kindly blast a hole in the far wall over there."

Worf looked confused. "In the wall?"

"In the wall."

Worf, not understanding, leveled his phaser and fired. The beam lashed out and blew a hole in the wall about six feet wide. From two stories below they heard the shouting of the crowd as people scattered to get away from the spray of falling debris.

Then the shouting and chanting resumed, filling the throne room.

"All you guards, step aside," said Stone sharply. "I want the praedor to hear that clearly. *Move.*"

The guards did as instructed, moving aside to allow a clear path between the hole and Ryne.

"That's the voice of the people," said Stone, low and tight. "Your people. They're expressing an opinion. A desire. As their ruler, you should be honoring their opinion."

"I've given you what you wanted!" shouted the praedor above the noise. "Now go!"

"Worf, contact the *Enterprise.* Tell them to beam us up."

Worf did so, and they all stood there, waiting.

"Let go of me!" shouted the praedor, but his legs and arms

were so numb from lack of movement that he could barely stand.

"I'll let you go," replied Stone calmly. He waited until the split second when the familiar hum of the transporter beams filled the air.

"Time to meet your people!" he shouted. He shoved the praedor across the room, toward the hole. The hole that opened over the crowd.

The praedor screamed, and the guards rushed towards him, trying to catch him before he tumbled through the hole, into the waiting arms of the crowd that would surely tear him apart. The open air loomed before the praedor, his arms pinwheeled as he teetered on the edge and the foremost guards leaped for him . . .

That was the last image the away team took with them as they vanished.

Chapter Twelve

"JACKSON?"

Riker walked out of his room, having pulled on his simple white robe. He called out again, then to Ellie and finally Stephy, but there was no response.

He checked the time and realized why. It was already just past noon; everyone else was already up and around and long gone. But they had let Riker sleep late.

He flexed his arms and smiled. Only slight next-day stiffness from the climbing. That was good to know. Jackson's ribbing about his being out of shape had hurt his pride. Riker worked out every day and was proud of that. So he sure didn't need one of his oldest, best friends to tell him that he was losing it.

He hopped into the shower and let the water massage the remaining muscle spasms. Then he dressed quickly and went out into Starlight to track down what was going on.

He went straight to Carter's office, but Carter wasn't there. The door wasn't locked—in Starlight, there were no locks. Too much depended on everyone trusting one another to start worrying about theft or invasion of privacy. Riker stood there, glancing around. The mess on the desk was as it was the last time Riker had been there. Which meant that Carter hadn't been in his office yet that day.

He sought out Mark Masters, who was busy rechecking a cracked forearm suffered by one of the colonists. Masters' hospital was primitive by Starfleet standards, and Riker feared that he was not able to disguise that sentiment particularly well when looking around the treatment room.

"Not good enough for you?" asked Masters dryly.

"If I was in need of medical help while on this planet, I can't think of any place I'd rather go."

"Which is a nice way of saying any port in a storm, right?"

Riker smiled. "That's one way of looking at it. So, can you tell me where Jackson went off to?"

"Sure could." He put down the scanner and patted the colonist on the shoulder. "Arm's fine. But try to stay off it for at least a week."

The colonist laughed throatily and walked out.

"Interesting bedside manner you've got there. So . . . Jackson?"

"Oh, right, right." He paused, as if in deep thought. "Haven't the foggiest."

"Before you said you did."

"Amnesia. It happens frequently on this planet. I once found a cure for it but I can't remember it now."

Riker stroked his beard and studied Masters for a moment. "Why am I getting such resistance from you? We're on the same side."

"No," said Masters. "You are on your side, and I'm on my side. Don't try to kid me that you have our best interests at heart."

"We have not interfered with you in any way."

Masters stabbed a finger at him. "You don't belong here."

Riker let out a laugh and sat back against the medical table. "Neither do you. None of you. This is an alien, hostile environment. What makes you think we have any less claim to be here than you?"

"We were here first."

"Oh, for pity's sake," said Riker, shaking his head. "Masters, do you have any idea how infantile that sounds?"

"Perhaps it sounds infantile to you, but that's because . . ."

Masters' voice trailed off and Riker stood there, arms folded. "Well?"

"That's because," Masters smiled sheepishly, "it is infantile, I suppose."

"All right then," said Riker. "Now that we have that out of the way, where the hell is Jackson Carter?"

Masters let out a sigh. "He told me not to tell you because he was embarrassed about it."

"Embarrassed? How?"

"It's a technical problem." He smiled, "It's that Terraformer pride. We have some S and A probes set up out there, and one of them . . . sorry, Surface and Atmosphere probes. They take readings, provide information on temperature, state of ionization, and so forth. They transmit back via an underground feed. Well, one of the probes stopped sending back readings, so Jack went out in a landrover to check it out."

"By himself?"

"Nah. Took Ellie and Stephy with him." At Riker's frown, Masters added defensively, "Everybody pulls their own weight around here."

"I don't doubt that Eleanor and Stephy are capable," said Riker. "Not for a moment. It's just that the thought of the whole family together out there . . . it's like asking for trouble."

Masters snorted. "No one terraforms a planet if they're planning to play life safely. Look, don't worry about it. Lord knows it's scary outside of Starlight, but it doesn't get to be really dangerous until nightfall, and in a landrover they'll be back way before that."

Riker nodded at that, still not overjoyed, but aware that what Masters was saying made sense.

He spent the rest of the day conferring with the scientific

116

team that he had brought from the *Enterprise*. Their reports thus far were mainly laudatory. The terraformers had been proceeding in an organized and competent fashion. Certainly, they had run into snags here and there, but the Federation would have to be insane to think that, with an operation such as this, everything would go perfectly.

The day wore on, and Riker kept a wary eye on the time. It dragged onward and, as each hour passed, Riker became more and more nervous.

He sat in the Carter home at 1600 hours, drumming his fingers on the arm rest of Jackson's chair and thinking about their time growing up in Valdez. Before he knew it it was 1630 hours and the alarm was beginning to build.

By 1700 hours Riker went outside and looked up at the darkening skies that swirled ominously beyond Starlight.

Something is wrong, his mind screamed. *Very wrong.* He turned away from the storms and began walking toward the hospital, determined to take some sort of action, whatever it might be.

By the time he arrived there, there were a half-dozen men milling about, looking nervous. They had all been mumbling to one another and talking in low voices, but the moment Riker walked in they fell silent. Riker slowly surveyed them, and the suspicion in their eyes did not dim for even a moment.

"You want to let me in on it?" he said.

Masters stepped forward, arms folded defensively. "We can handle it."

"No one is saying you can't," Riker began, "but—oh, the hell with this." His tone changed abruptly. "I am getting sick of this attitude problem. I've known Jackson Carter longer than any of you. That alone entitles me to know what's happening. And if that's not enough, then I'll remind you that this is an operation contracted with the Federation."

117

Masters was almost nose to nose with Riker now. "What's your point?"

"The point is that, since you have a contract with the Federation, and I'm a Federation representative, that gives me authority."

"Aha!" shouted Masters. "I knew it!" He turned toward the others as if vindicated, pointing at Riker. "I said they'd move in, take it all over, and now here they are. Typical! So typical!"

"I have had it with you, Masters," snapped Riker. "I've had it with your defensiveness, with your suspicion. With all of it. Now Carter is lost somewhere out there, and you're too busy fighting with me rather than going out there."

"Going out there is suicide," said one of the terraformers flatly. Riker glanced at him and turned back to Masters, who nodded briskly. "Taylor is right. Our telemetry was tracking them, but we lost contact, which means they're out of range. If they're out of range, there's no way that someone can get to them and back here again before nightfall."

"You must have more than one landrover . . ."

"Of course we do," said Masters, "but the weather can kill even the sturdiest engines, especially at night. It's insane to risk more men."

Riker looked from one to the other. "So that's it? You're just going to stand here?"

"We'll look for them in the morning. If their landrover is broken down—which is what I suspect happened—and they just stay inside, they should be fine."

"Should be?"

"Well . . . probably will be," said Masters uncertainly.

"I'm going, and that's all," said Riker, heading for the door.

Masters grabbed him by the arm. "You're not going anywhere! With Jack gone, I'm next in command here—"

Riker pulled away from him angrily. "I'm going after them."

Masters swung him around fiercely and said, "Not without my permission."

"I'm not asking for it."

"Oh yes you are!" shouted Masters, and he drew back and swung a furious right cross.

Riker brushed it aside, catching the forearm as it went past. He allowed Masters' weight to carry him forward and then yanked back on his arm sharply. Masters gasped as Riker twisted the terraformer's arm behind the small of his back. Riker shoved him forward, bending him at the waist. Masters tried to move to continue the attack, but any movement he made simply caused further pain to shoot along his arm.

He gritted his teeth as Riker leaned forward against him. "You mind?" Riker whispered sharply in his ear.

"What could I do about it if I did?" gasped out Masters.

"Nothing," Riker said. He released Masters then, shoving him aside and turning back toward the door.

Taylor helped Masters to his feet. "Who the hell does he think he is, anyway?"

Masters shook out his arm to try and ease the tingling. As he did, he watched Riker go out the door and said softly, "Well . . . maybe he's just someone who cares about a friend."

"What? Jeez, Mark, now you're talking the guy up too?"

Masters glanced at Taylor and said, "Man could have broken my arm. We both knew it. And God knows I was giving him enough incentive to. But he didn't. Maybe I have been getting on him a little too much."

"So all a guy has to do is almost rip your arm out of the socket and you're bosom buddies for life, is that it?" asked Taylor.

"Well . . ." Masters smiled. "Looks that way, doesn't it?"

Riker stopped briefly at Carter's home to get the proper equipment and, moments later, was moving quickly across the mazelike streets of Starlight. Coming around a corner, he almost ran over one of the *Enterprise* scientists, a middle-aged fellow named Vernon. As it was, he knocked Vernon onto his back and stopped to help the scientist up.

Vernon, pulling himself together, looked Riker over in mild surprise. "All bundled up, are we, Captain?"

Riker half smiled at that. To Vernon, rank meant little or nothing. Riker was in charge and, as far as Vernon was concerned, that meant he was Captain. Riker had corrected him on several occasions but had finally given up.

"Going out looking for some friends," Riker told him. "And I'm in a bit of a hurry."

Vernon looked doubtfully at the sky. "I can see why alacrity is important," he said. "That does not look pleasant."

"No," agreed Riker, pulling on his gloves. "It doesn't. Now if you'll excuse me."

"May I ask the nature of the problem?"

"The problem is that some friends of mine are out in that soup, and I want to make sure they get back in one piece."

"Even at the risk of your own life?"

There was no sense of melodrama in Vernon's voice. The scientist probably saw it as some kind of equation, Riker realized. What variable equals what other variable.

"That's right," said Riker. "Hopefully, though, everyone's life will be secure. Now I really have to be going," and with that he hurried off.

Vernon stood there, watching him go. Then with a faint harrumph, headed back to his quarters.

Riker, in the meantime, made it to the equipment center in record time. He was relieved to see that someone was on duty there, a dour-looking woman. She informed him that someone was always on duty there, a precaution he chalked up to Jackson Carter's foresight and attention to unpleasant possibilities.

Within moments he had an electronic map and had pinpointed the location of the S and A probe that Carter had been heading out to fix. Damn the man's pride anyway, that he couldn't admit to his oldest friend that something had broken down. As if that would have lowered him in Riker's esteem in any way. Riker shook his head and determined that he was going to have a very long talk with Carter about his curious attitude when he saw him.

If he saw him . . .

Riker promptly put that out of his mind and said briskly, "I need a landrover if I'm going out after him."

"We got one more," said the woman, whose named turned out to be Sylvia.

"That's all?"

"Normally we don't need more than one."

She led him through an irising door to another, larger room that was heavy with the aroma of lubricating fluids. Riker stopped and looked with amazement at what she was pointing at. "They still make those?" he said incredulously.

He walked slowly around the landrover, which was little more than a large, metal cab that seated up to four. More could fit if there was no equipment stored in the back. A phaser cannon was mounted on top, more for the purpose of blasting through obstacles than defending against menaces.

The cab was mounted on large, dutronium treads that were ideal for all terrain. There were windows on all sides, and Riker peered through to make out the impressive control board.

It was serviceable and dependable, but still, it was ancient. "You can't be serious," he said.

Sylvia frowned. "You got a problem with it?"

"It's an antique! It's got treads! It's not even antigrav."

She snorted disdainfully. "That's how much you know, Lieutenant."

"Commander." He should get her together with Vernon. Between the two of them they'd cancel each other out and he'd be at the correct rank.

"You want something that hugs the ground," she told him. "We tried one of those antigrav units once. Winds

121

knocked it to hell and gone. Overcame the sideboard stabilizers like they were nothing." She coughed loudly, raspily, and Riker winced. She rapped the side of the landrover. "You want something that gives you weight and traction. Plus, it handles like a dream. Once you've driven one of these, there's no going back."

Riker could very easily imagine going back, but at the moment he had no choice but to go forward.

He climbed inside the cab, sliding shut the door with a satisfyingly heavy thud. He scanned the controls a moment, familiarizing himself with what was where.

Hell, if he'd handled the manual docking of the *Enterprise* saucer section with the stardrive section, this should be easy.

He nodded to himself in satisfaction, reached over and flipped a switch. The motor roared to very noisy life, in sharp contrast to the quiet elegance of antigrav, or even warp engines.

He held up the electronic map and then shoved it forward into an open receptacle in the Ops board. A screen to his right flared to life, and a small, glowing spot appeared that beeped repeatedly. That was him. A distance away, with a kilometer reading to the side indicating just how far, was a steady glowing light that represented his destination. Somewhere between the two was the Carter family.

"Hold on, Jackson," muttered Riker, pulling his parka hood up over his head. "The cavalry's on the way."

He threw forward a lever and gunned the engine.

The landrover rolled backwards.

Sylvia screeched and darted out of the way as the landrover hurled back, crashing into shelving and sending tools and equipment clattering to the floor. Profanities spewed from her mouth like water from a faucet.

Riker pulled open the driver's side window and stuck his head out. "Sorry," he said.

Sylvia was waving her arms about madly. "Who's going to clean this up?"

"If I live to make it back, I will."

"You damned well better!"

Riker turned back to the controls. It had seemed simple enough. Push the lever forward, that makes it go forward. Except some design genius had made it the reverse. He hoped. Muttering a prayer, he drew the lever towards himself and the landrover obediently sped forward.

Riker was grinning as the walls sped past him. He was definitely getting the hang of it. Then he looked ahead and his face fell.

The exit bay doors were closed.

Riker tried to slam on the brakes. The treads locked, and the landrover skidded forward. Riker realized with sinking heart that momentum was going to carry him forward whether he liked it or not.

At that moment the doors irised open. The front of the landrover shot through three feet before finally stopping. By then, of course, there was no danger.

From behind him, Riker heard Sylvia shout, "You owe me, Lieutenant!"

With a sigh, and a quick check to make sure everything was in place, Riker rolled out through the doorway. Within seconds it had shut behind him.

Ahead of him, somewhere in the rapidly growing dark, were his friends.

Vernon paced his quarters, nervous and uncertain.

He tried to balance the equation—Riker risking his life for his friends. Riker's pride versus the need for safety. Riker's expendability versus the need to act.

He looked out the window toward the skies, where lightning was crackling invitingly, teasingly. Clouds were swirling in their perpetual storm.

He imagined what it would be like out there, imagined Riker's growing concern, the possible trouble that could result if he didn't find his friends immediately. Certainly, Riker was the best officer that Starfleet could produce, but no one should have to go it alone if they didn't have to.

But Riker might be mad if he interfered. But if he didn't interfere and Riker never came back, Vernon would carry that guilt with him. That sense of "I could've done something but didn't."

The equation then—which was greater? The concern for Riker's being upset with him? Or the concern for Riker's safety.

When phrased that way, there was no question.

Vernon crossed quickly to his computer terminal and sat in front of it. "Communications," he said briskly.

Several seconds passed, reminding him how inferior this particular model was when compared to the super sophistication of the *Enterprise* computers. Then again, these were primitive conditions.

"Working," the computer replied helpfully. "Destination and message please."

"U.S.S. *Enterprise*," he said, "or any ship within range of terraforming colony Paradise. We have an emergency . . ."

Chapter Thirteen

PICARD WAS LOOKING AT Deanna Troi in a way that he had never looked at her before: with flat-out disbelief.

"You *still* claim he's not insane?" he asked incredulously.

They were in the captain's ready room. At that moment, Data was seated serenely in the command chair on the bridge. Ordinarily, that was where the second-in-command would have been. However, Commander Stone was, at that moment, in his quarters, pending the outcome of the inquiry Picard was making into Stone's actions.

Deanna felt a flash of disappointment that the captain would, at this stage in their relationship, display any form of doubt in her abilities.

"Yes, Captain," she said calmly, "Commander Stone is not insane."

"Yet both you and Worf concur." Picard looked back at the transcript of his earlier conversation with the lieutenant. "Stone threatened homicide and suicide," he said incredulously.

"He would not have killed himself," said Troi flatly.

"How do you know?"

"I just do. The feelings I was getting from him were not in that vein."

Picard circled his desk to face Troi. "And what feelings were you getting from him?"

"Calm," she said. "Inner peace."

"Counselor, are you familiar with the concept of *kamikaze* pilots?"

She frowned, trying to recall it. "No, Captain."

"Japanese pilots," he said, "particularly during the Second World War on earth, who were perfectly willing to sacrifice their lives. I'm quite certain that they were calm and had inner peace as well, just before their planes exploded into fireballs."

"Be that as it may, Captain. I am certain that Commander Stone would not have killed himself."

"How can you be certain?"

"Because," she replied simply, "it's my job."

Picard regarded her for a long moment. "Counselor, I have always trusted your judgment. We have an understanding, you and I, that goes beyond mere surface. In many ways, we share a relationship intimate in all ways except physical. And, to be honest, sometimes I have felt closer to you than with women I have been . . . physical with."

She smiled slightly at that. "I am flattered, Captain."

"I didn't say it to flatter you," he said. "I said it because I have to ask you now whether you think your personal feelings for Commander Stone might be interfering with your ability to make calm judgments about him."

She blinked in confusion. "Personal feelings?"

"It was . . ." Picard cleared his throat. "It was Lieutenant Worf's opinion that perhaps you may have feelings for Commander Stone that transcend normal counselor/crew relations."

Her eyes narrowed at that and, for the first time in their relationship, Picard felt anger from her. "Was *that* his opinion?"

"You are as subject to the pull of emotions as anyone else, Counselor," said Picard, holding his ground.

"And what, may I ask, led Worf to this conclusion?"

Picard ignored the icy tone of Troi's question and glanced at the viewscreen. "Worf stated that Stone seemed particularly irate over the praedor's manhandling of you. He seemed to take personal affront. Is that correct?"

"Whatever Commander Stone might feel about me is not necessarily a reflection—"

"Granted," Picard said quickly, "but according to Worf, you addressed Commander Stone by his first name, and seemed extremely upset over his threats against the praedor."

"Of course I was upset," said Troi in frustration. "He was threatening to kill himself."

"But you told me he wasn't going to."

"Yes, but—"

Picard clicked off the viewscreen, letting Troi's protest hang there a moment. "But what?" he asked quietly. "But . . . you weren't 100 percent sure?"

Troi took a deep breath to steady herself, to relax her mind. "I was reacting," she said quietly, "to the urgency of the moment. I was not thinking properly. Undoubtedly, that momentary sense of disorientation is attributable to the human part of me."

Picard almost smiled at that. From anyone else it would have sounded insulting. From Deanna Troi it was simply an attempt at a reasonable explanation. "You still maintain that there was never any danger."

"Yes."

"That Stone would not have really killed the praedor, or himself."

"That is correct."

"Even though you, at that moment, thought he might."

She took a long breath. "Even though, yes, Captain."

"Thank you, Counselor. Oh, Counselor," he added quickly as she started to turn away. "I am curious about something. I asked about the final disposition of Praedor Ryne. Lieutenant Worf said that the last he saw of the praedor, he was alive, although shaken, and that there was a chance the praedor would be . . ." He clicked on the viewscreen to note Worf's exact words. "That there was a chance the praedor would be 'stepping down.' Is that correct?"

Slowly, Troi nodded. "Yes."

"Anything to add?" He seemed to be regarding her carefully.

"No sir."

She turned away, then stopped and turned back. "Captain." She cleared her throat. "What the lieutenant said . . . is correct. But clearly he did not volunteer certain information."

"Such as that the commander had Worf blast a hole and then shoved the praedor toward it so the crowd could have a whack at him."

Her eyes widened. "How did you—?"

"That's *my* job," said Picard. "But I am relieved you were going to be honest with me, Counselor."

She drew herself up stiffly. "I should think, Captain, that I would have earned that consideration by now." She turned and walked out of the ready room.

Picard leaned back against his desk and shook his head.

Moments later, he walked out onto the bridge to see Troi seated primly in her place at Data's left of the command chair. Data saw Picard coming and silently rose from the seat in deference to the commanding officer.

As Picard eased back down into his chair, his mind racing as to what to do about Stone, Worf said abruptly, "Captain, receiving a transmission from the planet."

Culinan still spun majestically beneath them, an image of calm that was a sharp contrast to the unrest and anger that boiled on its surface. *If only its inhabitants could see it like this,* thought Picard as he said briskly, "On visual, Lieutenant."

128

Moments later, an image came on the viewscreen, the image of someone new. His features were soft and pleasant, even a bit tired. "Captain Stone?" he asked politely.

Picard coughed slightly. "This is Captain Picard," he said. "Whom do I have the pleasure of addressing?"

"This is Ebunan A'T'siva," he said. "I am the people-elected praedor of Culinan."

"My congratulations to you," said Picard carefully.

"And my thanks to you," said Ebunan. "My thanks to the Federation for the fine ambassadors who supervised the election. And my special thanks and commendations to your Captain Stone for his superb handling of a difficult and regrettable situation."

"You mean Commander Stone."

"Oh." Ebunan shrugged. "Well, I am certain a promotion is in the offing for him."

"I'm certain something is," Picard said neutrally.

"I have already sent a message to your Federation and Starfleet Command praising the commander's actions. My predecessor's display was most unseemly, and threatened to hold up an advancement for our people that was long in coming."

"Indeed," said Picard, feeling a bit uncomfortable. "May I ask about the fate of the previous praedor?"

"Praedor Ryne?"

"That's correct."

Ebunan paused a moment. "He . . . stepped down."

Picard heard a sound behind him from Worf that might actually, incredible as it may have been to conceive, have been the beginning of a Klingon laugh. A brief, deep-throated barking sound that was just as quickly cut off. He did not turn to look at his security chief, but instead asked Ebunan, "Where is Ryne now?"

"Oh, quite well. He has retired from public life."

So they were covering for Stone too. Or maybe they weren't. Maybe Ryne had been caught by his guards, but had been so shaken by events that he had indeed decided to bow to the will of the people. Picard was relieved that he had spoken to the ambassadors first, or he might never have found out the real story.

But the Prime Directive. Dammit, Stone had violated the Prime Directive . . . hadn't he? And that could not be overlooked . . . could it?

"We will be in touch with the UFP shortly to inquire about formal admission," said Ebunan. "I want you to know, Captain, that the name of the *Enterprise,* and of Commander Stone, will be taught to school children on our planet for generations to come. Already they are singing songs about him."

"Is that a fact?" Picard managed to get out.

"Do you think," Ebunan asked, looking quite serious, "that we could obtain some sort of holographic reference on the commander? We would like to erect a statue to him."

His voice barely above a whisper, Picard said, "I'll take it under advisement. *Enterprise* out."

There was dead silence on the bridge for a time after that. Then Picard said, "Mr. Crusher, take us out of orbit."

"Heading, sir?"

Picard sighed. "A command decision, Mr. Crusher. Pick a direction." He stood up. "I have things I must attend to. Mr. Data, you have the conn." He went over to the turbolift and left the bridge.

The moment he was gone, Troi rose and looked up at Worf. "Lieutenant," she said tightly, "I would like to speak with you."

From his elevated position, Worf looked down at her. "About what topic?" he rumbled.

"I think you know."

He paused. "As you wish."

Troi and Worf started to head for the conference lounge when Data suddenly spoke up, saying "Excuse me, but . . . since I am in command of the bridge at the moment . . . should you not ask my permission to leave?"

The Klingon turned slowly and stared at Data, who met him with unblinking yellow eyes. Data's gaze then shifted to Troi's frozen mask of an expression.

"Permission granted," said Data quickly.

Blood . . .

Stone turned, twisted in his sleep. His body shivered and convulsed. Images flew at him. *Blood . . . Pain, so much pain . . . the screaming. Agony. Do something. Can't do anything . . . something, anything . . .*

His back arched and he cried out, gasping. *The baby . . . somebody save the baby. The lash . . . the beating. Blood on his clothes, on his back, on his hands.*

A door tone exploded in Stone's head and he sat up, gasping, his body covered with sweat.

He reoriented himself. Stone's knees were drawn up to his chin, and he looked around to see that he had twisted up the sheets on his bed again. His boots stood over in a corner.

The door toned again. He let out a long, trembling sigh. "Yes." He managed to sound perfectly calm as he said it.

"Commander Stone," came Picard's crisp, no-nonsense voice, "We have to talk. Now."

Stone nodded slowly. "Can I have a moment, Captain. Please?"

On the other side of the door, Picard realized that this was the first time Stone had ever asked him for anything. "Take your time," said Picard. "I'll wait."

Troi barely waited for the doors to close before she turned on Worf and said, "You had no right to imply to the captain that I was letting personal feelings interfere with my ability to function. No right at all."

Worf's expression never changed. "I did not imply it."

"What, then?"

"I came out and said it."

She stared at him and shook her head. "I do not understand you."

"Prevarication is not the Klingon way."

"Oh, you prevaricated well enough when it came to Commander Stone," she pointed out. "You did not tell the captain how Commander Stone pushed the praedor toward the wall."

"He did not ask."

"I see. So you tell the whole truth when it serves your purpose," said Troi.

"Of course. That *is* the Klingon way."

"You tried to embarrass me in front of the captain."

"No."

"You like Commander Stone more than you do me."

Worf looked at her curiously. "'Like'? I would not use that word. To *like* someone is not a term easily employed by Klingons."

"What would you say, then?" she asked, interested in spite of herself.

Worf ran through the Klingon vocabulary, searching for the closest equivalent. "Tolerate," he said at last.

"Tolerate?"

"Yes. You clearly do not understand the Klingon frame of mind, Counselor. For example, when humans encounter each other, they say *hello* or *greetings.* Klingons do not."

"What do Klingons say?"

"We say *nuqneH.*"

Troi tried to roll that around in her mouth. *"Nook-nekh."*

"Yes."

"And that means? . . ."

"'What do you want?'"

She sat down, shaking her head. "I do not understand an entire people who are always on the defensive."

"And I do not understand," he replied, "why it should make any difference to you whether I 'like' one person or the other."

She paused, trying to find words. "It is simply, Lieuten-

132

ant, that after the time we have served together, I thought that I deserved better treatment from you than your questioning my abilities. I expected more loyalty somehow."

"You have my loyalty," said Worf. "If someone tried to kill you, I would stop them."

"Really," said Troi. She shook her head. "Frankly, Lieutenant, it seems to me that you are always rather quick to turn on me. I don't think you trust me."

"And I do not think," replied Worf, "that your powers give you any feelings for Klingons. You get no empathic readings from me. And because of that, you do not trust me."

"I know enough about Klingon thought patterns," said Deanna. "More than enough. I'm sorry for wasting your time, Lieutenant." She rose and started for the door. "I'll waste no more of it."

Just as Deanna got to the door, Worf said from behind her, "Klingons do not eat babies."

She stopped and slowly turned, looking at him, her dark eyes wide.

His expression hadn't changed. "One of the many stories," he said. "That Klingons eat their runts . . . or the young of their enemies. An ugly tale that predates the Klingons joining the Federation. Such stories do not die easily, and are still perpetuated among gullible children. Correct, Counselor?"

She nodded slowly.

In the softest voice she had ever heard him use, Worf said, "Counselor . . . we have never spoken of this. But it is important to me that you understand. I regret . . . the fate of your child."

Troi staggered slightly. He knew, she thought. My God, he *knew*. All this time . . .

"Your pregnancy threatened the ship," he said. "It was of unknown origin, and the child you gave birth to . . . the child whose growth was accelerated . . ."

"Ian," she whispered. It was the first time she had been

able to bring herself to mention the name out loud since his death.

"Yes," he said. "I was doing my duty, acting to maintain the lives and security of the ship and crew. But I want you to know that never have I regretted having to fulfill that responsibility—never before or since—as in that encounter with your child."

"I—"

"Perhaps you thought I wanted to eat him," said Worf with a touch of dark humor. "Please understand—I had to treat him the same way that I would any potentially hostile life force."

"All life forces are potentially hostile, Worf," she said. "Just as all life forces are potentially benevolent."

"It is difficult to know when to take the chance," he said. "My position requires me to block any threat."

"Just as my position," she replied, "requires me to be open and receptive."

"It is small wonder that there is friction between us," Worf said thoughtfully. "Our duties to the ship are opposite."

"Opposites can attract, as in magnetism."

"Or explode, as in matter and antimatter."

"True," she said. "I guess we shall have to tread carefully to prevent further explosions."

He nodded curtly and started for the door. Now it was Troi's turn to stop him as she said, "Lieutenant Worf—"

"Yes?"

"If you were aware of all of this . . . and of my feelings on the matter, why did you not bring it up earlier?"

Troi thought she saw the merest hint of the impossible—a smile playing across his lips. Then it vanished, if it had ever been there.

"You didn't ask," he said.

"Excuse me, Lieutenant. I know I don't have Data's gift for memory, but I don't think I asked this time either. Not about baby eating and such."

"Yes, well." He shrugged his large shoulders, "*somebody* had to mention it." He walked out, leaving Deanna shaking her head.

The doors to Stone's quarters hissed open and Picard stood there, hands folded behind his back. Stone was seated on the edge of his bed, looking calm and collected. But there was a thin film of perspiration on his forehead. Nervous, was he? Well, he certainly had reason to be.

Then again, Picard could not shake the feeling that, whatever was on Stone's mind, it was only partly related to Picard. If at all.

"We have to talk," said Picard.

"We? Or you?" There was no snideness in the question. It was fairly neutral.

"We." Slowly Picard walked in, the door closing behind him. Stone did not rise, Picard did not sit. "What you did on Culinan was totally inexcusable."

"Inexcusable."

"That's right."

"Totally."

"That is correct."

"Not partially inexcusable, or mildly. Totally."

Picard let out a long breath. "Commander, I did not come here to engage in word play."

"No, you didn't," said Stone sharply. "You came here to read me the riot act. To relieve me of duty. To tell me the definitions of the world according to Picard. Isn't that right?"

"That's right," said Picard. He was calm and collected. There was absolutely no way he was going to let Stone get under his skin again.

"Even if it's a lie."

"I do not lie to my officers."

Stone's gaze wandered to the far side of the room. "Really. How about your saying that what I did was totally inexcusable."

"That is hardly a lie."

"Did you get any complaints from the ambassadors?"

Picard said nothing.

"Or how about the residents of Culinan?" he continued. "Did they complain of my actions? No, they excused it. So it wasn't total, was it?"

"No," Picard admitted softly. "But the Prime Directive—"

"States no interference with the development of a society. The society was developing in the direction of a new ruler. The old ruler was standing in the way of that. I helped the Prime Directive. I always help the Prime Directive. I always support the goddamn, beautifully pure, wonderful, all-is-holy, all-is-wonderful Prime Directive."

It was the longest series of sentences Picard had ever heard Stone utter. And yet, despite the inflammatory nature of it, Stone spoke in a flat monotone. As if he were discussing the feelings of someone else, someone he barely knew.

"You held a phaser on a man," said Picard, "and threatened to kill him."

"So?"

"And yourself."

"What's your point?"

Picard shook his head in disbelief. "The point is that it is not the behavior of a sane man."

Stone's eyes seemed to refocus on Picard.

"Sane?" he asked.

"That's right."

"It is your opinion that I acted in a manner that was insane, because my life and the praedor's life were in danger."

"That's correct."

"That is your reason for thinking that."

Picard had absolutely no idea where the conversation was going, but he did not wish to communicate his uncertainty.

"I had said that's correct, yes. I am not accustomed to repeating myself."

Stone's phaser was suddenly in his hand. It was the fastest draw that Picard had ever seen. But the speed of Stone's draw was actually only secondary to Picard's priorities right then. The main concern was that Stone's phaser was pointed at Picard.

Picard considered reaching up to tap his communicator to summon security, but the slightest movement might provoke Stone into firing.

"What," said Picard in his lowest, deadliest tone, "do you think you're doing?"

"What does it look like?" replied Stone affably.

"It looks like you are threatening your captain with a phaser, which is a court-martial offense, Commander."

They stared at each other, neither backing down.

"Is that what it looks like?" It was clear that Stone liked to repeat himself a great deal, as if laying groundwork for a legal defense. Picard tried to see some hint of insanity, some sign of desperation in Stone's eyes. But there was nothing except the cold, icy glimmer of someone who was in complete control of his decision.

My God, thought Picard, he's psychotic. He's totally psychotic. Deanna missed it. The psych profiles missed it. He is completely out of his mind, and no one realizes it. Now he's going to kill me.

And slowly, in response to Stone's question, Picard said, "That's what it looks like."

"Now," Stone's voice had a surprisingly conversational tone to it, "what if I were holding, say, a block of metal at you. Would that be threatening?"

Picard frowned. "What?"

"A block of metal. About this size." He waved the phaser slightly. "Would that be threatening?"

"Not especially, no."

Suddenly, Stone reversed the phaser, and for a brief moment Picard thought Stone was going to shoot himself.

Then, with a sidearm toss, Stone flipped the phaser to Picard, who sure-handedly caught it.

"Looks can be deceiving," said Stone. He leaned back on the bed, hands folded behind his head. "Shoot me."

Picard looked incredulously at the phaser and then at Stone. "No."

"Shoot the wall then," Stone said carelessly. "Or that small bust over there. Light stun, whatever. Go ahead."

Picard stared at the phaser. Paranoia flashed through his mind. Had Stone somehow rigged the phaser to blow up when triggered? Was that it? He was planning to kill Picard and make it look like an accident?

Then Picard's gaze noted the power level indicator on the phaser. It was at the bottom of the red.

"It's out of power," said Picard, and the truth slowly began to dawn on him.

"That's the phaser I was holding on Praedor Ryne," said Stone, still staring at the ceiling. "Before we beamed down I had a pretty clear idea of what I might have to do. So I took a phaser with me that was nearly drained. The two shots I fired finished it. I was holding an empty phaser to the praedor's head."

Picard's mouth opened and then closed again. Then he said, "You blasted the hole in the wall . . . no," he suddenly remembered, "Worf did that."

"At my order," said Stone. "Worf blew the hole. My phaser didn't have enough power to blow my nose."

"And if he'd called you on your bluff?"

Stone shrugged. "I'd have come up with something else."

"You shoved him toward the hole."

"Not too hard. Guards had more than enough time,"— now he actually smiled slightly—"presuming they wanted to catch him. Perhaps they decided to let him fall, or even gave him a push. That's more or less their decision, isn't it? Noninterference."

Picard stood there, nodding slowly. "You're rather pleased with yourself, aren't you."

"I did the job."

"You went outside procedures."

Stone propped himself on one elbow. "When you go outside procedures and it blows up in your face, you're an idiot. When you go outside procedures and it works, you're an original thinker."

"You're oversimplifying it."

"Am I? At the Academy we were taught *the Picard maneuver*. If that maneuver had cost you your ship, it would have been called *the Picard blunder* or *Picard's folly*. You're only as good as your results, Captain. Success forgives everything."

"Perhaps. But *I* don't," said Picard, even as the truth of Stone's words crept through him. "Your behavior was alarming. Commander Riker would not have behaved in such a fashion."

Slowly Stone sat up, and the temperature in the room seemed to drop twenty degrees. "You know," he said slowly, "I am constantly being compared to Commander Riker. By you. By other crew members. It's really starting to bother me."

Picard said nothing for a moment, and then said slowly, "How do I know that this is the phaser you were holding on the Praedor."

Stone's mouth twisted into that unpleasant smile. "Would you take Commander Riker's word?"

"I wouldn't have to. He would never have done what you did."

"No, of course not. He would have played by the rules, and perhaps the ambassadors would be dead, and Ryne would still be in power, but at least the rules would be satisfied."

Picard studied Stone carefully. There was so much anger in this young man. So much passion. He cared about everything so very much, and yet everything he did, the most minute gesture, indicated total control.

He did have the makings of a captain. A brilliant captain, the kind of grand strategist that could be legendary.

But there was something eating him up inside, Picard was sure of it. Troi had intimated as much. But what was it? And could it be worked out?

Whatever it was, it certainly couldn't be worked out if Stone were relieved of duty. Picard was positive that such a move would create another barrier of anger and resentment. Picard could block him out, but then Stone would block Picard out. And Picard was getting the distinct impression that Stone needed him—whether Stone was going to admit it or not.

"Considering the results of your handling of the Culinan difficulties, I am more than happy to restore you to your post," said Picard. If Stone was surprised he didn't show it. "However," continued Picard, "This matter has not been dropped. I will defer my decision on its final disposition pending your behavior in the future. Your reinstatement has two conditions."

Stone waited patiently.

"First," said Picard, "that you give Counselor Troi your full cooperation. We both feel that you have a great deal of pain you're not dealing with. She can help you."

Picard waited for a smartass reply. Instead, Stone said simply, "That would be fine. Second?"

"Second is, that you are never to threaten anyone, *anyone*, with a phaser, loaded or unloaded, except in extreme cases of self-defense. Is that clear?"

"Don't worry, Captain. I would never do that again."

"You wouldn't?" For some reason Picard did not feel mollified.

"Of course not." Stone smiled that smile of his. "I never repeat a tactic."

There was silence for a moment more, and then Stone

said, "I'll be on the bridge momentarily, sir. If that's all right."

Picard nodded, headed for the door, then stopped and said, "My ship, Stone. My procedures. My rules."

Stone said nothing. When he spoke it was with passion, but he didn't speak when it wasn't necessary.

Picard walked out of the cabin, and as the doors closed behind him, he couldn't get a thought out of his head.

Stone might have switched phasers. How did Picard know—*really* know—that the phaser Stone had been holding on Ryne was out of power? He couldn't be sure of anything about Stone, not yet. Picard considered ordering some more psych tests on the man. And he would definitely watch him carefully, very carefully.

Picard stood in the lounge, the models of earlier incarnations of the *Enterprise* decorating the wall. They looked so clumsy and inefficient compared to the sleekness of the NCC-1701-D. Still, their accomplishments were legendary. Historic.

What would history have to say about Captain Picard, he wondered. And what would it say about Stone?

He stared at the field of stars outside.

Troi said Stone was sane. Everyone else said he was crazy. Some of the world's greatest, most advanced thinkers were considered crazy by their peers. People dreamed of a round earth, or a vaccine that could prevent disease by giving people that same disease. And they were considered mad or foolish—or dangerous.

Would he, Picard, had he existed back then, have been one of those who would have supported the demented dreams of the visionaries? Or would he have been one of those who would have been howling for their lives?

Where would history have found Picard? Would it have been in clinics, syringe in hand, trying to help inoculate children against smallpox, despite all conventional wisdom?

Or would he instead have been in the Sistine Chapel, brush in hand, painting clothes on Michelangelo's masterpieces on the ceiling, covering up the glory of the artist's vision.

Picard had been confronted with genius before, certainly. Wesley Crusher was one example, and his initial reaction was to brush Wesley off and ignore his contributions because of his age. It had taken the influence of an alien being for Picard to realize Wesley's true potential.

After that he had sworn to be less judgmental of things merely because of superficial considerations. Yet here he was, doing it again with Stone.

If Picard got in Stone's way, he might be viewed with the same disdain as those who claimed the world was flat. Or he might be preventing disaster at the hands of a lunatic in a Starfleet uniform.

Troi said he was sane, dammit.

Perhaps he was. Perhaps Stone was sane. But Picard was starting to wonder about himself.

At that moment Picard's communicator beeped. He tapped it and said, "Picard here."

"This is Lieutenant Worf. We're receiving a transmission, sir."

"From whom?"

"A relay through Starbase 42, sir. Regarding Commander Riker."

Picard suddenly felt a chill. "What's wrong?"

"Trouble in Paradise, Captain. And Commander Riker is in the middle of it."

Chapter Fourteen

THE CHANGE IN WEATHER was startling to Riker. He was aware within seconds that he had passed out of the friendly confines of Starlight. Even the dim sunlight that was allowed through the revitalized atmosphere vanished, to be replaced by bleak nothingness. It was not pitch black. Faint glimmerings of moonlight managed to stab through. Nevertheless, the area surrounding him looked like property that Hell might consider developing.

Hell in Paradise. The kind of humor that Jackson Carter would appreciate.

He still remembered the first joke Carter had told him, when they were kids. Carter had run up to him full of excitement and said "Did you hear? They're going to be sending a ship to the sun!"

"The sun's too hot," young Will Riker had pointed out.

"Yeah, but," Carter had announced in a conspiratorial voice, "they're going at *night*." Then he had roared tremendously at Riker's confused expression.

It had been years later when Riker left, at the age of seventeen. His departure was a combination of frustration over his father, and an urge to get moving in the direction he was certain his life would take. His friend Jackson had been nineteen. They had sworn up and down that they would keep in close touch and never lose track of each other. It was the kind of promise you make that you know you won't keep, despite your best intentions, even as you're making it.

Fifteen years, thought Riker. My God, fifteen years, going on sixteen. Where had the years gone?

Riker's years had gone into his career, that he could see. And Carter's? There were his years in the form of Stephy. A willowy, joyful yardstick measure of his life.

What kind of a father would I be? he wondered. Better than his own, of that he was sure.

Then again, the way things were going with him, he had trouble envisioning ever taking the time to find a woman, marry her, and produce a child. So where did he get off, criticizing his own father, when he didn't even have the driving need to become a father in the first place?

All this went through his mind as the landrover rolled forward across the unpleasant terrain of Paradise. The treads crunched over a harsh land covered with snow. Here, the layer was thin, only a couple of inches thick. Snow had been falling on and off much of the day, but as the temperature dropped the snow ceased. Now a fierce wind came up, blowing the snow all about, creating a continuous white haze. Riker squinted, trying to make out the territory in front of him, but it seemed abandoned and lifeless. No sign of his friends, or their landrover.

He snapped on the headlights, and the powerful beams cut through the haze. The land here was completely flat, and his view was clear, at least as far as the headlights covered.

The temperature inside the cab had remained constant, despite the rapidly growing chill outside. Still, Riker drew his coat closer around himself, burrowed his head deeper into his hood. He let out a breath and watched the mist collect in front of his face. He shaped his mouth into an O and puffed several times, watching with distant amusement as his breath formed lazy circles in the cab.

In the beginning the grinding of the motor had been deafening. Now, more than an hour into the trip, it had become nothing more than a steady background drone. He was hardly aware of it. When he did give it thought, it was along the lines of being thankful that at last the damned thing was working.

The droning had lulled him into a false sense of security when the landrover abruptly hit a crevice.

Riker had no idea where it had come from, and not even a full realization that it was there. All he knew was that suddenly the landrover was listing wildly to the right. He was hurled forward, smashing into the front windshield and rolling off to the side. His back hit the wall and the next thing he knew his feet were up over his head.

As Riker madly scrambled to right himself, the motor of the landrover zealously kept going, its treads pushing him forward.

The landrover slid sideways, catching itself sidelong across the crevice and momentarily balancing there.

Riker hurled himself toward the controls, not sure of how deep the crevice was and having no desire to sample its mysteries firsthand. He had a brief glimpse out the front windshield of huge blackness staring up at him, and then he slammed the joystick forward. Obediently, the treads reversed direction, an aching, grinding noise sounding through the landrover. It slid forward slightly and for a moment Riker thought they were going to be pitched headlong into the crevice.

Then the treads caught and the landrover backed up. Riker saw the crevice recede. He remembered a time on the *U.S.S. Hood* when the ship's sensors had detected, at virtually the last moment, an uncharted black hole dead ahead. The ship had screamed into full reverse. Riker had seen an outline of the monstrosity—not on the viewscreen, but in a computer-generated image—of what was ahead of them. Riker had felt at that point as if he were staring straight down into the throat of destruction and had been coughed up at the last moment.

He felt like that again at this moment.

He waited until he was some meters away before he slowed the landrover and brought it to a halt. It idled there, and Riker slid the door open, tricorder in hand.

He staggered under the buffeting of the wind and raised his nose/mouth shield, his pleximask, up over the lower half of his face. His eyes now squinted through goggles that attached to the hood of his parka.

He walked slowly up to the crevice, tricorder operating. Winds whipped snow around him, and he jumped once as lightning ripped overhead. He glanced skyward and wondered, not for the first time, not for the last, just what in hell had possessed Carter to live on this of all planets.

Because he didn't want to get soft. Like you.

Riker dismissed that answer as he consulted the tricorder. Instrument readings were not reliable on Paradise unless done from proximity. Aided by the steady readings of the tricorder and the headlights of the landrover that cast eerie shadows across the landscape, Riker went up as close to the crevice's edge as he dared. He scanned for some sign of the other landrover, praying that he would find nothing.

Which is exactly what he found: Nothing. There was no reading for the other landrover at the bottom of the crevice, and Riker breathed a sigh of relief.

But if they weren't there, they had to be up ahead. Hopefully.

Using the tricorder, he determined how far to the left and right the crevice ran. Then he returned to the landrover, threw it into forward gear, and drove fifty feet to the left to give himself plenty of clearance around the crevice. He circled the edge and started forward once more.

He had been hurrying too much. Urgency had made him sloppy. He was not going to be doing Carter a damned bit of good if he got himself killed in the process of rescuing his friend.

The landrover rolled on through the growing darkness.

"You called the *Enterprise!*"

Masters was a study in frustration and anger. Vernon sat in Masters' office, arms folded calmly.

"How could you do that!" shouted Masters. "Look, maybe you don't understand something here." He tried to rein himself in, speak rationally to this obviously rational man. "Everybody who comes into a situation like this . . . we all know the risks. We all know what has to be done. We all know what can happen. And we've learned to consider the whole of the colony for what's best. Risking more people to rescue people, especially with night falling—we just couldn't do it. The odds were too great."

"Not too great for Captain Riker," said Vernon calmly.

"Exactly! There's no way to make someone who doesn't live on a terraforming world understand the risks and demands."

"The *Enterprise* can help."

"And what are we supposed to do!" yelled Masters. "Every single time we run into difficulty, we're supposed to yell for help? Is that what you expect?"

"I expect," said Vernon, "that the *Enterprise* will be along as soon as possible. And as soon as it is, you can address all your questions to Captain Picard. Let me make it clear, Mr. Masters, I admire your pioneer spirit, and your determination. It's dedication and pride such as yours that enabled mankind to come as far as we have. But as much as I admire mankind's striving, I also admire the Bible. And in the Bible it says 'Pride goeth before destruction, and haughty spirit before a fall.' I will not let your pride and haughty spirit be responsible for the destruction and fall of Captain Riker. Or anyone. And if you disagree, I'm sorry, but you can discuss it with the *Enterprise.*"

147

Masters stabbed a finger at Vernon. "This is none of their concern."

Vernon looked at him calmly. "It is now."

Riker checked his bearings, to make sure that he was on target. The last thing he wanted to do was lose track of where he was supposed to be.

No, there he was. A persistent beep on his electronic map, with the probe still in the distance. He had covered about half the territory now, and he looked up into the sky with a mixture of fear and awe.

It looked alive, as if it was laughing at him.

He felt fear building up inside him, fear for his friends, fear for himself. He felt naked and alone in an empty wilderness. He envisioned himself, covered with frost, dead eyes staring outward at nothing, slumped over the wheel of the landrover. And evil red eyes peering in, floating over a pair of massive jaws that were licking teeth as long as his fingers.

And then, somehow, for no reason that he could fathom, the concern vanished. A small, peaceful fleeting image had darted through his mind like a butterfly, easing his fears, chasing off the fearsome vision. Just a flickering, and then gone. But it was enough.

Stay tight, Riker, he told himself. You'll find them and be back in time for dinner.

Ahead of him, something was rising up. No longer was there a vast expanse of swirling nothingness. Far in the distance, huge jagged shapes arose against the horizon line. Like the teeth of an open maw.

The Hidden Hills. The place that Carter had warned him of.

But the probe certainly wouldn't be in there. That would be madness. Riker skimmed the electronic map ahead and sure enough, there were the Hidden Hills with the probe location marked as being a few kilometers before it. Which meant that if he could see the Hills, then certainly the probe could not be much further.

And then, far ahead of him, the headlights picked up something.

The dim outline of the other landrover.

Lightning cracked, and the skies laughed.

Chapter Fifteen

As THE SINGING SKIES danced in their shimmering harmonies, Deanna Troi shivered as a chill gripped her. A chill of fear, an ugly vision of death and frozen nothingness.

Her reaction was immediate and instinctive. She reached out with her mind, taking the fear to herself, caressing it and shining a soft light of hope and fearlessness on it. Almost immediately, she felt the fear melt away, to be replaced by calm and serenity. And then, just like that, the soft stroking against her mind was gone.

No one knew Deanna Troi's mind as well as Deanna Troi. Not for a moment did she doubt the source of that flash of misery.

"Will," she whispered, although it might not have been out loud. But whisper it she did. She just knew that despite all the distance that the *Enterprise* was endeavoring to cover now at warp seven, somehow her mind had brushed against Riker's. Wherever he was at this moment, he was scared and alarmed—but not alone. "Never alone," she murmured now.

The beautiful chimes of the Singing Skies echoed through her mind, strong and strident. The image of Will Riker floated behind her eyes and gave her peace and balance. He was like a rock for her . . .

A rock. Unbidden, her thoughts drifted towards Stone.

She dwelled on him, the strength of his aura, the rampaging energy of his soul. When he moved he was like liquid glass, smooth and glittering. Not a bit of wasted motion physically, not a fragment of random thought psychically. Pure, controlled power.

What did she feel for him? She found, to her surprise, that she was still carrying the queen in the folds of her skirt. She held it up now, gazing at it.

What did she feel?

The queen had so much power, could do so many things, could accomplish so much.

But she was not the most powerful piece on the board. Her capture was not the endgame. It was the king, who could only move one lowly square at a time, that represented the true power on the chessboard.

So many ways she could move. So many things she could do, to capture the king . . .

Capture?

How had that word sprung into her mind? She did not wish to capture him. She wished only to help him. Didn't she?

That was when she realized that something was missing from her mind.

It was the music. The gentle music, the symphonic music, the glorious agglomeration of notes that was the music of the Singing Skies—the music that told her that her mind was at harmony with her body—had ceased.

She saw the rainbow patterns, but they did not call to her.

She tried to recapture her balance, and Stone's face appeared before her. She couldn't concentrate, could not reach into herself.

There was a soft footfall behind her. She turned, expecting to see that it was Beverly Crusher.

It was not.

A few minutes earlier . . .

The bridge of the *Enterprise* was tense, everyone unconsciously tilting forward slightly at their posts, as if the additional leaning could somehow speed the great Galaxy-class ship to its destination that much faster.

Only two individuals were not in that position. One was Data, of course, who performed his responsibilities at Ops with machinelike efficiency. He knew that the *Enterprise* was proceeding with all reasonable speed to aid Commander Riker. All that was required now was to stay in peak functioning condition, should he be needed.

The other was Stone. He sat back in his chair, fingers steepled, saying nothing. His thoughts were his own.

Picard bit off the impulse to check with Wesley as to the heading. He could tell by the lad's alert posture and constant checking that the starship was on course, on speed. He also refrained from asking Data about the ship's ETA, because the odds were that only five minutes had passed since the last time he'd asked.

He rose, pacing the ship and feeling a surge of helplessness. Once, centuries ago, it had taken settlers weeks, months, in covered wagons to traverse the length of the United States. Now they had technology that could create vehicles capable of crossing that distance in literally an eyewink.

It wasn't fast enough. Picard wanted to order warp eight, but that was for emergency maneuvers and, if maintained for a sustained length of time, could cause structural damage. The hell with warp eight, he realized, give me warp eighteen. William T. Riker, my second-in-command, my friend, is in trouble.

He thought of the Borg, and their incredible, star-spanning speed. He thought of Q, who could apparently accomplish anything with a random thought and a sneering wink. But the Borg were malevolent, soulless conquerors and Q was, quite simply, an idiot. What sort of cosmic unfairness was it that such unworthy beings had such power while the *Enterprise*, striving to do good, was hampered by the limits of technology.

Who knows? Perhaps the Borg had advanced too far, too fast, and had given up their souls for mechanical, inhuman approximations of spirituality. And Q . . . well, who knew? No matter his power, Q was still an idiot.

None of which made Picard feel any better.

"Play back the message, Lieutenant," Picard said abruptly.

Worf exchanged a glance with Picard. They both knew damned well that it wasn't going to accomplish anything, but it would at least make Picard feel as if he were doing *something*.

"Playing back, sir," said Worf evenly.

His fingers played across the smooth coolness of the board, and moments later a reedy, nervous voice piped over the speakers.

"U.S.S. *Enterprise*, or any ship within range of terraforming colony Paradise. We have an emergency. Three people are lost somewhere on the surface beyond the boundaries of the city Starlight, and Captain Riker is intending to—will have, by this point—commandeer another landrover and go out searching for them. The status of the weather and planetary conditions make his chances of returning less than promising. Your aid is requested. This is terraforming colony Paradise."

The message was repeated twice more, which Picard thought was amusing in a bleak sort of way. After all, if a ship was going to detect the call, it would be detected from the beginning. Still, the caller was undoubtedly feeling the same way as Picard—frustrated over inability to act and doing whatever was possible.

Captain Riker? "Data," he said briskly, "voice cross check. Identify."

Data ran it through the Ops board and, within ten seconds, had the answer. "Geophysicist Vernon Detwiller," he said. *"Enterprise* crewman."

"One of the three who went down to Paradise with Commander Riker," said Picard.

"Yes sir."

Picard nodded. "Well, that checks," although there had been little doubt of the message's authenticity.

He rose from the command chair, stretching his legs and trying not to let his nervousness show. The last thing you wanted your crew to be aware of was your own discomfiture.

He suddenly felt the need to talk to Troi. Perhaps she would be able to have some sort of new perspective on things. Perhaps—it seemed a stretch at best—somehow she could get a feeling for how Commander Riker was doing. It was not ordinarily a capability that he would have ascribed to her powers. But Troi and Riker had a very obvious . . . how did they put it?

He smiled. *Understanding*. That was the word they used. Perhaps that understanding might surpass the known limits of mental abilities.

It was not, however, something he cared to discuss openly.

"You have the conn, Commander Stone," he said briskly, and walked down and over to his ready room.

The moment he was gone, and Stone had positioned himself in the command chair, Worf walked down from his post and said softly, "I am impressed."

Stone looked up at him in genuine confusion. "About what?"

"Your presence on the bridge. I would have assumed, after the Culinan incident . . ."

"That I would be *personna non grata?* Yes, well," Stone half smiled, "the captain and I had a little chat. Tell me Worf, do you approve of the way I handled things?"

"You accomplished your goals. Your methods were straightforward and refreshingly devoid of—" and he paused and said with slight distaste, "human angst."

"Thank you. Whatever works, right?"

"The end justifies the means," said Worf.

"Machiavelli," nodded Stone.

And Worf shook his head. "QumwI."

"What?"

"QumwI. The son of Kahless the Unforgettable was QumwI the Eminently Quotable. QumwI developed many sayings that were the foundation of Klingon thought and are repeated to this day. Such as 'Revenge is a dish best served cold.' "

"A running man can slit a thousand throats in a single night?" asked Stone.

"Yes. Although some say four thousand."

From Ops, Data, who couldn't help but overhear, spoke up, with "only a fool fights in a burning house?"

"That was also QumwI," said Worf.

And Wesley turned and said, "Do not pass go, do not collect two hundred dollars?"

They stared at him.

"Steer the ship, kid," said Stone.

In the ready room, Picard endeavored to contact Deanna Troi. But there was no answer in response to his page.

He sat back and frowned. Where could she be? In the shower, he supposed. She would hardly be wearing her communicator there. Still . . .

"Computer," he said briskly, "where is Counselor Troi?"

"Holodeck three," came the prompt response.

So she was wearing her communicator. Well . . . this might be a good time to kill two birds with one stone. Summon Deanna to the bridge, and at the same time see that Stone spent some time with her. Time that could only be beneficial to the new number one.

He tapped his communicator. "Commander Stone. A moment of your time, if you please."

On the bridge, Worf and the others looked at one another as Stone walked into the ready room.

"You think he's in trouble?" asked Wesley.

"I do not know," said Worf. Then he paused. "Considering that he spoke less than highly of you the other day, I would think it would be of little concern to you."

"Yeah, well . . ." Wesley stared ahead at the starfield. "That's before I found out things. Like about his dad and stuff."

Worf frowned at that. "His mother, too."

Wesley turned in his chair. "His mom also? He didn't tell me about that. Oh, the poor guy."

Now that, thought Worf, was damned peculiar. If Stone was mentioning his past to Wesley, why was he describing his father's death and not his mother's when they both died at the same time during the attack. "Ensign Crusher . . ." he began.

At that moment Stone walked out of the ready room and said, "Be back in a few minutes."

His reappearance reminded Worf that he had promised not to talk of matters involving Stone's background. So when Stone left the bridge and Wesley said, "What is it, Lieutenant?" Worf simply shook his head.

"Nothing," he rumbled. "Nothing of importance."

Deanna clambered to her feet as Stone stood over her. He extended a hand.

"I am fine," she said, as she stood.

"More than fine," he said quietly, with meaning.

They stood there, facing each other for a moment, and Deanna felt distinctly uncomfortable. She had still not managed to retrieve her mental balance, and Stone's nearness was not helping. "What can I do for you, Commander?" she asked.

He chucked a thumb towards the air. "Captain wanted to see you. He tried to page you but there was no answer."

She glanced at her communicator. "My . . . mind was elsewhere," she said. "I did not hear the summons. I shall apologize when I see him."

"Wait," he said. "No need to hurry off."

"I think there is."

"I think," he stood partly blocking her way, "there isn't."

She stood there a moment, regarding him. "I do not appreciate threats, Commander."

His confusion looked genuine. "Threats? I'm not threatening."

"Then what are you doing?"

"I need counseling." He took a step towards her. "Serious counseling."

Deanna stood her ground. "What is your intention?"

"You tell me."

"To frighten me," she said. "To intimidate me."

He half smiled. "Am I succeeding?"

"No. Because I know you would not hurt me."

There was a long moment. Then, when he said nothing, Troi could garner nothing from him except that same, maddening calmness.

His hand moved quickly and Troi involuntarily started back. But all that was in his hand was the black king. Obviously, he had retrieved it.

He held it up, inspecting it thoughtfully. He seemed oblivious to the beauty that the holodeck had conjured up around them. "King," he said.

She held up her piece. "Queen."

"Check."

"And mate," she replied.

He nodded slowly and circled her. He did not come too close, nor wander too far. He was like a moon circling a planet.

"Answer me a question," he said.

"If you'll answer one for me," she replied.

"All right. Check and mate. Mate. Do you have one?"

It was not what she had been expecting. Her dark eyes narrowed. "You have obviously been conversant with ship's records," she said slowly. "You should be able to find out through there."

"Your background is sketchy," he replied. "Mysterious. Exotic. Like you. Do you?"

"Do I?"

"Have a mate?"

"Are you volunteering?" she asked the calm man, the dark king.

He stopped. "Yes."

She stroked her chin thoughtfully. "You are serious."

"Always."

"No, I do not have a mate."

"You do now."

It was said with such firm conviction, such certainty, that it was all she could do not to nod her head and say, "Of course, you're right." Instead, she stared at him and said, "Just like that?"

"That's how I do everything. Just like that."

"May I ask why?"

"Why you? Why me?" She nodded twice in response to both questions, and Stone, always calm, always thoughtful, said, "I don't know. Perhaps because when I look at your eyes, their darkness draws off some of my own. Perhaps because you carry yourself with pride. Perhaps because," he spun the king in his hands, "I want to see if I can hold you in check."

"The challenge."

"There it is," he sighed. "Yes. The challenge."

"You admit to the darkness you carry in you?"

"I embrace it. I love it. It's all that I love."

"Not even me?" she said. "You do not even love me, yet you are volunteering to be my mate?"

"A mate has nothing to do with love," he replied. "A mate is conquest. A mate is being able to say, 'I have taken over this person's life, and have supplanted it as the most important thing in that life.'"

She folded her arms and tilted her head slightly, her dark eyes sparkling in the colors of the Singing Skies. "Is that what you believe?"

He smiled, fully now, showing his teeth. "Maybe. Maybe not. Sounds damned good though, doesn't it?"

"It sounds frightening."

"Do I frighten you?" he asked.

"No. Only one thing frightens me."

"And that is?"

"Me."

He looked at her with interest. "Really?"

"Maybe. Maybe not."

He actually laughed, that disjointed, unpleasant laugh. "Sounds damned good, though."

"I cannot be your mate," she said.

"You want to help me, don't you? Want to cure," he made vague, finger waving gestures, "the darkness within me."

"Yes. But we cannot be that way."

"Why?" He was close to her now, well within her personal space. The strength of his personality was virtually something one could touch. "Do you have a commitment to someone else?"

"Not a commitment, no."

"Then what—?"

"There is . . ." Should she admit it to him? She could rarely admit it to herself. "There is . . . someone else. Someone who . . . occupies me. Once we were close. We might be again . . . when he is ready. And when I am. Until that time we live and grow, and perhaps we shall grow together. Perhaps we won't. But I cannot bring myself to cut off that possibility yet."

"You sound confused. Is the empath actually admitting she doesn't know her own mind?"

She smiled. "Where love is concerned, the most powerful of empaths can become the most mewling of helpless infants."

He nodded slowly. "Is he on this ship?"

"No."

"Do I know him?"

"In a way."

"Counselor," he sighed, "I don't want to play guessing games. Who is he?"

"Commander Riker."

His face didn't change, his expression locked in. She tried to feel what he was feeling, but all that was there was the same, steady pulsing of intensity. Was he angry? Was he accepting? She couldn't tell. But his control was magnificent.

"I see. Well . . . I'm very happy for the two of you," he said flatly. He even smiled slightly then. "From all that I've heard, he is an exceptional man."

"Yes."

"So exceptional that a number of women take interest in him."

Troi had an unpleasant feeling. "He is very popular."

"And a woman like you would not tolerate that."

She said nothing.

"I," said Stone softly, "would cherish you, and only you, forever."

"As your conquest."

"Does it matter?"

"Yes," she said. "It does to me."

He nodded slowly. "Yes. Yes, I imagine it would."

He turned and started to head for the exit of the holodeck and Troi called after him, "Commander, we had a bargain, you know."

He stopped and without looking at her, said, "Shoot."

"On the planet . . . you said you died years ago. What did you mean? Is it related to Ianni in some way?"

Now he looked at her, his eyes steady and gleaming. "Sorry. That's two questions."

He walked out of the holodeck before she could say anything else.

For a moment Troi wondered if she should have handled it differently, but then realized that she couldn't have. There was absolutely no way it would be remotely ethical for her to have encouraged any attachment to her on his part, even for the purpose of aiding in his recovery.

Recovery from what?

That was the question that hung unanswered in her mind. What was it that was inside him that had so closed him off from her? From others? What?

Stone sat in his cabin, his face an impassive mask. He stared at the computer screen mounted on his desk and said calmly, "Computer—service record, William T. Riker."

Obediently, Riker's specs appeared. Stone scanned it, committing it all to memory. Not that he cared all that much, but he couldn't help it. The joys and drawbacks of an eidetic memory: your mind became a storehouse for anything you've seen. Even things you'd rather forget.

He hadn't checked Riker's record before, knowing that Riker would be gone. He realized now that had been an oversight.

"Visual," said Stone.

Riker's image appeared on the screen. The picture, according to the stardate, had been taken when Riker first came on board the ship. He looked deadly serious, as if contemplating the great responsibility that would be his. His gaze was piercing, his smooth jaw was set and determined.

Stone stared at it for a time, and then envisioned Troi with him. Yes indeed, they made a handsome couple. Strong, confident.

He pictured Troi in Riker's arms, his mind's eye painting an elaborate portrait of intimacy.

His right hand drew back, tightened into a fist, and swung a punch at the small computer screen.

His fist stopped barely half·an inch short of Riker's smiling face.

Slowly, he re-established control, lowered his fist and said in a low tone, "Oh I can't wait to meet you. We're going to have lots to talk about."

161

Deanna Troi looked uncomfortable, which was odd to Picard, since she was usually the most composed individual on the ship.

"You wanted to see me, Captain?"

"Yes," he said briskly, putting his mind firmly back on track. "You know, of course, that our Commander Riker has gotten himself into a situation." She nodded. "My question then," he continued, "is just how directional can your powers be?"

"I don't follow, Captain."

He swung his computer screen around. It displayed a spherical image. "I've been studying the specs on Paradise. The atmosphere is virtually a nebula. Most of our sensory equipment will be useless unless we're on top of whoever we're searching for. Communications are virtually impossible outside of Starlight, where the atmosphere has been reconditioned. Even matter transmission is a very difficult business. It depends on the atmospheric conditions at any given moment. There is, I'm informed, an 80 percent success rate."

"Which means a 20 percent lack of success rate."

He nodded. "And when dealing with the transporters, lack of success translates to death. Or worse," he added, recalling a couple of instances when he had seen firsthand the unfortunate results that improper molecular integration could carry with it. "Frankly, the only possibility I see is sending down shuttlecraft to do visual scans of the area and hope we can spot him that way. And I was hoping—"

"You were wondering whether I could be a sort of bloodhound, is that it?" she asked, smiling. "I doubt it. I could sense the commander's general feelings if I were close enough, but I doubt I could point and say specifically, 'He's over there.' And that's what you really need."

She did not add that a full Betazoid could have tapped Riker's mind and garnered all types of useful information—practically see the world through his eyes and tell the

162

captain everything he needed to find the misplaced first officer.

But there was no need to bring it up, or highlight her only occasional feelings of inadequacy.

Picard was nodding. "I understand. Although I must ask, how close is close enough? For example—?"

"Can I sense him now? Even as we speak?"

"Yes," and after a pause, he added, "I'm not certain how personal a question that is, but it's important to know."

"Of course it is," she said slowly. "I feel . . . I'm not certain. There was a brief moment, when I was on the holodeck . . . I thought my mind brushed against his. It would be unlikely from this distance. If Commander Riker were a trained telepath, it would be different. As it is, it would be merest happenstance if a stray thought found its way to me."

"Happenstance? Or something more?"

At that she smiled. "Now, Captain, that *is* becoming personal."

"I didn't mean to pry," he said.

"Yes you did," she replied, but there was humor in her voice. "You don't like dangling loose ends. And you perceive the relationship between the commander and myself as one of those dangling ends that you would like to see tied together."

"Wouldn't you?"

She smiled and looked down, surprised that she felt a little self-conscious over that simple question. "The universe is a strange and wonderful place, Captain," she replied. "Many possibilities are there. Anything can happen."

"Anything," he agreed. "Including our finding Commander Riker. And we will, Counselor, you can bet on that."

Now she looked up, and she looked very vulnerable to Picard. "He feels very frightened and very alone, Captain."

He reached out and took her hand, squeezing it firmly.

"He's not alone, Counselor. Even though he's no telepath, Commander Riker . . . Will . . . knows that we are with him. That you are with him. Besides, Will Riker is one of the more self-reliant individuals I've ever known. He grew up in an environment that, while not quite as inhospitable as Paradise, certainly had its share of difficulties. He'll be fine until we get there."

"You truly believe that, Captain?"

"Absolutely," Picard replied with a firm nod of his head.

But even as he spoke, Troi supplied an answer of her own, the phrase that still echoed in her head. *No, but it sounds good, doesn't it?*

Chapter Sixteen

THE MOMENT THE HEADLIGHTS picked up the landrover, Riker floored it. His own landrover leaped forward as if jetpropelled. "Warp six, Mr. Crusher," he muttered to himself.

The distance between the two of them had not seemed great, but now it appeared to stretch out into a vast, unending vista. No matter how fast he drove, how much speed he urged from the ancient vehicle, it wasn't fast enough. "Come on," he said under his breath, "come on, move it. *Move it.*" He repeated that to himself over and over again, like some sort of a chant.

He pulled out the chronometer that he had taken with him when he had packed up at Starlight. There was still time. Time to make it back, although night was falling and the temperature was dropping with alarming speed. He did not look at the thermometer. He didn't want to know how cold it was, because he wouldn't be able to do a damned thing about it except get nervous.

After what seemed an unconscionable amount of time, the landrover pulled up behind the halted one. Riker looked at it from the safety of his cab, and to his alarm there were no lights. Nothing that indicated that there was any life within the landrover of his friend.

Riker shut off his engine to conserve power and slid open the door. He was hit with a horrific blast of cold before he could put his pleximask into place. Once he had, he slid out of the landrover, bracing himself against the vehicle for a moment as a massive gust of wind threatened to knock him flat. He was grateful for the insulated clothes he wore, but he was uncertain just how much good they would do him in the long run. Well, hopefully the long run wouldn't be too long.

He waited until the wind subsided a bit, then dashed the short distance between the two landrovers. He got to the other one just as another fierce gust came up. He leaned against Carter's landrover rather than try and fight it.

"Jackson!" he shouted. But there was no answer. Maybe they just couldn't hear him.

He slid along the side of the landrover and made it to the sliding door on the driver's side. He yanked on it and found that it was locked.

Confused, Riker pulled himself up, balancing on the tread, so that he could see inside.

The face of a Wild Thing looked back out at him.

With a yell, Riker tumbled off the tread and landed on his back. He grabbed for his phaser even as he fell, and as he hit the ground, held it up to blast at the creature.

But it wasn't moving. It was simply staring out the side window at him.

Slowly, never lowering his phaser, Riker got to his feet and watched the Wild Thing carefully. It was not reacting to his presence at all.

Then it slowly dawned on Riker that the creature was dead. Somehow, its head had become wedged against the door and it had died that way, its lifeless eyes staring out at the hostile world that was its home.

"Jackson?" he whispered, even as he made his way around to the front of the landrover.

The front of the landrover was crunched in, and the front window had been smashed through.

Riker did not want to look in, but he had to. Something compelled him, some morbid, vague hope that everything was going to be okay. That he was going to peer in and there would be his friend, holding a Wild Thing head up against the door and laughing and saying "Ha! Fooled you, Thunderball! You are so gullible." Behind him his family would be laughing at the wonderful practical joke. Then Riker would laugh along too, after chiding Jackson for making him worry this way. Then they would all pile into Riker's landrover and head back for Starlight, laughing and cheered over an adventure that had ended happily.

That was what Riker was hoping for.

He pulled himself up, looked in through the shattered window, and saw what he knew he would.

There was the Wild Thing, all right. Its body was slumped over the driver's seat. Where its torso should have been was a huge hole. Riker did not even have to look up to know that its guts were now decorating the ceiling. In its death throes it had wedged itself into the seat, its head shoved against the driver's side window where it had startled Riker.

There were not supposed to be anymore Wild Things. Jackson Carter had claimed that they'd gotten them all. Whether that was another instance of terraformer pride, or whether Carter had actually believed it and been wrong, Riker would never know.

For Carter was also still in the driver's seat, under the body of the Wild Thing. His skin was dead white, and had already taken on a slight blue pallor. His upper right temple was caved in, and his chest was . . .

Riker looked away, gagging. He dropped down from his perch on the front of the landrover and felt a vast wave of nausea. Quickly, he yanked off his pleximask, even the fierce, stinging air of the planet preferable to the sudden staleness in his filter. He breathed it in, causing sharp pain in his lungs that made him gasp when he tried to take a deep breath.

But at least he was alive, dammit. That pain reminded him of that. And reminded him that perhaps, somehow, Ellie and Stephy might be too.

Slowly, the nausea passed as he kept telling himself that, over and over.

Were they also in there? He had to look. No . . . he had to go in.

He took one more deep breath, and then replaced the pleximask.

He went around to the passenger side and, to his surprise, found the door was already slid open. Clutching his phaser tightly, just in the event that there was another one of those monsters hiding in the back, he pulled himself up and into the landrover.

The rapidly falling darkness outside had one benefit—his eyes were already adjusted to the dimness of the cab. He stepped slowly inside, looking around and listening as hard as he could. But he knew within the first seconds that nothing living remained.

He looked at the debacle of the front and knew instinctively what had happened. The creature had come at them, hurling itself against the front window and smashing through. Its weight, the ferocity of the attack, had destroyed the control board. Jackson had had just enough time to reach a blaster just as the thing had gotten to him. He had placed the muzzle point blank against its torso and fired. But the creature's death throes had been sufficient to kill Carter.

Ellie and Stephy must have fled the landrover. Who could blame them? Controls smashed, the landrover was useless. With the body of Ellie's husband and Stephy's father lying there in its grotesque condition, staying there was a torture they did not want to face. And the gaping hole in its front made it useless as shelter.

Shelter. They would have needed shelter. They would never have been able to make it back to Starlight, not on foot. Not with the amount of daylight left.

He started combing the inside of the landrover but found nothing. No paper or writing implements. Who would have thought to bring such things on a repair run, for pity's sake?

Then he found it. Propped against the wall, practically in plain sight if it hadn't been so dark inside the cabin, was a recorder log.

He picked it up and prayed that the fierce winds that had been whipping around within the landrover had not destroyed the mechanism. He pushed the playback button and was relieved to hear sped-up voices, like chipmunks chattering.

And then Ellie's voice. Forced calm, incredible control as she said, "If you hear this . . . we are about to head due east, toward the Hidden Hills. There are caves there, and we have some provisions so that—" her voice broke, and then recovered "—so that we can survive, for a time. We cannot stay here. If there are other Wild Things in the area, sooner or later they'll smell the . . . blood, and be here. We would rather be elsewhere. We will stay here until daybreak and then try for home. If you hear this . . . please . . . be careful. This is Eleanor Buch Car—Carter."

He listened for more, but the log clicked off, the entry having been played.

He paused a moment more to look around. It looked as if they had taken whatever things they could carry, so obviously their departure had not been the helter-skelter flight that Riker initially assumed it was. That was a relief. He should have known to expect level-headed behavior from Eleanor Buch.

Buch Worm.

He went toward his friend, locked in a mutual death-grip with the creature that was not supposed to have existed. He reached down, tried not to think about what he was feeling, and lifted the Wild Thing off him. He shoved the monster to the side, where it fell against the passenger seat and stayed there, propped up in a bizarrely convivial position.

Carter's hands were empty. The blaster was gone. Either he had dropped it to the floor and Ellie had picked it up, or she had actually pulled together her nerve and reached in to pluck it from her dead husband's hand. Either way, Riker did not envy her. But that blaster might represent the difference between life and death for her and her daughter. Nothing would stop her from doing whatever it took to increase the odds of their survival.

Particularly her daughter's survival, Riker realized. He somehow knew that Stephy's life would be even more important to Ellie than her own.

He recalled his own behavior as a teen, and how he had hardly given Eleanor Buch the time of day. How could he have been so blind as to not recognize the qualities that were within her. Chalk up another one to Jackson Carter for being able to see nature's treasures where they really were.

Carter . . .

He looked down at his friend, whose eyes stared hollowly into the darkness of Paradise. A man of vision who could see nothing anymore.

Riker reached over and passed his hands over Carter's eyelids. Mercifully, they had not frozen open. When Riker took his hand away, Carter's eyes were shut.

"I'll find them for you, Jackson," he whispered. "I'll bring them back. I swear I will."

And then the roar filled the cabin.

It came from behind him, and Riker didn't even hesitate as he threw himself forward through the broken window. He had no time to prepare and the ground came up at him too quickly. He slapped the ground to absorb some of the impact, but felt pain lance through his right shoulder.

He kept rolling even as he threw a glance at the landrover. A Wild Thing was perched in the window. A huge piece of meat was between its jaws, meat with a dark, furry look to it. It was devouring the dead body of its fellow creature. But even as it had begun its grisly feast, it was clearly considering the advantages of going after something living.

Riker skidded to a stop and swung his phaser up, even as the Wild Thing clearly decided that warm meat was better than cold meat anytime. It leaped through the window, and Riker was momentarily horrified by its size and power. Carter had been right. The monster that had come after them in Starlight was clearly old. This one was in its prime.

Riker fired without stopping to aim. But instinct had taken over and his shot was perfect. It struck the monster in midair and, with a screech of anger, the Wild Thing vanished.

The Starfleet officer scrambled to his feet and dashed for his own landrover. He did not know how many of the things might be in the area, nor did he care.

Please keep them away from Ellie and Stephy. He thought of mother and daughter, screaming in unison as a pack of those things bore down on them. Then he forced it away. Nothing was going to be served by thinking along those lines.

He dashed, stumbling once, back to his landrover and leaped in. He checked the electronic map and recalibrated to get an eastern bearing.

Then he flipped the switch to gun the engine to life.

Nothing.

"No," he murmured in disbelief, and then louder, *"No!"* He slammed a fist against the front window in frustration. He looked at the power level indicator to his left and the needle *(needle,* for pity's sake!) showed half power. That should still be more than enough. Still, just to play it safe, he tapped it with his finger.

The needle promptly fell over to the left, next to the Empty label. A red light flashed obediently, indicating a needed recharge.

"Oh that's just great!" shouted Riker. He'd gone out in a half-charged landrover. He was going to kill Sylvia when he got back. If he got back.

He dropped to the floor and raised up the panel that covered the power cells. Sure enough, the power cells' indicators were flatlined. There was a small amount of charge left, but not enough to spark the engine to life. Even if he did manage to start it, he wouldn't get more than a few meters.

He did not waste time cursing the fates that had brought him to this point, as much as he wanted to. Nor did he think about the possibility of more Wild Things heading his way. Instead, he quickly started to review survival procedures that he'd been taught in the Academy.

What do you do when *(your damned antiquated landrover leaves you high and dry?)* your primary power source has been drained?

Look for alternates. Any alternate source . . .

He scanned the inside of the cabin. Alternate power source . . . somewhere . . . was there an—?

Slowly, he looked down at the phaser he was still holding in his hand.

"Power," he nodded.

As he rigged the power cells to drain off power from the phaser, he knew he was taking an awful chance. Even if he could make the transfer without blowing himself and the landrover to kingdom come, it would leave his weapon dangerously depleted. He did not want to think what it would be like taking on a Wild Thing with less than a fully-charged phaser, but . . .

Slowly, he drained the power into the cells, having to stop every so often to make sure he didn't overload the couplings.

Eventually, the red light on the power cells blinked out, to be replaced by a soft, glowing amber light. Riker nodded briskly, then closed the small panel door and looked at the level on his phaser. Low, as he had expected. Not drained completely, but still . . . not the greatest situation to be in.

He attached the phaser to his belt and then seated himself in front of the control board. The needle was back to the far right and he tapped it, just to make sure. It stayed serenely in place, the final check.

Just as Riker pressed the ignition switch, there was a furious howl from behind, and the landrover shook as something thudded against it from behind.

Instinctively, trying to get away, Riker slammed the stick forward, and was only reminded of which direction was which when the landrover rolled violently backwards.

The landrover angled up slightly as something went under the left treads, an animal scream cut short. Riker glanced out the driver's side window and saw a quick flash of blood and gristle on the tread before it rolled out of sight.

Riker cherished all life, and yet his mouth pulled back into an animalistic smile of triumph. "Take that you bastards," he snarled, and then slammed the landrover into forward gear.

The blip on his map representing himself obediently turned with him, and he expertly spun the landrover in the direction of the Hidden Hills. Within moments, he was speeding in that direction, praying that the women would be able to survive until he got there.

He could practically hear Carter's voice in his head, a youthful Carter with no idea of what his eventual, unhappy destiny would be. *Kid,* Carter was saying to him, *you'll go anywhere, do anything, to get your hands on a female. And you go through 'em like lightning. I think we'll call you Thunderball.*

Okay, thought Riker. So now I'm going after two more women, Jackson. Two more who are dear to you, although not for the reason you would have ascribed to me. Not for the reasons Thunderball would have gone after them. I've got to save them because, if I blow it, you'll haunt me forever.

Chapter Seventeen

GUINAN LOOKED UP with mild surprise as Deanna Troi entered the Ten-Forward lounge.

The counselor rarely stopped by, and Guinan instinctively understood why. Large gatherings of people, particularly people who were feeling free and uninhibited in their emotions, could be somewhat emotionally buffeting to an empath. Certainly, Deanna had control over what she wanted to receive and how. But from so many sources it was sometimes overwhelming. Just as, for example, one could stop water from flooding the village by sticking one's finger in the dike. But if a dozen holes suddenly sprung up at the same time, then what?

Yet, here Deanna Troi was, sliding into a booth far away from the bar. Guinan regarded her a moment, then pulled out a bottle and measured out a portion into a glass.

She walked over to Deanna and slid it over to her. Deanna looked at it questioningly.

"It won't bite you, Counselor," said Guinan bemusedly.

"What is it?" asked Deanna.

"A special concoction of mine. I call it Ol' Sublight. One shot and you'll do everything on impulse."

Deanna smiled slowly. "I don't know . . ."

"You wouldn't want to insult the hostess now, would you?"

With a sigh, Deanna lifted it up and swallowed it in one gulp.

"No, wait!" said Guinan, "a little—"

Lights exploded behind Deanna's eyes and for one moment she was amazed by the fact that the stars were now inside the lounge and she was sitting outside the ship. Interestingly, the ship was going at warp speed and she was maintaining pace, pumping her legs furiously and skipping from one piece of floatsam to another.

In less than an instant, Deanna suddenly thudded back down into the seat. The rest of the room followed shortly thereafter.

"—at a time," finished Guinan.

Deanna coughed. "How does anyone drink that."

Guinan pulled the glass away. "Should have warned you. Sorry. Powerful stuff when it reacts with a powerful mind."

"It . . . makes my brain tingle."

"Yes, well, one more shot and your brain will be in your shoes."

"Thank you for the warning."

"So," said Guinan slowly, "how's Stone?"

Troi looked at her with surprise. "How did you know?"

"A hunch I had. He was thinking of putting moves on Dr. Crusher. So I steered him in your direction."

"You what?"

"You heard me. I made sure he kept hands off Beverly and refocussed his energies on you."

Troi's large, dark eyes—which looked slightly larger after a shot of Ol' Sublight—stared at Guinan. "You could have warned me."

"Do you think you needed a warning?"

Deanna considered it a moment and then slowly shook her head. "I suppose not. It is my job, after all."

"We all do our jobs. So, what are you down here for?"

"To try and consider information that I've learned about Commander Stone."

"And to have someone to talk to about it?"

Troi looked up and realized only at that moment that this was indeed the reason. She could have spoken to Beverly about it, but—

"But Beverly has a bit of a blind spot about Stone," Guinan completed her unspoken thought.

Troi tilted her head and regarded Guinan thoughtfully. Guinan merely smiled back in that peaceful and occasionally maddening way she had.

"Yes," said Deanna. "That's right."

"Okay, then. Shoot."

"Starfleet Command got us some records we had requisitioned—the captain's log for a ship that Stone served aboard—the *Moniter*. It was during his time on that ship that something happened—I'm not sure what. But I believe that it was connected with a planet called Ianni."

"And what did the log tell you?"

She paused, trying to think of the best way to sum it up. "In some ways," she said, "it was similar to what happened on Culinan several days ago. The government was in a state of disarray. Commander Stone and a landing party were sent down to establish diplomatic ties with the governmental heads. Apparently, while they were down there, there was some sort of coup."

"A coup?"

"Yes. The ruler was overthrown and a new governing board was brought in. Apparently, it was all very violent and unpleasant. But according to the captain's log, Stone kept his head and there were no casualties for the away team. Furthermore, Stone remained to establish ties with the new government, and not too long after they actually applied for membership to the Federation. The captain praised Stone's actions, citing his composure and his adherence to the Prime Directive under adverse conditions."

"That's all?"

"Almost," said Troi. "I did some cross-checking, because Starfleet sent us all the records for the *Moniter* for that time. Including medical logs."

"And—?"

"When Stone reported for duty on the *Moniter,* he was checked out as in perfect shape. There was no mention of any health oddities or imperfections. Yet now he apparently has severe scars on his body."

"That is the word around the ship," said Guinan ruefully, "thanks to Scooter."

"Yes. So the question becomes, where did they come from? Was he captured and tortured at some point? There's nothing in his records that indicates that."

"I don't know," Guinan said. "How much do you think that impacts on him?"

"You mean is that why he is the way he is?"

"And how is he?" was the hostess's reply.

"You mean how do I view him personally?" asked Troi. At Guinan's nod, she thought a bit and said, "I don't know. He's a very powerful personality."

"Like Commander Riker?"

"No," she said firmly. "Nothing like Commander Riker."

"You don't have to sound defensive, Counselor."

"I'm not defensive," said Troi defensively. "I just—"

At that moment, Guinan looked away. Deanna turned to follow Guinan's gaze and she saw Stone enter, barely two feet away from them.

He turned and smiled thinly. "Am I interrupting?"

"Not at all," said Deanna quickly. "We were just—"

"Discussing Commander Riker," said Stone with quiet conviction.

And Deanna, in spite of herself, was curious as to how he would react. She would try anything that would crack that veneer of his. "Yes, we were," she said. "I was just . . . expressing my concern for his safety."

Stone nodded, his control never slipping a fraction of an inch. "Well, don't you worry," he said. "We're getting there as quick as we can and, as soon as we hit orbit around Paradise, I'm going to be leading the away team personally to find him."

Deanna sensed total and quiet confidence radiating from him. "You're certain you'll be able to?"

"I've done it before," he said. "Ask some crewmen I saved while I was serving on the *Nimitz*. I have a knack . . . a sixth sense. After all, I seem to be able to find you when I want to, right?"

She shifted uncomfortably in her seat.

"Believe me," he added, "I'll get the job done. After everything I've heard, I'm very, very anxious to meet Commander Riker." He turned to Guinan, touched his finger to his forehead, and walked out of the Ten-Forward.

"Why am I not comforted by that?" said Guinan.

Chapter Eighteen

THE LEADER OF THE Wild Things sniffed around the fallen body. Once, the fallen one had been of the pack. Now he was no more. That did not make him less a Wild Thing.

He had been crushed beneath the monstrous beast from the city some time earlier. Now the scent of blood stuck on the trail.

The Leader turned and, as was the custom of the Wild Things, led a mournful howl in memory of the dead one. Then they ate.

As the pack gathered around, the Leader insisted the young eat first. The young ones had to be kept strong, for the time when the elders had to eat them. Then again, the young ones might eat them first. That was the way of the Wild Things.

He surveyed his pack as they ate. There were none to equal the Leader in strength or fierceness. Part of him regretted having no peer, for he felt alone even in the pack. Still, he knew that if he had a peer, he might himself be consumed. That also was the way of the Wild Things.

The Leader saw that the trail of blood led toward the

Hidden Hills—to their lair. Their prey was going directly to the home of the Wild Things. Good. He hurried the pack through their feast on their fellow and then set them off on the trail.

The Hidden Hills loomed in front of Riker, and he could see that he was not going to be as fortunate with the weather up there as he had been on the plain. It was colder in the Hidden Hills, Jackson had told him. And the snow never melted there, but only grew deeper and more treacherous.

He glanced toward the back of the landrover in the vain hope that something had materialized there that could be of some help. Antigrav boots, for example. But there was nothing. Mountain climbing had not been a consideration when he'd first set off.

It was not snowing now, for which he was grateful. But lightning and thunder rumbled across the sky, the air seemed to crackle and sparkle above the peaks of the Hidden Hills, and the clouds surged and rolled like spacegoing serpents.

The landrover rolled up to the base of the mountain, and there he stopped. Before him stretched upward a myriad of paths and byways, all of which were far too narrow and treacherous for the landrover to navigate.

He had found an air horn off to the right on the panel board and he pushed it now, hoping that the klaxon would catch the attention of Eleanor and Stephy. It sounded loudly and discordantly. Riker waited to see if there was a response.

There was a response, all right. A nearby rumbling, and Riker looked up to see a small wave of snow, ice, and rocks tumbling down toward him.

He slammed the landrover into reverse and it shot backwards, barely vacating the spot that was, within seconds, covered with icy debris.

Riker stayed where he was a moment, allowing his

heartbeat to return to normal. Where had his brain been, he wondered? On vacation?

Avalanche, you idiot, he told himself. Make very loud noise, get very large mess. Keep it quiet!

He slid open the door of the landrover and hopped out, fixing his pleximask over his face. The temperature had dropped so quickly that he was having serious doubts as to whether his insulated garb would be of use for very much longer.

He pulled out his tricorder and swung it slowly, carefully, in a gradual arc, trying to pick up life readings. After several long minutes, he came to the conclusion that this wasn't getting him anywhere.

Then he decided to switch tactics. He reset the tricorder for thermograph readings, and began the sweep again.

His heart jumped. Off to his right, at two o'clock, he was getting faint readings. Something warmblooded had passed that way. He saw from the angle that it had been heading for one of the higher points on the mountain.

He followed it quickly, his booted feet sinking ankle deep with each step. The wind was blowing the snow about so furiously that, within moments of Riker's passing, his footprints were filled in again.

Was it them? he prayed. Or was he picking up something else? A predator, for example.

Up ahead was the base of a ravine that seemed to lead up into the peaks. It would have been a reasonable path to go—after all, the ravine was sheltered on both sides. He made his way there and stopped, looking around for some sign, some clue that he was heading in the right direction.

Then he saw them . . . footprints. About three meters into the ravine. He dashed forward, slid, pulled himself up, and slid once more to a halt in front of them. His breath was already ragged sounding inside his chest.

Getting soft, his friend's voice said to him, but he ignored it. All that mattered were the tracks—definitely human tracks, rather than animal. They were faint, for the snow had done its job here as well. But the high, sheltering walls of the ravine had done theirs, and he looked on the two sets of tracks and rejoiced.

Riker started running up the ravine. The incline was very steep and steady, but he didn't let that slow him down. Instead, he kept before him the image of Ellie and Stephy, and somewhere in the back of his head Jackson Carter was urging him on, hurling insults and profanities and jokes at him.

He was not going to fail, dammit. He was going to find them. That's all. Don't think about the temperature. Don't think about the fact that you've lost the feeling in your toes. Just do it, that's all. Just do it.

He stopped.

The ravine had come to a halt, banged up against a wall of ice that seemed to stretch up to forever. He looked around left and right. They couldn't have circled back. They sure weren't there now. Perhaps—

Off to the left was a narrow crack, little more than a fissure. It had to be where they went—there was nowhere else. A brief feeling of claustrophobia swept over him. If he were inside that thing and suddenly the ground shifted, closing the fissure walls . . . Or perhaps another avalanche might come crashing down, burying him . . .

"Doesn't matter," he said. His breath was sounding loud to him in the pleximask, but this time he didn't remove it. He felt as if breathing the air now would sting so sharply that a lung would collapse.

He entered the fissure, which seemed barely wide enough. But sure enough, as he looked down, there were tracks. Tracks from Ellie and Stephy . . .

For a moment, his mind froze in horror.

There was a third set of tracks. Clawed tracks, deeper into the snow, indicating the weight of the creature that walked on them. They were fresher than the women's tracks.

Of course they were. It's natural that they would be fresher when something is stalking.

Where had it come from? Riker looked around, trying desperately to figure its place of origin. Then he spotted it. Just barely visible, under an icy overhang some meters away, was the faintest hint of a cave mouth. You wouldn't be able to spot it if you didn't know it was there. Ellie and Stephy had definitely not known. They had walked past the potential shelter in their quest for higher ground.

They had been lucky, incredibly so. If they had spotted the cave and gone in, the creature that was in there would have ripped them apart. Luckier still . . . when they had passed by, the creature was dormant. Even monstrosities like Wild Things must need their rest.

But their luck had run out. The creature was right after them now, having stirred from its slumber and realizing that potential prey had passed right by.

Riker bolted up through the fissure, running as hard as he could. The snow seemed to become deeper, determined to slow him down. He could tell that the climb was incredibly steep as had been the ravine slope before it. He was losing track of just how high up he was going, and didn't want to think about it.

His legs pumped, heart pounding against his chest, and he was saying over and over again, please, please, don't let it happen. Let me get close enough. Let me get there before it happens.

The fissure rose up on either side of him, like a rocky, snow-covered coffin.

High overhead, the lightning cracked, and mingled with it, Riker heard a scream.

He hoped that he had heard wrong.

Suddenly, the fissure opened up in front of him, and he hurled himself through it.

It opened up onto a vast cirque glacier, a huge expanse of ice that looked, from Riker's point of view at that moment, as massive as the saucer section of the *Enterprise*. It was flat, angled slightly downward.

At the far end were Ellie and Stephy.

Stephy was on her knees, crying hysterically, clutching at her mother's legs. Ellie was facing directly toward their oncoming danger.

Two Wild Things were approaching them. Their advance was not slowed at all, for here the snow had been blasted into a virtual sheet of ice. They walked with sure-footed precision, their claws giving them traction that was denied the humans. They were coming from two angles rather than together, to cut off any possible flight on the part of their victims.

"Mother, help me, help me, help me!" Stephy was screaming. Ellie was looking frantically from one beast to the other, trying to find a way out. She backed up slowly, grabbing Stephy by the back of her jacket, but there was only so far she could back up. Behind her was an ice cliff hanging off a sheer ice fall.

Above them, the Hidden Hills towered, majestic spires that were about to bear silent witness to slaughter.

Riker grabbed at the phaser that was clipped to his belt, and only at that moment realized how much of a toll the frozen temperatures had taken. His fingers had lost their flexibility and the phaser leapt out of Riker's hand and hit the ice. It started to slide away.

Suddenly, Ellie shoved Stephy to the side, as hard as she could. Stephy lost her grip on her mother's leg and skittered away, howling. One of the advancing Wild Things turned in her direction.

"No!" screamed Ellie. She started to run along the edge of the ice cliff. "Over here! Over here you bastards!"

Above her, the pinnacle started to shake as if being roused from its slumber.

Riker lunged towards the phaser, hit the ground on his belly and slid. For a brief moment his fingers grazed it and then he overshot it. Desperately, he slammed his fist into the ice and halted his forward slide. He felt pain shoot once again through that same shoulder.

The Wild Things turned towards Ellie, distracted by the shouting and screaming. They were drawn to the liveliness. In the wastelands of Paradise, life was rare, and special. Even Wild Things could appreciate that.

They advanced on her, growling, the sound of their controlled fury speeding up. Ellie was as far back against the ice cliff as she could go. The sheer drop of the ice fall lay right at her back. And from her belt, she pulled the blaster she'd taken from her husband. She aimed uncertainly; a marksman she was not.

Riker spun on his belly, grabbed the phaser and swung it at the Wild Things.

At that split instant he realized that it wasn't set on kill. Normally, it was a flick of his thumb to alter that, but his hands were numb and barely functioning. Besides, lethal setting would drain the phaser so fast that he might not be able to get both of them.

The Wild Things leaped at Ellie. Ellie fired, missed clean.

Stephy screamed out her mother's name.

Two of them, Riker's mind shouted, *get the one closer to her.* The beam lanced out.

Pinpoint.

Perfect. One in a million.

The beam lanced straight through the Wild Thing's left ear and out through the other side. Its brain fried instantly and the creature hit the ice, blown off course, and skidded down and off the ice fall.

Without pausing, Riker swept the beam toward the other Wild Thing which was in midleap.

Above, the snow rumbled, angry at the noise. Silent witness was one thing. This was intolerable.

The beam lanced out, blasted the creature's head.

One in a million. But not two.

The creature did not die instantly, or at least not fast enough. The blast snapped its head around, broke its collarbone, shattered its spine—

It hit the ground three feet from Ellie, who tried to dash out of its way.

Writhing in agony, the creature spun around, skidded across the ice, and struck Ellie. She staggered back and tred air, still clutching the blaster.

"Mother!" shrieked Stephy.

Riker had a brief, agonized glimpse of her expression, and then Eleanor Buch Carter was gone, plunging down the ice fall. The critically wounded Wild Thing tumbled after her.

Stephy continued to shriek hysterically, and her screaming almost blinded Riker to the newer, more immediate problem.

The spires had decided that, between the screaming and the roaring and the phaser blast, they had had more than enough.

Huge chunks of ice and snow began to tumble down from on high, a rumbling seizing the entire cirque glacier.

Riker hurled himself toward Stephy, shooting across the ice on his belly. In his childhood, it had been fun. Now it was desperation.

Off to their right, Riker spotted a crevice out of the corner of his eye. A crevasse in the side of the wall, a wide one. But it was far. Too damned far. They were going to be buried under frozen debris before they could get there. Probably.

"Mother!" Stephy was still shrieking, and she started to move as if she wanted to throw herself off the ice cliff after her.

Riker scrambled to his feet, fighting to keep himself upright. The noise of the avalanche grew louder and he had to shout to be heard. "Come on!" he shouted, *"Come on!"*

Stephy was struggling fiercely, completely oblivious to the danger. "Mother!" she shrieked again.

Riker spun her around and slapped her as hard as he

could. It was buffeted, of course, by her own pleximask, but it grabbed her attention.

She saw the fierceness in Riker's eyes, and then she saw what was behind him.

The entire mountain was collapsing on top of them.

"This way!" he shouted, yanking her arm with such force that it almost came out of the socket. She staggered after him, in a daze, and all around her the world was coming apart. Her emotional world, her physical world. Everything.

"Faster!" he shouted. They were almost to the crevasse. Snow and ice were falling all around them, the glacier starting to crack under their feet.

Stephy slid and cried out, and Riker was now pulling her entire weight. The crevasse was hardly the safest place, but it was the only place.

A piece of ice struck Riker in the back and drove him to his knees. Now it was Stephy who was on her feet, and she was pulling him by the right arm, and damn but his shoulder was killing him. One second she was the terrified teenager, the next strong and desperate to survive. A contradiction.

"Come on!" she was shouting now. They staggered and hurled themselves into the crevasse as tons of frozen waste rained down around them with a terrifying rumble that drowned out the thunder overhead.

Chapter Nineteen

IT WAS IN THE MIDDLE of a conference, as the *Enterprise* senior officers were trying to determine the best way to proceed upon reaching Paradise, that Deanna Troi suddenly cried out.

All heads snapped around as Deanna gasped, her arms flying up over her head as if to ward off some horrible fate descending upon her. Immediately, Picard was at her side, holding her by the shoulders to steady her as her dark eyes stared in uncomprehending fright at something she could only sense rather than see.

"Counselor," said Picard urgently. If she could hear him she gave no sign. But she clutched onto his hand, perhaps not even knowing what it was—only that it represented strength and confidence.

Slowly, she began to return to normal. Her breathing slowed and her heart eased from its triphammer pace. Her eyes began to refocus, and she saw Stone's concerned face looking into hers. From behind her, Picard was saying, "Counselor . . . was it Riker?"

She took one more deep breath, composing herself for a moment, and then said, "I . . . I don't know. It might have been. I sensed . . . something was falling. I felt chilled. Now . . . now there's nothing."

"You think he's still alive?" Stone asked.

She looked at Stone and felt dim frustration welling up in her. He was so in control of himself that she could not sense whether he would be pleased or upset at Riker's fate.

Would Stone hurt Riker if he had the opportunity? No, she was certain he would not. She was positive. Except . . .

What if she was wrong?

What if Stone was in even more control than she thought? What if he really was insane? If others were right and she was wrong? Would it be possible for Stone to protect his inner thoughts that much?

Should she warn the captain?

Warn him of what? That perhaps he shouldn't trust her opinions? How, in that case, could she possibly continue as counselor if she undercut her own advice?

She wasn't wrong. She had to trust her instincts, that was all. She was not wrong about Stone.

All of this went through her mind in the most fleeting of moments. Then she said to Stone, "Yes, I think he's still alive."

"Good," said Stone. That was all. Just good.

Except Troi, to her surprise, actually sensed relief from Stone. He was genuinely pleased that Riker was alive.

She hadn't misjudged him after all, she thought. A sense of satisfaction and relief swept through her.

"All right, people," said Picard, even as he released the now composed Deanna. He circled the room and said, "Opinions on the best way to proceed?"

"Data has given me the specs on Paradise," said Geordi. "It's not going to be easy. Transporters are not going to function properly through that soup. Communications would be so heavy with static that they'll practically be useless, and sensors will be unreliable."

"I only see one choice," said Picard. "Shuttlecraft and visual sweeps."

"Absolutely," Stone agreed. "This is up my alley."

"Indeed?" Picard raised an eyebrow.

"I've done it before," he said simply.

"Yes, so you have," said Picard, recalling the rescuing of the *Nimitz* crewmen that had sent Captain Borjas into such a tizzy. "Very well. We arrive in—Data?"

"Seven point three hours, sir," he said.

"Worf, signal ahead and let them know we're coming," Picard said. "We should be in instantaneous communication range before too long, so we'll be able to learn the full story of what happened. Who knows," he smiled, "perhaps by the time we get there, Commander Riker will be sitting safely back in Starlight eating a bowl of chicken soup."

Sometime later . . .

Stone slowly walked around Commander William T. Riker, who was standing straight and at attention. Stone studied him carefully, stroking his chin as he did so.

"You're very impressive, Commander," he said slowly. "Very impressive indeed."

Riker just stood there. Stone had not given him permission to speak.

"Everyone talks about you," said Stone. "Everyone thinks about you. You get yourself into trouble, the entire ship turns around and comes speeding to rescue you." He smiled. "I've gotten in trouble in the past. You know what people did for me?"

Riker turned and looked at him questioningly.

And Stone, his entire body suddenly locked in a rictus of fury, screamed, *"Nothing!"*

Riker made no reply.

As quickly as the anger had been there, it was gone. Stone was pleasant and calm once again. "You're a very popular man. You're just the kind of officer Starfleet likes. Cool. Calm. Always making the right decision. And I can tell just from looking at you . . . you never doubt yourself. No matter what kind of situation you're in, you have your cloak of righteousness draped around your shoulders.

"Oh yes," he smiled. "Oh yes, Commander . . . I am definitely glad we will have the chance to meet. We'll discuss all kinds of things. Success. Popularity. Deanna. All kinds of things. And you know? Sometimes talks like that can make all your troubles disappear, just like that."

He turned and spoke to the emptiness. "Computer—discontinue."

The image of Commander Riker promptly vanished, leaving Stone alone on the holodeck, the gleaming grids on the wall humming in expectation.

"Just like that," he repeated softly.

Stone returned to his cabin. They would be at Paradise in a very short time. He had to be prepared. Had to be ready for whatever he might have to do.

Riker was still out there. Stone could feel it. The good commander was somewhere in that frozen wasteland of a planet, and he was undoubtedly suffering.

He slid open the drawer of a cabinet and withdrew a weapon.

It was a long, vicious bullwhip, studded with small angry spikes. Stone held it up to the light, studying it with a curious detachment. It had obviously seen some action, for there were bloodstains all along its length.

He thought about what it represented, smiled, and put it back.

In her cabin, Deanna Troi, who had not slept in days, slipped from her meditative trance into slumber, and dreamed of Commander Riker.

Cold . . . so cold . . .
Riker stamped his feet, trying to restore some measure of feeling to them. From nearby, Stephy's hysterical sobbing had trailed off into soft, occasional sniffles.

Riker had been stooped over for so long he thought his back was going to go out on him. The cave that they had taken refuge in was not an especially tall one. But at least it was there, and at least it was unoccupied.

Riker looked back at the entrance that was now completely blocked with ice and snow. The avalanche had followed them into the crevasse, and for a moment Riker had had a brief vision of their bodies entombed in icy death. And then, off to the side, miraculously, had been a cave.

His mind had flashed a warning at him—what if there was something hideous and slavering waiting for them inside? But with the world crashing in around them, he didn't see where he had a lot of options.

He had yanked Stephy toward the cave. She hadn't seen it. Her gaze was riveted on the white death falling down toward them. Riker had virtually pulled her off her feet and thrown her headfirst into the cave. A split instant later he dove in after her. Moments after that, snow and ice covered the entrance.

They had scrambled back against the cave floor, afraid that somehow the debris might actually spread further in, encompassing the whole of the cave. That, of course, had not occurred. But they were now in pitch blackness.

Terrified, Stephy had thrown her arms around Riker, all the while crying for her parents. Riker had held her tightly and remained calm. Icy calm. Having two hysterical people in a lightless cave was not going to help matters.

He could understand her fear. He literally could not see his hand. *Is this what it's like to be dead?* he wondered. What if part of your brain never shuts down, if there's some small bit of consciousness left that's undetectable to normal instruments. If instead of brain functions ceasing, you're actually locked into blackness forever and ever and—

Well, *that* sure wasn't helping matters either.

They remained that way until the rumbling subsided. It seemed to take an eternity, but eventually it stopped.

"All right," Riker said softly. "It's all right, Stephy." He tried to ease her off him but her arms were locked around him. "Stephy," he said with a bit more firmness, "I have to do things to give us a better chance of staying alive. I can't do that if you won't let go."

"Mother," Stephy whispered. "Dad . . ."

"Your parents," Riker said with complete confidence now, "would not want you to freeze to death mourning for them. Not if there's something that can be done to avoid it."

"All . . . all right," she said slowly. Still, it took her a few moments more to unlock her arms from around Riker. He could understand her fears. It was like being afloat in the middle of an ocean and being told that the only way to survive was to let go of your life preserver.

His breath was sounding hollow in his pleximask and slowly he removed it. The air in the cave wasn't nearly as sharp as outside. Still, he couldn't see a damned thing.

He had deliberately traveled light, and now was beginning to regret it. "You don't have a light source on you, do you?"

There was a pause. "Hold on," she said.

He heard a rustling. She was removing something, but he couldn't see what. Then, a few moments later, there was a sudden flare.

He squinted against the abrupt harshness of it, automatically holding up a hand to shield himself against it. Then slowly, he lowered his hand and squinted.

Stephy was holding up what appeared to be a lanternlike device that gave off a cheerful glow, lighting up the cave and giving Riker his first opportunity to clearly see their haven. For a moment he dreaded the thought of looking down the maw of a Wild Thing, but he realized that, were there a creature like that in the cave, chances are it would have made its presence known by now. They weren't exactly subtle.

"Prometheite," she said, raising the lamp. The shadows it cast danced about her face. Next to her, on the floor, was an open backpack with some rations and other useful things. "Provides light for ten hours."

"More than enough," said Riker. He raised a hand in front of it, then removed his glove and put his hand closer. "Light. No heat."

"Can't have everything," she said.

"Yes, but heat is something I think we're going to need fairly quickly," he replied. "But . . . not to worry."

"Commander, if I wasn't worried right now, I think I'd have to be crazy."

He half smiled at that and nodded. She was speaking quickly, nervously, obviously hoping that talking would chase away the vivid memories she had of her parents' deaths.

Both of them. Still . . . was there a chance that Ellie had survived? Riker was uncertain just how far down the ice fall went. If she'd landed in a drift then maybe . . .

But it was pointless to speculate over such things with Stephy. First, she would say that he was just saying that in order to make her feel better, which would essentially be correct. And second, why build up her hopes over a one in a million shot?

"You're probably right," Riker said, stretching his legs. He rose and found that the ceiling of the cave would only allow him about three-quarters standing room. Well, better than nothing.

"How are we going to get out of here, Commander?" she asked.

"Right now, we aren't," replied Riker. "Night's fallen. Temperatures out there are below freezing."

"Then . . . then what are we going to do?"

"Stay put." He walked over toward the ice covering the entrance and rapped it. It was solid. "Definitely stay put. Sure this is blocking us in, but it's also giving us shelter. Have to take the bad with the good."

"Well," she snuffled, "so far most of it's been pretty damned bad."

"Could be worse."

"How?"

194

"You could be alone."

She nodded. "I think I'd die."

"Look," he held up a finger, "let's make an agreement. No more talking about death or dying. That's the _D_ word. I don't want to hear the _D_ word. And since I'm the ranking officer on hand, what I say goes. Got that?"

She tossed off a bemused salute. "Aye-aye."

"We don't salute in Starfleet."

"Oh." She put her thumb to her nose and waggled her fingers. "Aye-aye."

"That's better," he smiled. "We'll have you ready to join Starfleet in no time."

Even as he spoke he was making his way to the back of the cave. It didn't extend too far, not more than a couple of meters. Still, it wasn't too bad. It was about the size of the quarters he had when he'd been an ensign, just starting out . . . except the cave's ceiling was a lot lower.

Riker remembered the captain of that vessel, who had decided that Riker had entirely too much confidence and poise for a mere ensign, and vowed that during the voyage he would cut Riker down to size. Riker fleetingly wished that captain were here now. Shortness would definitely be an asset at this moment.

He pulled out his phaser and checked the power levels. Not promising, but still enough to serve the purpose of survival, at least for a while. He turned and aimed the phaser at the barrier of ice and snow that covered the exit.

"I thought you said—" began Stephy.

"Never question a superior officer," Riker replied, and fired a pencil-thin beam.

It drilled a small hole straight through the ice, and Riker quickly snapped off the beam, hoping that he'd been fast enough. He listened carefully. There was not so much as a slight rumble.

"Air hole," he explained.

"Oooohhh," said Stephy, nodding. "That's helpful. Now all we have to do is worry about freezing to death."

"You have a portable furnace in that thing?"

Stephy shook her head. "No, that was in my . . . mother's . . ." Her voice trailed off.

I'm going to have to walk on eggshells with her, Riker thought.

But Stephy looked up, determined to show that she could be as strong as Riker. "It was in my mother's pack," she said. "That's the breaks, I guess."

Riker nodded. "I guess so. Still . . . it's nothing we can't handle. Give me a hand."

Moments later Riker had gathered a small pile of stones. He adjusted his phaser to the lightest setting and fired steadily at the rocks. In seconds the rocks had heated up, and provided a comfortable, glowing warmth.

Stephy, who had removed her pleximask long before, crouched in front of the rocks and held her hands in front of them. "Great!" she said. "How long will they stay like this?"

"I'll have to keep rewarming them every hour or so."

"I hope you've got plenty of power in that phaser."

He didn't even glance at the indicator to note how low it was. "More than enough," he lied.

Stephy cracked out rations from her backpack, and she and Riker ate in silence. He knew what she was thinking about, and he wished that Deanna were there to console the girl. Riker didn't have the words to assuage the pain she had to be feeling.

At any rate, his mind was racing ahead to what would be the next likely move. He glanced at the chronometer he had taken with him from the landrover . . .

He winced. The landrover. It was at the bottom of the mountain. There was a better-than-even chance that it had been buried in the avalanche. So even presuming they survived the night, the daytime promised only a very long, very difficult walk back to Starlight, pursued by who knew what?

Back to the chronometer. He knew roughly when sunrise, such as it was, occurred on Paradise. So he would keep close tabs on that. He didn't want to remain in the cave any longer than he had to.

"I hear it's a good way to die," she said softly.

He looked up at her. "What did I say about the *D* word?"

She seemed barely to notice that he was even there. Her eyes were staring off at something he couldn't see. "Freezing to death. It's supposed to be very comfortable."

"Stephy, this is pointless . . ."

"You get all numb, and then you start to feel warm." Her voice was oddly distant. "This nice, relaxed feeling, and then you just go to sleep and you don't wake up. Very peaceful."

He took her by the shoulders and stared directly at her. "We're not going to die, peacefully or otherwise. The rocks are more than enough to keep us warm."

She nodded slowly, and was silent for a long time. Several times Riker tried to engage her in conversation about something innocuous—about boys back in Starlight, about simple things. But she was no fool. Hanging over all of it was the incontrovertible fact that they were in deep, deep trouble, and all the smooth talking and convivial chat from Riker was not going to alter that simple truth.

He reheated the rocks twice more and Stephy stared at him with distant curiosity. Something was going through her mind and he wished he could tell what it was. Dealing with teenage girls was definitely not his forte. Again his thoughts turned to Troi. It seemed oddly selfish that he was wishing Deanna was with him. That meant her life would be in jeopardy as well. Yet somehow, when she was there, he felt more capable of seeing . . . what? The big picture? The way things were? The true relation of Riker to the universe?

The hell with all that. He wished she were there just so he could hold her and take strength from her.

So that's where he was at this point: stooped over, walking about the cave. Sometime a while ago, Stephy had begun crying again, and he could think of nothing to do to ease her pain. What was he supposed to say? That everything would be all right? That mommy and daddy were in a better place now? Let's make some cocoa and pretend we're really camping? So he had said nothing, allowing the girl as much privacy for her grief as the cramped quarters would allow. Slowly, her crying had eased to an occasional sniffle.

He sat back down, leaning against the wall. The rocks were once again starting to cool off, but he didn't want to fire on them too soon. He had to apportion the small amount of phaser power he had left.

He felt a soft warmth coming over him and forced himself back awake, Stephy's words echoing in his head. Hours had passed according to the chronometer, hours more until daylight.

He had to stay awake. If he didn't, he wouldn't be able to keep the stones heated and the temperature in the cave would undoubtedly drop to a dangerous level.

Stephy was curled near the stones. She half opened her eyes. The glow of the stones reflected in them as she said, "Commander . . ."

"Yes?"

"Why did my father call you Thunderball?"

He laughed softly. "When you're older," he said.

"I'm not going to get any older."

He sighed. "Don't talk like that," he said tiredly.

"Dave Mosley likes me."

He was having trouble following the conversation. "What?"

"Dave Mosley. He's this guy back at Starlight, a couple years older than me. He's always trying to spend time alone with me."

"He's your boyfriend?" said Riker, fighting to keep his mind on the subject. His thoughts kept wandering from fatigue. Where the devil was the girl getting the energy?

"No. He's a drip."

"Oh."

"He only wants one thing."

Riker looked at her through slitted eyes. "Oh."

"I've never done it, you know."

"It?" He paused, trying to figure out what they were talking about, and then the obvious snapped into place. Obviously, his brain was starting to freeze over. He leaned forward and phasered the rocks, bringing them up to a pleasing heat again. "Oh . . . *it*."

"Yeah. I was . . . kind of waiting. For someone who was special."

"Oh."

"Fat lot of good waiting did me, huh?"

"You're only a teenager, Stephy," he said. "You'll have lots of years. Lots of time."

"Not if I die."

"You're not going to die, Stephy, now go to sleep. Get some rest. We'll have a busy day tomorrow."

He felt something on his knee and looked down. It was her hand.

"You're special," she said softly.

He sighed. "Stephy . . . I know you're scared, and frightened . . . and you think that the only thing that can chase your fear away would be . . . *it*. But running never helped anything."

"You're not interested," she said, her voice laced with disappointment.

"Stephy . . . it would be . . . inappropriate."

"Because of the age thing?"

"The age thing, the parents thing . . . how do you think your parents would feel?"

"They don't feel anything, they—" Her voice choked, and she started to cry all over again. She sagged against Riker, but there was nothing of the would-be teen seductress about her now. Now she was once again the frightened girl. Riker held her to him and stroked her hair gently, telling her that everything would be all right (which he didn't completely believe himself, but you had to say whatever worked). Eventually, the crying subsided once more, and without a word she slid away from him and curled herself around the rocks once more.

But before she fell asleep she said softly, "Dave Mosley would kill to be in your shoes right now."

"Yes, well . . ." and he thought of the relative comfort and safety of Starlight, "I wouldn't mind being in his right now either."

The only sound in the cave now was Stephy's slow, relaxed breathing.

Riker was floating, half-slumbering in an in-between world. It was peaceful there, comfortable. A pleasant haze was falling around him.

The quiet of the cave seemed very loud, as if a low roaring were filling it. He was slumping down, his spine becoming stiff, and he forced himself up and stared at the lantern. A gentle glow suffused it, and Riker felt completely at ease.

Stephy lay there, asleep. If Riker had followed Carter's path, he realized, he might have had a daughter about her age. He tried to envision what that would be like and failed.

He speculated on the oddness of it. On the *Enterprise,* the ship was specifically designed to accommodate families. No longer was it necessary to abandon the hopes of a personal life, of a family and loved ones, to go off into space. Yet no one on the bridge crew—not Picard, nor Geordi, nor Worf—was part of a nuclear family. They had no spouses, no children. Despite the option that was now open to them, none of them had availed themselves of it. Why?

"You're all gutless," said Jackson Carter.

Riker looked over at Stephy's sleeping form, and Jackson Carter was seated next to her, stroking her hair lovingly. Riker did not question Carter's being there. It seemed right.

"How can you say that?" Riker asked. "Every single moment of our life is filled with the unknown. With danger."

Carter snorted disdainfully. "That's easy. That's glamorous. Everyone says space is the great frontier. Nonsense. Human relations—that's where the true adventure lies. What's your life like, anyway? You go to planets, you look around, you leave them as they are."

"It's a hell of a lot more complicated than that, Jackson," replied Riker.

"You know nothing about nothing," said Carter.

Riker leaned forward, his eyes glimmering. "I've seen the stars, so close I could reach out and scoop them up. I've seen suns going nova and suns being born. I've stood on planets with life just beginning to crawl out of the primordial ooze, knowing that millions of years into the future, something great and majestic might be there, and I've rejoiced. I've stood on planets where the only things remaining were vast radioactive wastelands, buildings bombed into oblivion, and I've wept. I've seen the wonders of the universe."

Carter smiled and shook his head slowly. "I," he said, "have known the peaceful joy of lying in a warm bed, next to a woman who was there yesterday and is there today and will be there tomorrow. And if I felt a chill, I would place my body against hers, and I would be warmed. I've been up at two in the morning to feed my crying infant, sat with her in my lap, holding a bottle for her to still her sobbing. And she would look up at me, focus only on me, with those magnificent, innocent eyes. In the silence of the early morning the galaxy slept and there was only us. And to her, I *was* the wonders of the universe."

Riker sat back and stared at his friend, who he could never recall having spoken like that before. "You lucky bastard," he said softly. "I feel happy for you."

"Would you trade?" asked Carter.

"No."

"Then I feel sorry for you."

Riker closed his eyes, slowly shaking his head. "I . . . am so sorry, Jackson. If I'd done something differently, I could have saved you all. Sometimes I think my whole life consists of second-guessing myself." He sighed. "What the hell am I doing here? A stranger in a Godforsaken place, fighting for my life."

"We're all strangers, Will."

Now Riker opened his eyes, and Deanna Troi was there. Of course she was. Where else would she be?

"Meaning what, Counselor?"

"Meaning everyone has feelings of desolation, of being alone. Even in a crushing crowd, we are all of us alone. What is the true test of the spirit is how that spirit copes with that aloneness."

He smiled and said, "I'd rather be alone with you."

"You must be strong, Will. You are needed to be. Regrets over might-have-beens can only blacken your soul."

"Even if the regrets involve lives I might have saved?"

"Even if."

"I miss you, Deanna."

"And I you, Will."

He paused. "So I should not even have regrets about the way I've handled our relationship?"

Now she was smiling. "It has been a two-way path, Will."

"Maybe. Still—" He sat up fully. There was a soft haze covering Deanna that seemed to be growing. "If I get out of here, I've been thinking. Maybe we should—"

She put up a hand. "Don't think things you'll regret."

"I wouldn't regret it," he said.

"No. There's an old earth saying, Will: 'There are no atheists in foxholes.' What seems clear now can become very unclear once the danger has passed."

"Maybe this was what I needed to see clearly."

"Then," she said softly, "that point of view will most certainly be present after you have been saved. I suspect, though, that once you are back in the comfortable surroundings of the *Enterprise,* you might see things differently."

"I don't want to die with regrets, Deanna."

She shrugged. "Then don't die."

Don't die.

Riker suddenly sat up, his body fully awake. The rocks—almost chilled to uselessness. He quickly aimed his phaser and heated them up once again. Stephy half turned in her sleep, murmuring something incomprehensible.

Riker stood, flexing his muscles. His recollections of fleeting dreams were already growing dim, although he couldn't shake the feeling that it would have been something he wanted to remember. All he knew was that he felt warm, but the warmth wasn't just from the heated rocks. It was a warmth that came from within.

He checked the chronometer and saw that daybreak would be coming soon. He sat back, softly tossing the phaser from one hand to the other to keep his fingers flexed, and waited.

Stephy turned and looked at him through half closed eyes. "Commander," she murmured, "have you ever been in worse trouble than this?"

"Stephy, William T. Riker has been in far worse than this," he smiled, "and always survived. Trouble is my middle name." And with a wink he added, "What do you think the 'T' stands for?"

She went back to sleep with a confidence that Riker didn't feel.

Chapter Twenty

"I'M COMING WITH YOU."

Stone looked at Troi blankly, and she waited for some sort of protest. Instead, he remained as impassive as ever. The two of them were standing on the shuttlebay landing deck as others on the team that Stone had assembled prepared to leave.

"Are you sure that's wise?" he asked at length.

"I think it is what I must do."

He tilted his head slightly and studied her. "Because you don't trust me?"

"It has nothing to do with that," said Deanna, which was the truth. "And of course I trust you."

"Well, that is good. That is certainly good. For a moment I thought the white queen was trying to keep the black king in check."

He smiled that same, maddening, disturbing smile, and then said, "If you're coming, I suggest you get some gear on. This isn't a day at the beach."

Troi nodded curtly and went off to supplies, to pick up some of the heavy gear that the other crew members were wearing.

Moments later, Picard had entered the shuttle bay, and was surveying the away team that Stone had selected. Worf, of course, as head of security. Three more security men, all heavy and muscular. Clearly, Stone was anticipating trouble.

Geordi La Forge hurried in, closing his jacket. The chief engineer practically seemed to disappear within its folds. Picard looked at him curiously and said, "Mr. La Forge, why are you going along?"

"Since the atmosphere can play fast and loose with our instruments, Commander Stone wanted me along because of my VISOR," and he touched the metal device encircling his face. "His feeling was that the components of my device might be less susceptible to interference."

Picard nodded slowly and looked approvingly at Stone. "Good thinking, Commander," he said.

Stone's expression did not change as he said merely, "Thank you, Captain."

Troi entered briskly, putting on her gloves. "All right," she said, looking even more lost in the equipment than Geordi. "I'm ready."

"Counselor?" said Picard in surprise.

"We're bringing her along to give the group some style," Stone said.

"It was at my request, Captain," said Troi, ignoring the ripple of laughter from the security guards (although not from Worf, of course). She, in turn, looked to Worf, to see what sort of reaction he had to her coming along on the potentially hazardous mission.

Worf said nothing, naturally. Worf rarely wasted words. But he tilted his head slightly toward her, acknowledging her presence, and she smiled. That was probably the most she could hope to get out of him as far as cordialities were concerned.

"All right," said Picard. "All of you be careful. I want you to stay in touch with the ship as much as possible."

"That's pretty much what you said when we went down to

Culinan, sir," said Stone mildly. "Aren't you satisfied with the way things went down there?"

Picard did not take up the open challenge. "If you wish to discuss that further, Commander, we shall upon your return. Good luck."

They nodded and climbed into the shuttle.

Stone seated himself in the pilot's seat and glanced around at the shuttle's make-up. "All the comforts of home. Get ready people. We're going to have some fun."

As the others prepared for the takeoff, Stone's hands moved confidently across the controls. The check systems came to electronic life, and Stone powered up the nacelles. The shuttle began to turn, slowly and majestically, in order to face the bay door.

La Forge, seated next to Stone, tapped the comm link and said "La Forge to shuttle control. Open bay door."

Smoothly the great doors opened in front of them, clicking into place. Geordi thought the door movement seemed less smooth than it should, and made a mental note to check on it.

Before them was a vast array of stars, and to the lower right, the calmly turning sphere that was Paradise.

Stone finished running through the last minute checks and said briskly, "Everybody ready?" There was a murmur of assent. "All right then. Let's—" he hit the forward thrusters, "blast."

Picard, who was standing far to the side of the shuttlecraft, jumped back in shock as the shuttle seemed to leap forward, as if shot from a sling. Normal liftoffs were smooth and slow. With this launch, however, the shuttle had gone from no speed to cruising speed in the blink of an eye.

"He drives like a maniac," said Picard to no one. "Naturally."

The shuttlecraft practically blew out of the back of the *Enterprise,* and everyone inside except for Stone and Worf gasped with shock. Stone was grinning ear to ear, and he banked the shuttle at a sharp, dizzying angle that seemed to drop them toward Paradise totally out of control.

"Stop!" pleaded Deanna Troi.

"I don't think you'd like that, Counselor," said Stone cheerily. "I slam on reverse, everybody winds up a smear on the front."

"Commander," Worf intoned just behind him, his voice unmistakably ominous. "Slow down the descent."

"That an order, Worf?"

"Think of it as a request that should not be ignored."

"I thought we were in a hurry," said Stone. His fingers flew over the controls and the reverse roared to life. The shuttle obediently began to slow down, but still the planet was coming at them quickly.

Stone said, with all trace of amusement gone from his voice, "This is going to be a tough one, people. If you're going to be shaken by something as relatively minor as my piloting, you're on the wrong assignment and I'll be more than happy to return any of you. By the way—I'm rated class 1 AAA by Starfleet. I've never so much as scraped the hull of a shuttle. So ease up. And think happy thoughts."

Then, in a low voice only Worf heard, Stone said, "Oh, Worf . . . we might run into some re- nowned terraformer stubborness. If so, here's what we'll say . . ."

Riker nodded approvingly at the chronometer. "Stephy," he said in a soft voice, and shook her shoulder. "Time to get up."

She yawned, blinked, and then sat up abruptly. Riker recognized it as the common sort of disorientation you feel when you're waking up in a strange place. And Riker had trouble picturing any place stranger than this.

"I'm not dead," she said in wonderment.

"Neither of us are," replied Riker. "And it's morning.

Time to start thinking about getting out of here." He pointed at her backpack and said "Anything else useful in there?"

She upended it and the contents spilled out across the floor: Some more rations, which might come in handy, a collapsible knife and fork, a—

"Now this could be handy," he said, and picked up an ice axe. It was worn but still sturdy. The pick appeared sharp and, on the other end of the shaft, was a spike.

"Mom had some other mountain climbing equipment, including a rope," said Stephy matter-of-factly. Riker was relieved by the calm way the girl had said that. It showed that if there was any grief left in her, she was clearly going to deal with it at a more appropriate time. On the other hand, he wished to hell Stephy had the rope.

"Ah well," said Riker, sticking the ice axe into his belt. "We deal with what we can."

He touched the stones, the heat of which was pretty much worn off by this time. But there would no longer be any need to continue heating them.

Riker moved over to the ice wall and tapped it. Still solid. He pulled the ice axe from his belt and gave it a whack with the pick edge, and managed to chip off a few pieces.

"Good," said Riker. "At that rate we'll be out sometime next month."

He took out his phaser, checked the power level. There wasn't enough for a full disintegration blast, that much he knew. Besides, he'd be concerned about the noise level.

But a pencil thin beam would be a lot less noisy, and less of a drain.

"This may take a little while," he said, as he positioned himself in front of the ice wall.

"It's okay," said Stephy. "Today is laundry day back home anyway, so I'm in no particular hurry."

Riker put the phaser right up against the upper left hand corner, checked the calibration, and fired.

* * *

The shuttle made a quick stop in Starlight, touching base with Vernon and the other scientists. They quickly pumped the townspeople for as much information as they could.

As first the terraformers were reluctant to cooperate, but Stone settled that issue rather quickly.

"You're such hotshots," Mark Masters was saying. "The Federation comes in here, all hot to trot. It's daylight now, and we'll go out and find our people, thank you very much, without any help from you."

"I see," Stone replied—slowly, thoughtfully. Then he turned to Worf and, chucking a thumb at Masters, said, "Lieutenant . . . kill him."

"Quickly or slowly?" Worf asked on cue.

"Surprise me."

Worf nodded, and crossed quickly toward Masters, placing a hand on the scientist's arm. Masters gasped, "You're bluffing!"

"You bet your life?" replied Stone.

"What . . . what do you want to know," said Masters.

The shuttlecraft lifted off from Starlight and shot out in the direction of the probe.

Stone skimmed the surface with dazzling ease, and even Geordi had to admit to himself that Stone was one hell of a pilot. "Nice bluff you guys used on that terraformer back there."

As one, both Stone and Worf said, "Bluff?"

Geordi decided that it would be best not to pursue the matter. As he did, Stone said briskly, "Counselor . . . you getting any reading on Commander Riker?"

"I sense his presence," she said. "He seems calm, at peace. Determined."

"That's our Riker," said Stone, and Deanna knew that she definitely did not like the sound of that. But Stone was, as always, controlled, and Deanna couldn't make headway.

Except . . .

He felt agitated. She sensed something stirring within him. Certainly some degree of concern would be a natural thing for someone spearheading a rescue mission to have. But what specifically was he agitated about? Something positive, or something negative?

He was sane. He would not hurt Will. She kept telling herself that over and over again, and she was starting to wonder if she was doing so to remind herself, or to convince herself.

The ice steadily melted away under the heat of the phaser. But it wasn't enough, not nearly. The depth of the snow and ice had been greater than Riker could have surmised.

He stopped, realizing that he was not going to get through. He checked the power level and it was pathetically low.

"What's the problem?" asked Stephy, fighting to keep down alarm. "What's wrong?"

"What's wrong is that this isn't working," he said. "I was essentially hoping to cut a hole for us to climb out of, but look." He pointed to the border that he had cut away, with the intention of shoving the snow through like a giant plug. But when he put his hands against it and shoved with all his strength, the plug showed not the slightest interest in moving.

Stephy got up and, without a word, added her strength to his. But it made no difference.

"So . . . so what do we do now?" she asked.

He sat back, stroking his beard. "You haven't got a thermite bomb in there by any chance, do you?"

She shook her head.

He stared at the phaser, and then an idea struck him. It was desperate, but then again, so were they.

"Get to the back of the cave," he said, "as far back as you can."

"What're you going to—"

"Just do it. And grab your things."

She did as he instructed, stopping just briefly enough to

scoop her belongings into the backpack and sling it onto her back.

Riker, in the meantime, began adjusting settings on his phaser. Sweat beaded his forehead as he hoped that what he was doing would work without killing them.

"What's going on?" she asked from the back.

"Nothing important," he said grimly. "I'm just going to try and blow open the front door."

"Oh." She didn't sound overly thrilled. Then again, neither was he.

Riker took the ice axe and started chipping furiously, pieces flying, until he had created a small hole in the center of the ice wall. Stephy watched uncomprehendingly. "We're getting out through there?" she said doubtfully.

"That's the general plan," he said, and didn't add that there was also a good chance he might bring the entire cave down on them, if not the mountain. After all, even the best plans had their drawbacks.

He made the final adjustment and then pressed the trigger. Slowly a high-pitched whining filled the cave, growing sharper and louder.

Riker shoved the phaser into the hole as deeply as he could, and then darted back toward the rear of the cave.

He covered Stephy with his body as she said fearfully, "What's going on?"

"I set the phaser to overload. It's like sticking your finger in a faucet and letting the water get backed up. Sooner or later it blows."

"We'll be killed!"

"Hopefully not," said Riker. "I didn't tell you that the phaser was almost out of power. It should only cause a low level explosion, hopefully enough to blow that snow and ice out."

"It was almost out of power and you didn't tell me?" screeched Stephy above the noise. "Is there anything else I should know!"

"Yeah. Duck!" He shoved her head down.

Behind them, the phaser reached critical and blew. Huge chunks of ice and snow flew out from the cave as if jetpropelled. Stephy screeched, clinging more tightly to Riker, and a fine spray of ice fell on them, giving them a light, dusty coat. Air rushed in, blowing out the stale atmosphere that had collected in the cave.

Riker lifted his elbow and peered around at the blockage. Where once there had been a mass of snow, a huge hole gaped at them.

"Come on." He yanked her by the arm as they stumbled toward the opening.

Truthfully, Riker wasn't certain whether they weren't leaping from the frying pan to the fire. They had no phaser. And although the explosion had been muffled, it might still be enough to trigger another avalanche, in which case they might be crushed by falling debris moments after making the break to freedom. But anything was better than staying in the cave.

They burst out of the cave, Stephy's backpack banging against her back. Riker threw them against the far wall of the crevasse, putting his back against it and looking up nervously. Stephy did likewise.

They waited. Waited for an answering rumble, and for the world to start falling in around them.

Nothing. The Hidden Hills seemed momentarily unsettled, but when no further noise or vibration arose, it was as if the Hills let out a slow breath and settled back to normal.

Riker glanced down the crevasse, the direction from which they had come. A small mountain of snow had fallen and blocked the path. He realized that they'd been damn lucky that only a coating, several feet thick, had fallen over the cave front. If the avalanche had completely filled in the crevasse, they'd be dead.

It was as if the Hidden Hills were toying with them, giving them some measure of hope before snatching it away from them.

Up. The crevasse path open to them angled up. They

wanted to go down, but at least they had a direction in which they could go. Take the good with the bad. Dwell on the pluses, use your advantages, and all the other wonderful homilies they teach you at the Academy. All of which seem like nice, cozy words when you're seated behind a desk studying scenarios.

Scenario: Your childhood friend and his wife are dead; their daughter is keeping herself together with spit and bailing wire; you have no phaser, short supplies, an ice axe, and genetically spawned monsters prepared to leap out at you at any time as you make your way through a mountainous, cold, hostile environment.

Funny how this one had slipped past the Academy trainers. Hell, happens all the time, right?

"Come on." He patted her on the back. "Let's go."

They started up the crevasse.

The shuttlecraft located the Carters' landrover.

"What do you see, Lieutenant?" Stone asked Geordi as they stood in the hatch of the shuttle, poised on the edge. "Picking up anything warm? Tricorder says no life, but . . . you never know."

Slowly, Geordi shook his head. "Nothing. But I'm picking up objects through that window there."

Stone squinted, but the inside of the landrover was dark to him. "Like what?"

"From the mass, shape, I'd say a body. Maybe two. One of 'em seems like an animal of some sort."

"One of the Wild Things that Masters warned us of," said Worf.

"And didn't he warn us gladly?" said Stone with oddly out of place cheer. "You sure they're dead, Lieutenant?"

"Getting no warmth at all, Commander."

Stone nodded briskly and hopped out of the shuttle. "All right. Let's check it out. Troi, stay here."

From behind him, Deanna felt a bit of annoyance. "I might be needed," she said.

He turned and looked at her square in the eyes—one of the few times he had ever done that. "If that's your boyfriend's body in there, and he went three rounds with a Wild Thing, you really want to see it?"

She paused, her expression saying all.

"Stay here," said Stone. "Tinker, stay with her." The security guard Stone had selected was not anxious to possibly see a gutted Commander Riker, and so was only too happy to obey.

They crossed to the landrover, Stone in the lead. The passenger door was open and without hesitation Stone hopped in. Worf was right behind him but La Forge hung back because, in reality he wasn't thrilled about examining corpses either. *I'm an engineer,* he thought, *not a doctor.*

Worf watched as Stone went straight and unflinchingly to the bodies. He glanced at the man briefly and said loudly, "Not him. I think it's Carter."

His voice carried across the short distance to the shuttlecraft and Deanna Troi, upon hearing it, let out a long sigh of relief.

How did it make Stone feel?

The answer, the possibly telling answer, prompted Troi to reach out to him. Sure enough, Stone had relaxed his guard just long enough for her to sense a basic feeling—Stone was pleased that it wasn't Riker.

She took a great measure of confidence in that, for to her that proved that Stone bore no ill will against Riker.

Worf, meanwhile, was impressed by Stone's implacability. The body was not a pretty sight, even by Klingon standards, but Stone did not seem the least bit phased by it. Instead, he said briskly, "Let's look around. See if we can find some clue as to where they went."

Short moments later they located the recorder log. However, when Stone tried to play it, it jammed up because of its long exposure to the cold.

"No problem," said Geordi calmly. "Let me get back to the shuttlecraft and I'll have it up and working in no time."

As they stepped out of the landrover and started back toward the shuttle, Geordi glanced over to his left, then to his right, and it was the latter observation that prompted him to say, "Commander Riker—I mean, Commander Stone."

If Stone took offense at the slip, or even noticed, he gave no sign. "Yes, Lieutenant?"

"Something over there," and he pointed. "I think it's another one of those creatures, but it's half-buried under the snow."

"Okay, Lieutenant. I'll check it out. You get back to the shuttle and get that recorder working."

Without waiting for response, Stone turned and ran over to where La Forge had indicated. He didn't even have to glance behind him to know that Worf was right there. He got to the spot and waited a moment for Worf to catch up. Still, Stone was feeling winded and Worf was not even working up a sweat.

"Your sash still uncomfortable, Lieutenant?" he asked as he crouched over the remains.

"Very."

"As long as you're happy." He studied the remains carefully. "This was picked clean," he said. Then he held up a leg bone. "Look at this. This thing was crushed. And . . ."

He felt along the ground, looking for some sign of tracks, but could detect nothing. The wind and swirling snow had more than done its job. Stone went down on one knee and pondered a moment, bearing a resemblance to the statue of The Thinker.

"Okay," he said slowly. "Here's what happened. Riker finds the landrover. Before or after he finds it, he's attacked by a Wild Thing. He runs the bugger over. Then he heads off . . . where?" He paused. "He didn't head back to town. We would have found him between here and there."

"Unless he got lost."

"There's that." He paused. "I think he went after somebody. Didn't Carter have his family with him?"

Worf nodded slowly.

"And the family wasn't in the landrover, so they must have headed off somewhere, and Riker found out where. And he's off after them."

"The log."

"Has to be," said Stone, and he stood. "Hope La Forge can get that fixed quick." He turned and started for the shuttlecraft.

"And what consumed the remains of the Wild Thing?" said Worf slowly.

"Other Wild Things, I would imagine," said Stone. "They're supposed to be good trackers. So after they ate their pal, they immediately set off on the trail of blood left by the treads of Riker's landrover. Which was lucky for Carter there," and he chucked a thumb at the landrover, "or he would have been dessert."

"But if that's the case," rumbled Worf, "then a pack of bloodthirsty monsters is on Commander Riker's trail."

Stone nodded. "Stimulating, isn't it?"

Stephy looked up. "Oh God, I can't."

"It's the only path open," Riker said.

"Then let's stay here," she almost begged.

The crevasse had narrowed further and further, and Riker had been concerned that their passageway would vanish altogether. Fortunately, though, it started to widen out, and then opened out onto . . .

A sheer drop.

Riker had almost stepped off before catching himself and looking down. It was not pleasant. Wind rushed far beneath them, and for a moment he fancied he could hear the mournful voice of Ellie far below them.

Then he had looked off to his left and there was another path, a narrow one hugging the side of the mountain. In order to get to it, they would have to virtually step over nothingness to make it.

"I'll go first," said Riker.

"No! Then you'll fall and I'll be all alone here!"

"All right. You go first."

"What if I fall!"

"Stephy, we don't have a lot of time. I'll go first and help you over."

Riker stood there a moment, gathering his strength, pulling together his resolve. It wasn't a particularly far distance. If there were no drop, he wouldn't even give it a second thought.

But there *was* that drop.

Don't look down. *That* they had taught in the Academy. It also happened to be the first rule of life.

Riker leaped.

Stephy gave a little shriek as Riker landed on the path. He slipped momentarily, then stood and put his back against the mountain. The path was four, maybe five feet wide. Not a lot. But not too little.

Riker stretched his hand out and called, "Come on, Stephy. Your turn. You can do it."

She looked down, thereby violating rule number one.

"Don't look down," said Riker urgently. "Just look at me. See? Look straight into my eyes, Stephy. You can do it. Come on. Just step over. No problem. Easiest thing in the world."

She stretched out a hand to him, still bracing herself against the edge.

"That's it. Now just step over."

From behind Stephy there came a low growl.

She was afraid to turn, for she knew what she would see.

It was coming toward her slowly, red eyes glowing with a furious light. Its mouth was open and snapping in anticipation.

Ten feet away, closing fast.

"Stephy!" shouted Riker. "Come on! Move!"

She was frozen, paralyzed. She couldn't take her eyes away from that hideous face.

"Move it!" Riker yelled. "Don't look at it! Come on! Just

217

jump! Just come to me!" He stretched out as far as he could, his fingers barely inches away from her.

Her mouth moved and no sound came out.

Eight feet, and a full roar built in its chest as it paused and then let loose with a bloodcurdling howl.

"Stephy! Move it, damn you, move it. Jump, *jump, and damn you, move!"*

The monster reared back on its legs and then leaped toward the terrified girl.

The move broke her from her paralysis and Stephy lunged blindly toward Riker, flailing out. He snagged her and swung her up onto the path next to him.

The Wild Thing sailed by, looking puzzled and furious, and then it arced past them and down. It howled all the way as it plummeted, until it struck the mountain face once and then was silent for the rest of the plunge.

Riker and Stephy stayed there a moment, backs against the mountain, letting their breathing settle back to normal.

Slowly, Stephy turned toward Riker and said, "You didn't have to curse at me."

Under the pleximask his mouth twisted into a bemused grin. "I'll try to watch that."

The shuttlecraft did a slow, high turn around the eastern portion of the Hidden Hills as all of them looked out nervously.

"We're picking up some life readings," Worf said, scanning the instruments. "Difficult to be precise as to the nature. It could be Commander Riker. Could be those animals. Either way, I'm having trouble pinpointing them."

"Well, we can't skim too close," said Stone. "Noise of the shuttle engines will cause an avalanche for sure." He paused thoughtfully. "I'm bringing her down about a quarter mile away and we'll go on foot. Unless any of you see some alternatives?"

Troi let out a shriek.

Their heads turned as one and Geordi said, "Counselor! What is it?"

She paused, letting her pulse return to normal. "Near miss," she said.

"From down there?"

"I . . . think so. I'm not certain though."

"All right," said Stone. "Let's make certain."

Riker and Stephy made their way along the ledge for what seemed an eternity. Several times the wind gusted at them, threatening to pluck them off and hurl them down to join the Wild Thing. Each time, though, they stopped and rode it out, and felt grateful when the wind slowed and passed them by.

"I'm not sure how much longer I can do this, Commander Riker," Stephy said. It was the first words she had spoken in some time.

"Well, we may not have to much longer. Look up."

She did, craning her neck.

The path had been working them steadily upward, and now above them was what appeared to be a ridge that flattened out into a summit. It was difficult to tell from the angle they were at, however.

"Care to take a look?" said Riker.

Stephy wasn't thrilled with the idea of climbing up, since she had no idea what might be waiting for them on the summit. On the other hand, the ledge didn't seem much more promising.

"Okay," she said, and stepped close to Riker. He put his hands around her waist and hoisted her up. Stephy's fingers closed on the ridge and, with an additional boost from Riker, she scrambled upward.

There was what seemed an incredibly long pause, and then Stephy called out, "Oh, this is great! Come on up." She leaned over and extended her hand.

Riker jumped, his fingers catching the edge, and then with

Stephy's aid he hauled himself up. He realized that the wind and chill was taking a lot out of him. Ordinarily, he would have been able to pull himself up without any help.

He flexed his right shoulder and felt a twinge. It was still bothering him from yesterday, but at least it wasn't as bad as he had thought.

They had made it to a summit, not particularly large, but large enough to be a comfortable resting point. Protected by taller mountains around them, the summit was not a sheet of ice, but instead, about a foot deep in snow.

Riker crunched through it, walking the edge and looking down. To his combined alarm and relief he saw that the ledge they had been walking along had come to an end just around the bend from where they had been. They had clambered up just in time.

"Commander!"

Riker turned, grabbing for his ice axe, thinking they were under attack.

Instead, Stephy was calling and pointing. "Over here! There's a path over here that goes down.

He went over and saw that she was correct. On the opposite side of the summit was a very short, but not remotely dangerous, slide down to a notch. And off to the left of the notch was a ravine.

"I think you're right," he smiled. "Maybe things are improving at that."

The away team made their way slowly around the base of the mountains, searching for some sign of where Riker and whoever he had managed to find had gone.

Geordi made a slow, careful sweep with his VISOR. Nothing. "Come on," he muttered, "be something. Be somewhere. Come on . . ."

And suddenly he shouted, "Commander!"

"Shhh!" hissed Stone. "Keep it down. If you shout, the mountains may get angry and shout back. What have you got?"

"Over there!" he pointed.

"Over where?"

"There!" La Forge was pointing to a large embankment of snow. "Look!"

Then Stone saw it too. A hand, wearing a white glove that had caused it to be lost against the background.

They dashed toward it, the rest of the away team right behind them. Stone skidded to a stop and said, "My God. She almost made it out."

It was clear what had happened. For there, just barely peering out from the snow, was the agonized face of a woman.

"She tried to dig her way out," said Stone, looking up. "And she almost made it. And then her strength must have given out."

In a low whisper, Deanna Troi said, "She's alive."

"Are you sure?" demanded Worf.

She nodded, her face ashen. It was like the smallest, fading glimmer of light, and there was fear. Fear of the darkness, fear of being alone. "Help her," she whispered hoarsely, "help her. Please."

Stone and Worf tore at the snow and ice, Worf ripping out massive chunks. Within seconds they had pulled her out of the snow.

"Not breathing," said Stone sharply, and touched her neck. "No pulse."

"She doesn't want to go!" Deanna's voice was almost a shriek. With surprising fury she pounded on Stone's arm. "Help her!"

"Okay, let's move!" said Stone. "Come on! Get her back to the shuttle."

Worf lifted her up and began to run. He was amazed at the stiffness of her.

Stone was barking orders as he ran full throttle to keep up with Worf. "Tinker, you'll fly the shuttle back to *Enterprise*. It's her only shot—the med lab facilities at Starlight are worth shit. Troi, you'll go with her."

"But I—"

"Just do it, dammit!" He didn't even slow down. "There's a first-aid kit with everything you'll need in there to keep her going, if she is going, that is." He was shaking his head. "She looks long gone. Are you—?"

"Yes! Yes! I'm sure!"

"Fine. The second you've dropped her off, Tinker, haul your butt back down here, got that?"

"Yes sir."

"Good. Someone who doesn't question orders."

Within moments they had loaded her into the shuttle and the remaining away team stepped back as the shuttlecraft roared to life, turned and angled sharply upward toward the waiting starship.

"Gentlemen," said Stone slowly, "we're up a creek. Let's paddle."

The pack had been hiding, sleeping within the caves. They had followed the trail of blood, but it had ended against a mass of snow. Useless. Still—there was not a serious problem. It would not be time for them to eat for many days yet. But—

The Leader raised his head in curiosity when he heard faintly the machines of man, far overhead. But that was out of their reach. The men could not be eaten if they were out of reach. And so he had placed his nuzzle down on his paws and gone back to sleep.

Later (who knew how much later? for time was irrelevant to the Wild Things except in cases of time for food) he heard voices, urgent harsh whispers carried echoing up from the canyon below.

Voices. Which meant that the humans were within reach.

The voices faded, but now it was too late. The Leader began to move around their cave and rouse the pack.

At first they did not wish to go, for they had eaten well as of late and felt no desire. But the Leader urged them on, for meat was not plentiful from sources other than themselves and should not be wasted.

For they were the pack, the pack from which all other Wild Things came. There were scavengers, rovers, loners—but they had all come from the pack. The pack was all. The pack was everything.

The pack was hunting.

Riker and Stephy Carter could not believe how easily it was going. This path was practically a godsend, taking them straight down.

At the bottom of the path, Stone, Worf, Geordi, and the two security guards, D'Angelo and Scully walked carefully around. Worf swung his tricorder in a slow, gradual arc.

Suddenly he stopped. "Up there," he said.

At the same moment, Geordi said "Over there."

But they were pointing in two different directions.

They looked at each other, and then a low, angry growl alerted them.

They were coming from all sides, the Wild Things, hideous and slavering. From above them, poised on overhangs. From their level, approaching slowly.

As the away team drew closer together, putting their backs against each other, Stone did a quick count. "About fifteen, maybe twenty, I'd say," he commented in a low voice. "Suggestions, gentlemen?"

"Let's kill them," said Worf.

"Good idea. But if our phaser fire is too loud, we bring the mountain down on us."

"Then we will die honorably, in combat," Worf observed.

Stone glanced at him. "Trust you to find the up side of any situation, Worf. All right, gentlemen . . . phasers on full. But short, controlled bursts. Not anything too noisy. Wouldn't want to bring the Hidden Hills out of hiding. Understand?"

There were brief nods and Stone said, "Go."

They started firing.

The pack was caught by surprise at first. One moment their prey seemed helpless, the next their fellows were vanishing.

The Leader howled in fury and the Wild Things attacked en masse.

From high in the mountains, Riker heard the sound of phaser fire, mingled with the sounds of furious roars.

He figured it out instantly. "Come on!" he shouted and started running toward the source of the sounds.

The away team managed to pick off a half dozen of them before one of the creatures that they hadn't spotted leaped from an overhang.

Geordi saw it at only the last second and fired off a fast burst. But it was a clean miss and the creature landed squarely on top of Worf.

The massive Klingon went down. Stone spun, saw it, and flicked his phaser to heavy stun before firing point-blank. The creature was hurled off, but scrambled to its feet, shaking off the impact.

Before Worf could get to his feet, the Wild Things came at them, one sailing through the air and smashing broadside into D'Angelo. The back-to-back formation was shattered.

"Fall back!" shouted Stone, tossing off bursts left and right. "Fall back!"

D'Angelo screamed as a Wild Thing clamped its massive jaws onto his arm. Worf, giving absolutely no thought to his own safety, jammed his fingers into the animal's mouth and pried its maw off of D'Angelo. Blood fountained from D'Angelo's torn arm as Worf yanked the monster's upper and lower jaw in opposite directions. The creature's head split with a resounding snap.

Geordi fell back, laying down a suppressing fire. The

creatures were fast, incredibly fast. For every one that he picked off, another seemed to spring into its place.

Overhead, the mountains began to rumble in irritation.

Stone fired off blast after blast, and the creatures vanished in howling fury one by one. Worf had picked up D'Angelo, slung him over one shoulder, and was continuing to fire from a crouching position.

The Leader turned and spotted the other leader, the human leader. He raced toward him to greet him with death.

Stone caught it, out of the corner of his eye—the largest of them. Damn, the thing was massive, with streaks of gray and black running through its fur and a mouth the size of a shuttlebay.

Stone, his back against the wall, turned and fired. The Wild Thing actually seemed to twist in midair and avoided the shot. It dropped to the ground six feet away from Stone.

From behind the Wild Thing, Scully jumped in and shouted "I got it, Commander!"

The Wild Thing turned with blinding speed and leaped toward Scully as Stone's shot blasted the ground where the creature had been. The Wild Thing's jaws opened wide and clamped across Scully's torso.

Scully screamed, dropping the phaser, and such was the strength of the Wild Thing that it didn't even slow down. As if Scully's weight were nothing, the Wild Thing dashed up a nearby path, bearing off its prize.

"Commander!" screamed Scully, and then they were gone.

Stone cast a quick glance at the others. Worf, with incredible precision, was picking off the monsters one by one. Geordi now had his back against Worf and they were working smoothly, efficiently. D'Angelo was clutching at his arm, moaning, but otherwise everything was under control.

In the distance, Scully's screams were fading.

Stone fired off two more shots, atomizing two more of the monsters, then turned and ran up the path after Scully.

Riker almost fell into a narrow crevice as they dashed down the ravine. It wouldn't have been fatal, but if he hadn't spotted it he could have snapped his ankle. He vaulted over it and Stephy did the same.

The Leader charged up the path, the human squirming in his grasp. Blood filled the Leader's teeth, slid down his jaw, and he rejoiced in it.

Then, from behind him, more of those blasts from the weapons the humans wielded. One of them was pursuing him.

The human leader. It had to be. None other would have the nerve, or the stupidity.

The Leader saw a kinship in the eyes of the human leader. They were very much alike.

The human leader would not stop. That was obvious. And although the struggling human in his jaws was not slowing the leader down much, it was slowing him down enough.

He turned and spat the human out.

At that moment, he caught another scent. More humans, from farther up the path.

Let the human leader stop and attend to this one. The Leader would, in the meantime, feast on whatever was up the hill.

It seemed to Riker that the roaring and phaser blasts were diminishing. It was just in time, for the mountains around them were getting remarkably fidgety, and he did not care to try and beat the odds against another avalanche. Then he skidded to a stop.

He heard the growling, much closer, like the engine of the landrover, but alive and angry and vicious.

Stephy banged into him from behind. "What!" she gasped. "Why did you stop—"

"Back up the ravine," he said curtly.

"But—"

"Now!"

Stephy obeyed, turning and running. Riker was right behind her, hurrying her along.

For a moment he thought he caught a glimpse of it in the shadows, and then it was gone. Then it was there. It was huge, bigger than any Riker had seen.

Stephy had already figured out what was going on. Now, though, she did not cry or scream. All the panic had been leached out of her, to be replaced with a dull, steady ache. She was reaching the point where she accepted the fact that she was going to die, soon and horribly. It was just a matter of how.

The Leader followed, slowly and steadily. There was no need to rush. The Leader knew where they were heading, knew there was no escape.

Stone dashed up the path, his phaser held out in front of him. Every so often he thought he heard something and stopped, waiting for it to come at him, phaser poised. But nothing did.

And during one pause, he saw blood trickling down the path.

He ran full tilt and almost tripped over the body of Scully.

Stone had arrived just in time to see the light flicker from Scully's eyes and vanish. His wounds were horrific. He had been trying to hold his torn stomach together and had not succeeded.

Stone mentally flashed through Scully's service record: Two commendations for valor, ten year veteran, wife, two daughters back on board the *Enterprise*.

"Damn," he said softly. "Damn."

He looked up the path and envisioned the monstrosity that had done this to a man who had been trying to save him.

"All right, you bastard," he said softly. "You and me."

Riker and Stephy got to the notch and clambered up, heading for the summit from which they'd been coming. Riker had only one hope—to reach the opposite side of the summit and work their way back across.

The creature was right on their heels. Riker could practically feel it breathing down his neck.

From the notch to the summit, it had been a short slide downward. Now it seemed an insurmountable haul back up. Riker grabbed Stephy and shoved her upwards. Her questing fingers grabbed the ridge of the summit and she pulled herself up.

Riker yanked out the ice axe and slammed the pick into the rock wall. It caught and he pulled himself up behind her.

They dashed across the summit, clumsily staggering through the snow, hoping to reach the other side. Then a deafening roar crackled through the air.

The ground seemed to shake under them as the Wild Thing charged across the summit. Riker spun, ice axe in hand, and swung desperately. The Wild Thing leaped over the blade and smashed into Stephy, crushing her to the ground. Her head struck the ground with a hideous thud, and only the cushion of the snow saved her skull from caving in.

The Wild Thing paused over her, roaring, and Riker slammed the ice axe down into the creature's back.

Pain! shrieked the Leader.

"Will!" shrieked Deanna Troi, as the shuttle slid into the docking bay.

The Wild Thing spun, the ice axe still in its back, and yanked it from Riker's grasp.

Riker did not back off, knowing he was dead if he did. Instead, he leaped forward, wrapping his arms around the

228

creature's midsection and grabbing at the ice axe. His fingers brushed the handle and then it fell out and into the snow.

The Wild Thing reared up on its hind legs, howling its fury. Riker held on desperately, keeping his hands away from its jaws, locking them around its throat instead.

It dropped to all fours and shook furiously, trying to hurl Riker off. Riker clutched, grabbing desperately. Suddenly, he was sailing through the air. He landed, snow leaping up around him, and just out of reach was the ice axe.

The Wild Thing charged.

Riker lunged, grabbed the ice axe and swung it as hard as he could. The pick slammed into the Wild Thing's left eye and it screamed, a scream almost human, and fell back. Riker scrambled to his feet, swinging the axe back and forth, trying to keep the creature at bay.

Blood was pouring down the side of its face as it snarled and snapped at him. Blinded in one eye it still kept at him, swinging right and then left as Riker steadily backed up.

Its tail went straight out, and the Wild Thing leaped.

It came in too fast for Riker and the side of its head slammed into his stomach. He fell to the ground, tumbling over and over, the creature's claws raking him up and down. Then Riker struck back with his own claw, the ice axe slamming over and over into the creature's side, its underbelly, wherever Riker could strike it. The massive jaws snapped closed barely inches from Riker's face, and Riker slammed a fist up into the creature's throat, held its knotted neck still for the shortest of moments, and sent the pick furiously into the creature's other eye.

The creature screamed, completely blinded, and rolled off Riker, writhing in pain. Riker started to stagger to his feet.

The creature lunged toward him, blind and dying. When it crashed into Riker it had no clear idea anymore of what was happening.

It didn't matter. The impact sent Riker staggering back, and then his brain screamed, *the edge! The edge!*

It was too late, and Riker fell backwards off the cliff.

He grabbed out desperately, certain it was going to be his last act, but his fingers caught on the edge. His body swung down and slammed into the side of the cliff. That was it for his shoulder as he heard an awful *pop*. Pain ripped through him and it was all he could do to stay conscious.

He heard the creature above him, howling and moaning, and then it stopped. It was dead. It had to be. It had better be.

He hung there by his fingertips, trying to pull himself up. He groaned in agony. His shoulder was completely stiff. He couldn't move it, and he was starting to lose feeling in the arm.

He had no strength, and was bleeding from a dozen wounds.

He hung there, cursing his lack of strength. Cursing that he had become soft.

And then—a footfall. He looked up.

Above him stood a man he had never seen before, but he was wearing Starfleet gear.

"You must be Riker," he said, and smiled. "I'm glad you're not dead. I've been looking forward to this."

Chapter Twenty-one

THE MED TEAM skidded into sickbay with the frozen body of Eleanor Carter. They had already applied resusitative measures and they slid her off the antigrav gurney and onto the bed. Beverly Crusher quickly slid her medical equipment into place.

Behind her, Deanna Troi came in, not having been able to fit into the same turbolift with the med team. "Beverly . . ." she whispered, "she's in there . . ."

"Not now, Deanna," Beverly said crisply as she scanned the instrument board. "I'm getting brain wave activity. Faint, but there. And a very faint pulse."

"She doesn't want to go."

"No one goes from my sickbay unless I tell them to." Beverly was all business, calm and collected, and thrilled to be back where she belonged—behind a diagnostic table instead of a desk. She snapped out orders with cool efficiency. "Stabilize the vitals, Jansen. Sweeney, get the R.D.T., both units. I'm going to need them." She shook her head as she studied the thermofac schematic. "Right hand isn't going to make it," she murmured. "Left leg is iffy. Thank God for prosthetics. Sweeney, move it!" She glanced over at

Troi, who looked like she was in a trance. "Deanna, what is it?"

Troi seemed as if she were ready to split in half—confused, bewildered—as Data would look if he were flooded with too much information. "I . . . I . . . don't know where to . . . she'll need me if she awakes, but . . . Will . . ."

"Will?" said Crusher, never taking her eyes from the readings.

Suddenly the pulse flatlined.

Beverly Crusher was already in motion, making adjustments on the large, pyramid-shaped device that covered Eleanor's torso, and affixing a neural stimulator to her head. Jansen was assisting, and Sweeney was rolling up the R.D.T. units.

"Don't go," Deanna pleaded softly.

"Jansen," Beverly shouted, "eighty-five microvolts, now!"

"Now" he affirmed. Eleanor's body convulsed from the combination of cordial and neural stimulation. The pulse remained flat.

"Resetting," she snapped. "Ready?"

"Ready," he said again.

Again her body arched. Deanna gasped, feeling darkness gripping her, gripping them.

For long moments Beverly Crusher worked on the unmoving body of Eleanor Carter, and then—

"We've got a pulse," said Sweeney excitedly.

"I see it," said Crusher calmly. "Stabilize her."

"Pulse is getting stronger. Heart beat up, respiration up."

"Atta girl," said Beverly, patting her frozen cheek. "Some bionics and a few skin grafts, you'll be fine."

"I haven't had a chance to work with you before, Doctor," said Sweeney as he prepped the first R.D.T. "I came on when Dr. Pulaski did. It's a pleasure to watch you."

"Always keep your head, and never think of the worst,"

she said. As she said it, the audios played Eleanor's heart-beat throughout the sickbay.

Beverly smiled thoughtfully. "That really applies to a lot of things in life, doesn't it? Including poker."

"Poker?" said Jansen.

"Uh huh. Deanna . . . is it cheating if I hear someone else's heartbeat in—Deanna?"

Troi looked like she had lapsed into a coma, except her eyes were wide open. Crusher went to her quickly, took her by the shoulders. "Deanna!" she said. "What is it? What's wrong?"

"I . . ." she tried to find the words. "Will . . . he's in terrible trouble. All emotion scrambled, mixed in . . ."

"Where is he?"

"On the planet," and then she said, "Oh, Beverly . . . what if I've made a horrible mistake? What if Stone wanted to find Will himself so that he could kill him?"

Riker hung there against the sheer cliff face and looked up at the newcomer.

"Quintin Stone," he introduced himself. "No no . . . don't get up." He paused, studying Riker's situation and then said, "Looks like you need some help."

He crouched down and grabbed Riker firmly by the right wrist. Riker released his grip on the cliff side. He clutched Stone's right hand in his and put his left hand around Stone's forearm. A precarious grasp, especially if Stone should become tired, but it didn't matter since Stone would now haul him up and everything would be fine. Except . . .

Stone wasn't pulling. Instead, he was laying there, on his stomach, holding Riker suspended over the drop. His grip was firm, but it couldn't be tireless.

Riker looked up into his eyes and saw something frightening there. *My God . . . he's insane,* he thought.

Riker glanced down. There was nothing below him to break the fall that would be hundreds of feet. The ledge they had used to climb on was far off to the left, woefully out of reach.

His shoulder throbbed.

He should never have let go of the ledge. At least he had had some modicum of control over his fate. Now his future was entirely in the hands of the man supporting him. A crazy person in Starfleet gear.

Stone surveyed Riker's predicament coolly. "Now it looks like you've gotten yourself into trouble, doesn't it?"

"Like to get . . . out of it."

"I'm sure you would," said Stone. He was not showing any sign of the strain that supporting Riker's weight must have been causing him. "Looks like this planet hasn't been too kind to you."

Riker forced himself to remain calm. Tried to affect a reasonable tone. If he sounded desperate, which he was, then this nut might let go. The only thing that he could do was play for time. His right shoulder had now lost all feeling.

"It's had its moments," Riker grunted. He tried to put his feet against the rock to give himself additional purchase.

No chance. The rock crumbled out from under him.

"It's not easy," commiserated Stone. "Trapped in a savage, unpleasant environment. We're both in the same situation, I suppose. You here. Me on the *Enterprise*. Oh, that's right. You don't know. I'm your replacement. Could be temporary." He looked thoughtful. "Could be permanent."

Riker said nothing, gritting his teeth against the pain.

"You hurt?" asked Stone.

Riker nodded.

"Pain's a bitch, isn't it? Doesn't do anyone any good."

As he sought to resolidify his grip, Riker quickly ran through what you were supposed to do when dealing with an unstable personality. Sympathize with him. Ask about his side of things. Make him believe you're on the same side. Gain his confidence.

He looked up at Stone, who seemed to be staring off into

234

the distance somewhere. Stone was still holding him firmly, but he could release Riker at any second. "I've heard so much about you," he was saying. "From everyone . . . especially Deanna. She's quite a woman. You've really been wasting time not firming up your relationship with her. You should never waste time. You never know when it might run out."

"That's . . . that's very true," said Riker. He noticed that there was a scar on Stone's cheek, and it was flushing bright red. "Nasty scar you have there . . . where'd you . . . get it? . . ."

Stone stared down at him and uttered a short laugh. Then he held up his free hand and started to count off on his fingers. "Sympathize with him," he said. "Ask about his side. Make him think you're on the same side. Gain his confidence. What do you think, Will, that I didn't go to the same laughing academy that you went to? That I wasn't taught what to do? What are you saying, Will, that I'm unstable?" He uttered a strange laugh.

He smiled down at Riker. "But you know what? I like you. And because I do . . . I think I'll tell you how I got this scar. And a whole bunch of other scars, all over.

"You ever hear of Ianni, Will?"

Riker shook his head. The fingers on his right hand were starting to slip off their grip.

"They sent us there to meet with the government head," Stone said, sounding remarkably pleasant. "Wanted to apply for membership in the Federation. Planet had a history of barbarism, but the UFP was anxious because Ianni was strategically situated near the Neutral Zone.

"So the head guy invites us down, and he introduces us to his family. He had a huge family, like about a million wives and kids. And his pride and joy is his oldest daughter." He glanced at Stephy's unmoving form. "A few years older than that one, but heavily pregnant with the head guy's first grandchild."

Riker felt as if his fingers were in a permanent clawlike

position. His body was trembling with the strain. Aside from preventing him from falling, Stone was doing nothing to pull him up. What in hell was his game?

"So anyway, while we're there, suddenly all hell breaks loose," Stone said. "Suddenly everyone's screaming. Everyone's shouting, people are running all over, bodies are piling up. We're in the middle of a coup d'etat, can you believe that? Enough people decided that they didn't like the way the guy was doing things, and got together and decided that he had to die. People were being cut down before our very eyes. And you know what we did?"

"Wh—what?" stammered Riker.

"Nothing." said Stone. "Kept our noses clean, kept to the Prime Directive. Oh we talked to them, tried to reason with them, but we did not interfere, even though we could have stopped the whole thing. Now, here's where it gets interesting. The new people are in power, and now they say *they* want to join the UFP. But first, they say, they have some business to attend to." He paused. "You know what a purge is, Will? Where they make sure they get rid of anyone associated with the folks in charge? Well, that's what they did.

"They brought out the family members of the former leader, one by one." Stone's voice seemed almost surreal. "They brought them out, and they tied each of them to a large stake, one by one. And then they had a guy come with a whip, and he beat them to death. Every single one. Every damned one. The uncles. The aunts. The wives. The . . ." His jaw set. "The children. And I stood by. Couldn't interfere. I could try to talk them out of it, plead with them but I couldn't *do* anything. And then they brought out the daughter . . . the one I mentioned before? The pregnant one? And they beat her to death."

Almost singsong, he said, "And then you know what? Just to play it absolutely safe, they got a guy with a big knife, and he delivered the baby C-section, and then they killed the baby. The blood splattered onto my nice clean Starfleet uniform. And you know what I did? You know what I goddamn did?"

In a furious voice Stone hissed, *"Nothing!"*

Riker's right hand slipped out of Stone's grasp, but with blinding speed Stone's other hand was now wrapped around Riker's forearm. With both hands he was supporting Riker by the left arm. Riker's right arm was throbbing so badly that he couldn't bring it back up over his head. He was now completely at Stone's mercy. He cried out in pain.

Deanna he thought.

"And the people," Stone was saying, "The people in charge were so pleased that we 'approved' of the way they did things, which they judged by our beloved noninterference, that they did indeed sign up to be in the UFP. And the UFP, nonjudgmental lovers of different lifestyles that we are, we let them. And you know what the people did before I left? They gave me the whip as a souvenir. Insisted I take it. And I smiled, and said thank you, and kept telling myself that I should understand and cherish different lifestyles. I told myself and told myself, lying there in my cabin. All I could think of was the death and blood and pain. I couldn't sleep, couldn't eat. It hurt to live. I stood there in my cabin one night, with the voices of the dead screaming at me, and I grabbed the whip. The first place I hit was between my shoulder blades. Then my lower back, my face, all over, again and again and again until I was numb all over. And I haven't hurt since. Isn't that great, Will? I learned how to overcome it."

Stone looked down at him and shook him slightly, as if to jostle him awake. Riker knew, knew beyond any doubt, that within seconds he was going to be plunging to the bottom of the cliff and probable death.

"And you know what else I learned?" asked Stone.

He dangled there, the only thing between himself and

oblivion being Stone's steely grip around his forearm. Riker felt himself starting to fall . . .

Except he wasn't. Stone was readjusting his grip.

"Always," Stone said, "lend a hand when things go down." He laughed that odd laugh as he hauled Riker up to the top.

Riker sat there for a moment, catching his breath. Stone watched him, completely calm, even bemused. "You're nuts," said Riker at length.

"No I'm not," said Stone. "You're making a common mistake, Will. You're confusing insanity with style." He smiled and seemed to look over Riker's shoulder. "Just doing you a favor. Giving you a taste of death. Making you that much happier to be alive."

"Why?"

He shook his head. "If you have to ask, you'll never understand. Just like I don't understand what I'm doing in Starfleet anymore.

"I was kind of wondering what you're doing here myself," said Riker.

Stone got to his feet. "I checked on the girl, by the way. A nasty crack to the head, but she'll be fine. Let's get out of here."

He stood and was suddenly slammed to the ground by a blur of gray and black.

The Leader knew that he was dying. But something called him back from death. It was the scent, the scent of the human Leader. He was here. He was close by. And so the Leader waited until he had just enough strength, and then harnessed it in one final attempt to bring the human leader with him into death.

Stone went down beneath the crushing weight of the Wild Thing. The creature's claws ripped Stone up, and Stone shut out the pain, trying desperately to keep the creature's maw away from his face.

Where the hell was his phaser? he thought desperately. Then he realized he had put it down when he'd spent time with Will. Well, that was a brilliant maneuver. Bet they'll be studying that one at the Academy real soon.

The Wild Thing roared over him, trying to hurt him, trying to kill him. *There it is,* thought Stone. Finally the challenge. Finally the death. But not without a fight. That wouldn't be right.

He drove his knees up into the creature's underbelly, pounding on the side of its head. Its jaws snapped blindly to the right and left and then suddenly it drew back, ready to slam its head forward with all its strength, and Stone knew that there was no way he was going to be able to avoid it.

A moment passed between them. A moment of mutual respect for an enemy.

The Wild Thing's head started to descend, stopping short just inches from Stone's face.

Stone gasped as he saw a sharp point emerge from under the creature's jaws. The Wild Thing howled in fury and pitched backward, rolling on the ground in death spasms.

Quickly, Stone got to his feet and noted with interest the ice axe, the spike of which had been driven through the top of the Wild Thing's head, into its brain and out the bottom. Crouching nearby was Riker, gasping at the exertion.

Stone looked at Riker and said, "You could have used the phaser over there."

"Oh," and he glanced where Stone was pointing. "I didn't spot it. Sorry."

"It's all right."

Slowly, the Leader of the Wild Things stopped moving, drawing a last, tremulous breath that ended in a low rattle.

Stone walked over to the Wild Thing. Then he sat down next to it and just stared at it.

"Stone?" said Riker.

Stone ran his fingers through the fur that was matted with blood.

"Stone?" Riker repeated. "Are you okay?"

Slowly, Stone looked up at him. A single tear rolled down his cheek. "You don't get it, do you?"

"Get what?"

He held the creature's muzzle in his hand and said softly, "I finally find someone who understands me, and he had to die. Does that stink, or what?"

Chapter Twenty-two

"THAT'S IT," said O'Brien in disgust, throwing down his cards. "I've had it. I want Troi back."

Riker looked at the transporter chief in sheer disbelief. "You want Deanna back? Since when?"

He stabbed a finger at Beverly Crusher, who was seated opposite him and was busy serenely gathering her chips. "Since Dr. Jekyll over there started getting good, that's when. I do not, repeat, do not like being bluffed out of three of a kind by a charming little ship's doctor who's holding a lousy pair of threes!"

"Can't take it, O'Brien?" smiled Beverly.

"Obviously," Riker observed, "you picked up some pointers while I was away."

"Just exercising my bedside manner," she said ingenuously, and began to stack her chips.

"And that's another thing!" ranted O'Brien. "She makes little piles with her chips. I hate people who make little piles with their chips! When can Troi come back?"

"You practically chased her away with a stick last time," Riker pointed out. "Why do you want her back?"

"Because at least if I lost to her, I could blame it on her being an empath. Losing to her—" and he pointed at Crusher.

Data said helpfully, "Are you frustrated because she bluffed your socks off?"

"Oh, go pop a microchip."

"That would be most unlikely."

"I think," said Riker, rising from his chair, "that Dr. Crusher is going to be fitting in just fine."

"And where do you think you're going?" demanded O'Brien. "I still have to get even."

"Not in this lifetime," murmured Beverly with a smile.

"Oh, ha ha ha."

"I must leave early," Riker said. "I promised someone I'd meet them."

"I'll just bet," said O'Brien.

"See you and raise you five," said Crusher.

The Singing Skies were in full volume today.

Deanna Troi sat in her favorite spot and looked out at the dancing musical lights. Then she held up a chess piece. A white queen.

"Thinking of taking up chess?" Riker asked from behind her.

She half turned, smiled, and patted the ground next to herself. Riker sat down.

"No," she said. "Just thinking of the maneuvering that goes on in life."

"And about Stone."

"Yes." She paused. "I am sorry that he decided to resign. I could have done a great deal more for him."

"Not *resign*," he corrected. *"Leave of absence.* And I can tell you quite frankly, I think he'll be right at home on Paradise. An entire city filled with people who don't take any crap from anybody. Who knows? Maybe he'll be back. Or maybe he'll have found his niche."

She nodded and then said softly, putting her hand on his,

"I wanted to tell you again how sorry I am about your friend."

He nodded in return. It was a private grief, and one that he was dealing with. What had impressed him was how, given the option to stay aboard the *Enterprise,* Eleanor (with her brand new prosthetic hand—Crusher had saved the leg—that had enough strength to shatter marble, which delighted her no end) had decided firmly that she would stay on Paradise and follow her husband's dream. And Stephy had backed up her mother one hundred percent. He was going to miss them both. Still, with Stone staying there with them, he felt that much more confident about their safety.

Confidence in Stone? Now wasn't that crazy? Still, Stone had saved him, albeit it in his own strange way. And Riker had seen fit to keep some of the details of their encounter private. Somehow, Riker instinctively knew that he had never been in danger—that Stone really did intend all along to help him, and was indeed in control. But explaining that to Picard was a task even the first officer did not care to take on.

"You know what frightens me?" said Riker. "When I think about what Stone went through, on that planet, Ianni . . ."

Troi shivered. Riker had shared with her what Stone had told him, and somehow, despite all the contradictions in Stone's nature, she was certain that this was indeed true. "Horrible," she said.

"Yeah, well . . . I keep thinking. All the psych profiles of Stone, the Academy tests, all of it, said he was as fit a candidate as myself or the captain or anybody. But what he went through—seeing that hideousness, and being helpless to interfere—I wonder what it would be like—"

"If it happened to you?" she said.

He nodded. "There but for the grace of God go I. I'd like to think I could handle it better than he did. But in a way, I'm afraid to find out."

"Let us hope it never comes to that," she said.

He stared out with her at the shimmering lights. "So . . . what is this thing again?"

"The Singing Skies."

"I don't hear anything."

"You have to be at peace. Balanced in mind and spirit."

"Oh. Well . . . all right. I'll give it a try. But first, I wanted to ask you . . ."

"Yes?"

"There were a couple of times, when I was on the planet . . . I thought somehow we were . . ." He gestured helplessly. "Talking. Thinking to each other. Is that possible?"

"What was it we were thinking to each other?" she said in bemusement.

"I don't remember."

"Well then . . . I guess it didn't happen."

"I guess not."

"Now then," she placed her fingertips to her forehead, "Relax. Breathe in and out slowly. And I should warn you right now, Commander . . . the chances are slim that you will actually be able to hear more than the faintest murmurings of the Singing Skies your first time out."

He grinned at her and said, "You know something, Counselor. I'll bet you that on the day that I can remember what we didn't discuss . . . that will be the day we'll be able to make beautiful music together."

She smiled at him and said, "Oh Will . . . that's so . . . what's the word? . . ."

"Romantic?" he said.

"Sappy," she replied. "Now . . . clear your mind."

"That shouldn't take long."

And the Singing Skies chimed a harmony overhead.

Coming soon from Titan Books

STAR TREK
THE NEXT GENERATION
PERCHANCE TO DREAM

by Howard Weinstein

On a routine mission to survey Domarus IV - a class M world with no intelligent life - an *Enterprise* shuttle crewed by Data, Troi and Wesley Crusher is captured by a race called the Tenirans who claim the world for themselves. As Captain Picard tries to negotiate with the captain of the Teniran ship, the shuttle suddenly disappears in a blaze of colour and light.

Picard demands to know what's happened to the shuttle and its crew, but the Tenirans deny any part in their disappearance. Suddenly, Captain Picard vanishes from the bridge and finds himself alone on the planet's surface with the Teniran captain. As the two captains begin to work together, they realise that they are not alone on Domarus IV as they confront an incredible alien force with the power to transform a world - or to destroy it.

THE RIFT
by Peter David

Every fifty years, a rift in space connects the Federation with a mysterious race called the Calligar who live on a planet hundreds of light years away - much too far to travel in a Starship. Captain Kirk and the U.S.S. *Enterprise* are dispatched to transport a Federation delegation of diplomats, scholars and scientists who will travel to Calligar directly during the brief period of time that the rift will be open.

Mr. Spock leads the Federation party as they travel by shuttle through the rift just as a group of the aliens arrive in Federation space. The meetings go smoothly until the Calligar take Spock's party hostage and Kirk discovers that the aliens are keeping a deadly secret. With angry Tellarite and Andorian fleets ready to attack the Calligar, Kirk must save Spock and the others before war breaks out and the rift closes for another fifty years.

Also available from Titan Books

STAR TREK GIANT NOVELS

For a complete list of Star Trek publications, T-shirts and badges please send a SAE to Titan Books Mail Order, 19 Valentine Place, London SE1 8QH. Please quote reference NG 10.